Dear Reader:

Nora Roberts, Ann Major, Dallas Schulze—each of
these wonderful authors possesses a gift for telling
stories that will tug at your heartstrings and bring a
smile to your face. Life doesn't always turn out quite
the way we'd planned, and these stories explore the
"what ifs" of love, motherhood and babies in three
unique and wonderful ways.

I am delighted to have Nora, Ann and Dallas in this
year's *Birds, Bees and Babies* collection. Over the
years each of these authors has contributed the kind
of stories readers call "keepers" to Silhouette Books,
stories that can be read and enjoyed over and over
again.

Each writer has also demonstrated that for them, a
romance novel is not just a "boy meets girl" story,
but a complex and compelling celebration of the
potential for joy in our lives—and the power of love.

Happy reading,

Isabel Swift
Editorial Director
Silhouette Books

Please address questions and book requests to:
Reader Service
U.S.: P.O. Box 1325, Buffalo, NY 14269
Canadian: P.O. Box 1050, Niagara Falls, Ont. L2E 7G7

Birds, Bees and Babies '94

NORA ROBERTS
ANN MAJOR
DALLAS SCHULZE

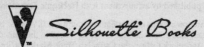

Silhouette Books

Published by Silhouette Books

America's Publisher of Contemporary Romance

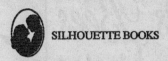

SILHOUETTE BOOKS

Birds, Bees and Babies
Copyright © 1994 Harlequin Enterprises B.V.

ISBN 0-373-48285-X

The publisher acknowledges the copyright holders of
the individual works as follows:

THE BEST MISTAKE
Copyright © 1994 by Nora Roberts

THE BABY MACHINE
Copyright © 1994 by Ann Major

CULLEN'S CHILD
Copyright © 1994 by Dallas Schulze

CONTENTS

The Best Mistake

Nora Roberts

A Note from Nora Roberts

I always wanted to be a mom. And not just because you get presents and pampering on Mother's Day— though it's a pretty cool side benefit. Really, I don't know why I thought it would be such a terrific idea. I was the youngest of five, and my mother was always working. Ironing, cooking, hanging the wash, running to the store, to school, to dentists' offices. She was especially always running to the emergency room with one of us bleeding.

We liked to keep things interesting.

Despite all of this, I thought motherhood was a wonderful thing. I believe I mistakenly saw myself in charge, setting the rules, making the plans, snapping my fingers and being obeyed.

Obviously my two sons changed my rose-colored outlook. But what didn't change, and never will, is the wonder of it. This small person belongs to you, depends on you, loves you without reservation. This human being isn't perfect, isn't always obedient or sweet, and rarely is he quiet. But this is your child, and no one else ever had one quite like him.

They grow and they change and they develop. When that boy, whose nose you wiped and whose shoelaces you tied, becomes a man, it's a shock. Somehow the years that pass never quite prepare you. With my oldest, the moment of truth came when I was chasing him around the kitchen, seeing red over some infraction he'd committed. When I caught him and began the usual heated lecture, I suddenly realized, I was looking *up* at him. Fortunately, this didn't occur to him, and the balance of power remained with Mom.

Because it still seems right, I believe I made a good choice in opting for motherhood. It's a tough road, full of pitfalls and sharp turns, but it's an incredibly interesting ride. I may have taken the step because my own dear mother often wished for me to have a dozen children just like me—although she may not have meant it as a blessing at the time. In any event, I stopped at two and it turned out just fine.

Chapter One

No one answered the door. Coop glanced at the scrawled note in his hand to make sure he had the right address. It checked out, and since the tidy two-story Tudor in the neat, tree-lined neighborhood was precisely what he was after, he knocked again. Loudly.

There was a car in the drive, an aging station wagon that could use a good wash and a little bodywork. Somebody was in there, he thought, scowling up at the second-floor window, where music pumped out—high-volume rock with a thumping backbeat. He stuffed the note and his hands in his pockets and took a moment to survey the surroundings.

The house was trim, set nicely off the road behind clipped bayberry hedges. The flower garden, in which spring blossoms were beginning to thrive, was both colorful and just wild enough not to look static.

Not that he was a big flower lover, but there *was* something to be said for ambience.

There was a shiny red tricycle beside the driveway, and that made him a little uneasy. He wasn't particularly fond of kids. Not that he disliked them. It was just that they always seemed a kind of foreign entity to him, like aliens from an outlying planet: they spoke a different language, had a different culture. And, well, they were short, and usually sticky.

Still, the ad had talked of quiet, privacy, and a convenient distance from Baltimore. That was exactly
what he was looking for.

He knocked again, only to have a thundering wave
of music wash out the window over him. The rock
didn't bother him. At least he understood it. But he
wasn't a man to kick his heels outside a closed door for
long, so he tried the knob.

When it turned, he pushed the door open and
walked in. In an old habit, he pushed back the dark
hair that fell over his forehead and scanned the none-
too-neat living room he'd entered.

There was a lot of clutter, and he, a bachelor who'd
spent a great deal of his thirty-two years living alone,
wondered over it. He wasn't fussy or obsessive, he often told himself. It was simply that everything had a
place, and it was easier to find if it had been put there.
Obviously his prospective landlord didn't agree.

There were toys that went along with the tricycle
outside, piles of magazines and newspapers, a pint-size
fielder's cap that declared for the O's.

At least the kid had taste, Coop decided, and moved
on.

There was a small powder room done in an amazing combination of purple and green, and a den that
had been converted into a makeshift office. File
drawers were open, papers spilling out. In the kitchen
dishes waited in the sink to be washed, and lurid
drawings, created by a child with a wild imagination,
decorated the front of the refrigerator.

Maybe, he thought, it was just as well no one had answered the door.

He considered backtracking and wandering upstairs. As long as he was here, it made sense to check the rest of the place out. Instead, he stepped outside to get the lay of the land. He spotted open wooden steps leading to a short deck. The private entrance the ad had mentioned, he mused, and climbed.

The glass door was open, and the music rolling through it was overwhelming. He caught the smell of fresh paint, one he'd always enjoyed, and stepped inside.

The open area combined kitchen and living space cleverly enough. The appliances weren't new, but they were gleaming. The tile floor had been scrubbed recently enough for him to identify pine cleaner beneath the scent of paint.

Feeling more hopeful, he followed the music, snooping a bit as he went. The bathroom was as scrupulously clean as the kitchen, and, fortunately, a plain glossy white. Beside the sink was a book on home repair, open to the plumbing section. Wary, Coop turned on the tap. When the water flowed out fast and clear, he nodded, satisfied.

A small room with definite office potential and a nice view of the yard was across the hall. The ad had claimed two bedrooms.

The music led him to it, a fair-sized room that fronted the house, with space enough for his California king. The floor, which seemed to be a random-width oak in good condition, was covered with splattered drop cloths. There were paint cans, trays, brushes, extra rollers. A laborer in baggy overalls and bare feet completed the picture. Despite the hair-concealing cap and oversize denim, Coop recognized a woman when he saw one.

She was tall, and the bare feet on the stepladder were long and narrow and decorated with paint splotches and hot-pink toenails. She sang, badly, along with the music.

Coop rapped on the door jamb. "Excuse me."

She went on painting, her hips moving rhythmically as she started on the ceiling border. Stepping across the drop cloths, Coop tapped her on the back.

She screamed, jumped and turned all at once. Though he was quick on his feet, he wasn't fast enough to avoid the slap of the paintbrush across his cheek.

He swore and jerked backward, then forward again to catch her before she tumbled off the ladder. He had a quick, and not unpleasant, impression of a slim body, a pale, triangular face dominated by huge, long-lashed brown eyes, and the scent of honeysuckle.

Then he was grunting and stumbling backward, clutching the stomach her elbow had jammed into. She yelled something while he fought to get his breath back.

"Are you crazy?" he managed, then shot up a hand as she hefted a can, slopping paint over the sides as she prepared to use it as a weapon. "Lady, if you throw that at me, I'm going to have to hurt you."

"What?" she shouted.

"I said, don't throw that. I'm here about the ad."

"What?" she shouted again. Her eyes were still wide and full of panic, and she looked capable of anything.

"The ad, damn it." Still rubbing his stomach, Coop marched to the portable stereo and shut it off. "I'm here about the ad," he repeated, his voice loud in the sudden silence.

The big brown eyes narrowed with suspicion. "What ad?"

"The apartment." He swiped a hand over his cheek, studied the smear of white on it, and swore again. "The apartment."

"Really?" She kept her eyes glued to his. He looked tough, she thought. Like a brawler with those broad shoulders, lean athletic build and long legs. His eyes, a light, almost translucent green, looked anything but friendly, and the faded Baltimore Orioles T-shirt and battered jeans didn't contribute any sense of respectability. She figured she could outrun him, and she could certainly outscream him. "The ad doesn't start to run until tomorrow."

"Tomorrow?" Nonplussed, he reached into his pocket for his scribbled note. "This is the right address. The ad was for this place."

She stood her ground. "It doesn't run until tomorrow, so I don't see how you could know about it."

"I work at the paper." Moving cautiously, he held out the note. "Since I've been looking for a place, I asked one of the girls in Classifieds to keep an eye out." He glanced down at his note again. "Two-bedroom apartment on second floor, private entrance, quiet neighborhood convenient for commuters."

She only continued to frown at him. "That's right."

Realizing his inside track wasn't strictly ethical, he winced. "Look, I guess she got a little overenthusiastic. I gave her a couple of tickets to a game, and she must've figured she'd do me a favor and pass the information along a little early."

When he saw that her grip on the can had relaxed, he tried a smile. "I knocked, then I came around back." Probably best not to mention he'd wandered through the house first.

"The ad didn't run the address."

"I work at the paper," he repeated. He was taking a good look at her now. There was something vaguely familiar about her face. And what a face it was. All slashing cheekbones and liquid eyes, that creamy porcelain skin women's face cream ads always raved about. Her mouth was wide, with an alluringly full lower lip. At the moment, the face continued to frown.

"They had the address for billing," he continued. "Since I had a couple of hours, I thought I'd come by and check it out. Look, I can come back tomorrow, if you'd feel more comfortable. But I'm here now." He shrugged. "I can show you my press pass."

He pulled it out for her, and was pleased when she narrowed her eyes to study it. "I do a column. J. Cooper McKinnon on sports. 'All in the Game'?"

"Oh." It meant nothing to her. The sports page wasn't her choice of reading material. But the smile had appeased her. He didn't look so much like a thug when he smiled. And the smear of paint decorating the lean, tanned face added just enough comedy to soothe her. "I guess it's all right, then. I wasn't expecting to show the apartment for a couple of days yet. It's not ready." She held up the can, set it down again. "I'm still painting."

"I noticed."

She laughed at that. It was a full-throated, smoky sound that went with the natural huskiness of her voice. "Guess you did. I'm Zoe Fleming." She crouched down to dampen a rag with paint remover.

"Thanks." He rubbed the rag over his cheek. "The ad said immediate occupancy."

"Well, I figured I'd be finished in here by tomorrow, when the ad was scheduled to run. Are you from the area?"

"I've got a place downtown. I'm looking for something with a little more space, a little more atmosphere."

"This is a pretty good-sized apartment. It was converted about eight years ago. The guy who owned it had it done for his son, and when he died, the son sold it and moved to California. He wanted to write sitcoms."

Coop walked over to check out the view. He moved fluidly, Zoe thought, like a man who knew how to stay light and ready on his feet. She'd had the impression of wiry strength when her body tumbled into his. And good strong hands. Quick ones, too. She pursed her lips. It might be handy to have a man around.

"Is it just you, Mr. McKinnon?" She thought wistfully how nice it would be if he had a family—another child for Keenan to play with.

"Just me." The place felt right, he decided. It would be good to get out of a box that was just one more box in a building of boxes, to smell grass now and then. Barbecue smoke. "I can move in over the weekend."

She hadn't thought it would be so easy, and she nibbled her lip as she thought it through. She'd never been a landlady before, but she'd been a tenant, and she figured she knew the ropes. "I'll need first and last months' rent."

"Yeah."

"And, ah, references."

"I'll give you the number of the management company that handles my building. You can call Personnel at the paper. Have you got a lease for me to sign?"

She didn't. She'd checked out a book from the library, and she'd meant to type up a scaled-down copy of a lease from it the next morning. "I'll have it tomorrow. Don't you want to look at the rest of the apartment, ask any questions?" She'd been practicing her landlady routine for days.

"I've seen it. It's fine."

"Well." That deflated her a bit. "I guess I can cancel the ad."

There was a sound like a herd of rampaging elephants. Zoe glanced toward the open door and crouched to intercept the missile that hurtled through.

It was a boy, Coop saw when she scooped the child up. He had glossy golden hair, red sneakers, and jeans that were streaked with some unidentifiable substance that looked like it would easily transfer to other surfaces. He carried a plastic lunch box with a picture of some apocalyptic space battle on it, and a sheet of drawing paper that was grimy at the edges.

"I drew the ocean," he announced. "And a million people got ate by sharks."

"Gruesome." Zoe shuddered obligingly before accepting his sloppy kiss. She set him down to admire the drawing. "These are really big sharks," she said, cagily distinguishing the shark blobs from the people blobs.

"They're monster sharks. Mutant monster sharks. They have teeth."

"So I see. Keenan, this is Mr. McKinnon. Our new tenant."

Keenan wrapped one arm around Zoe's leg for security as he eyed the stranger. His eyes were working their way up to Coop's face when they lit on the T-shirt. "That's baseball. I'm gonna learn. Mama's getting a book so's she can teach me."

A book. Coop barely checked a snort. As if you could learn the greatest game invented by a man from a book. What kind of nerd did the kid have for a father?

"Great." It was all Coop intended to say. He'd always thought it wise to avoid entangling himself in a conversation with anyone under sixteen.

Keenan had other ideas. "If you're going to live here, you have to pay rent. Then we can pay the mortgage and stuff and go to Disney World."

What *was* the kid? An accountant?

"Okay, old man." Zoe laughed and ruffled his hair. "I can handle it from here. Go on down and put your stuff away."

"Is Beth coming to play with me tonight?"

"Yes, Beth's coming. Now scoot. I'll be down in a minute."

"'Kay." He made a dash for the door, stopping when his mother called him. It only took one look, the raised brow for him to remember. He looked back at Coop, flashed a quick, sunny grin. "Bye, mister."

The herd of elephants rampaged again, then there was the crash of a door slamming. "He makes an entrance," Zoe said as she turned back to Coop. "The dramatic flair comes from my mother. She's an actress, off-off-Broadway." Tilting her head, Zoe rested one bare foot on the bottom rung of the stepladder. "You look like you're ready to change your mind. You have a problem with children?"

"No." The kid might have thrown him off, but Coop doubted it would be a problem. The boy would hardly be beating a path to his door. And if he did,

Coop thought, he could send him off again quickly enough. "No, he's, ah, cute."

"Yes, he is. I won't claim he's an angel, but he won't make a nuisance of himself. If he gives you any trouble, just let me know."

"Sure. Look, I'll come by tomorrow to sign the lease and give you a check. I'll pick up the keys then."

"That'll be fine."

"Any special time good for you?"

She looked blank for a moment. "What's tomorrow?"

"Friday."

"Friday." She closed her eyes and flipped through her messy internal calendar. "I'm working between ten and two. I think." She opened her eyes again, smiled. "Yeah, I'm pretty sure. Anytime after two-thirty?"

"Fine. Nice meeting you, Mrs. Fleming."

She took his offered hand. "It's Miss," she said easily. "I'm not married. And since we'll be living together, so to speak, you can make it Zoe."

Chapter Two

No one answered the door. Again. Coop checked his watch and saw that it was quarter to three. He didn't like to think he was a man obsessed with time, but as his living centered around deadlines, he did respect it. There was no rusting station wagon in the driveway this time, but he walked around the back of the house, hoping. Before he could start up the stairs to the apartment, he was hailed from across the chain-link fence.

"Young man! Yoo-hoo, young man!" Across the yard next door came a flowered muumuu, topped with a curling thatch of brightly hennaed hair that crowned a wide face. The woman hurried to the fence in a whirl of color. It wasn't just the dress and the improbable hair, Coop noted. The face itself was a rainbow of rich red lipstick, pink cheeks and lavender eye shadow.

When she reached the fence, she pressed a many-ringed hand over the wide shelf of her breasts. "Not as young as I used to be," she said. "I'm Mrs. Finkleman."

"Hi."

"You're the young man who's going to live up-stairs." Mrs. Finkleman, a born flirt, patted her curls. "Zoe didn't tell me you were so handsome. Single, are you?"

"Yeah," Coop said cautiously. "Miss Fleming was supposed to meet me. She doesn't seem to be home."

"Well, that's Zoe, flying here, flying there." Mrs. Finkleman beamed and leaned comfortably on the fence, as if she were settling in for a nice cozy gossip. "Got a dozen things on her plate at once, that girl does. Having to raise that sweet little boy all alone. Why, I don't know what I'd have done without my Harry when our young ones were coming up."

Coop was a reporter, after all. That, added to the fact that he was curious about his landlady, put him in interview mode. "The kid's father doesn't help out any?"

Mrs. Finkleman snorted. "Don't see hide nor hair of him. From what I'm told, he lit out the minute he found out Zoe was expecting. Left her high and dry, and her hardly more than a child herself. Far as I know, he's never so much as seen the boy. The little sweetheart."

Coop assumed she was referring to Keenan. "Nice kid. What's he, five, six?"

"Just four. Bright as a button. They grow them smarter these days. Teach them faster, too. The little love's in preschool now. He'll be home any minute."

"His mother went to pick him up, then?"

"Oh, no, not her week for car pool. Alice Miller—that's the white house with blue trim, down the block?—it's her week. She has a boy and a girl. Little darlings. The youngest, Steffie, is Keenan's age. Now her oldest, Brad, there's a pistol for you."

As she began to fill Coop in on the neighborhood rascal, he decided it was time to draw the interview to a close. "Maybe you could tell Miss Fleming I was by? I can leave a number where she can reach me when—"

"Oh, goodness." Mrs. Finkleman waved a hand. "I do run on. Nearly forgot why I came out here in the first place. Zoe called and asked me to look out for you. Got held up at the flower shop. She works there three days a week. That's Floral Bouquet, down in Ellicott City? Nice place, but expensive. Why, it's a crime to charge so much for a daisy."

"She got held up," Coop prompted.

"Her relief had car trouble, so Zoe's going to be a little late. Said you could go right on into the kitchen there, where she left the lease and the keys."

"That's fine. Thanks."

"No problem at all. This is a friendly neighborhood. Always somebody to lend a helping hand. I don't think Zoe mentioned what you did for a living."

"I'm a sportswriter for the *Dispatch*."

"You don't say? Why, my Harry's just wild for sports. Can't budge him from in front of the TV when a game's on."

"That's what makes this country great."

Mrs. Finkleman laughed and gave Coop's arm an affectionate bat that might have felled a lesser man. "You men are all the same. You can come over and talk sports with Harry anytime. Me, if it's not base-ball, it isn't worth talking about.''

Coop, who'd been about to retreat, brightened. "You like baseball?"

"Son, I'm a Baltimore native." As if that said it all. "Our boys are going to go all the way this year. Mark my word."

"They could do it, if they heat those bats up. The pitching rotation's gold this year, and the infield's tight as a drum. What they need—"

Coop was interrupted by a cheerful toot. He glanced over to see Keenan burst out of a red sedan and rocket across the side yard.

"Hi, mister. Hi, Mrs. Finkleman. Carly Myers fell down, and there was blood.'' The big brown eyes gleamed wickedly. "Lots and lots of it, and she screamed and cried." He demonstrated, letting go with a piercing yell that had Coop's ears ringing. "Then she got a Band-Aid with stars on it." Keenan thought it would have been worth losing some blood for such a neat badge of honor. "Where's Mama?"

"Little lamb." Mrs. Finkleman leaned over the fence to pinch Keenan's cheek. "She's working a lit-tle late. She said you could come stay with me until she gets home."

"Okay." Keenan liked his visits next door, since they always included cookies and a rock on Mrs. Finkle-man's wonderfully soft lap. "I gotta put my lunch box away."

"Such a good boy," Mrs. Finkleman cooed. "You come on over when you're done. Why don't you show the nice man inside so he can wait for your mother?"

"Okay."

Before Coop could take evasive action, his hand was clutched by Keenan's. He'd been right, he thought with a wince. It was sticky.

"We've got cookies," Keenan told him, cannily deducing that he could have double his afternoon's treat if he played his cards right.

"Great."

"We baked them ourselves, on our night off." Keenan sent Coop a hopeful look. "They're really good."

"I bet." Coop caught the back door before it could slam shut.

"There." Keenan pointed to a ceramic cookie jar in the shape of a big yellow bird on the counter. "In Big Bird."

"Okay, okay." Since it seemed like the best way to appease the kid, Coop reached in and pulled out a handful of cookies. When he dumped them on the table, Keenan's eyes went as wide as saucers. He could hardly believe his luck.

"You can have one, too." He stuffed an entire chocolate chip deluxe in his mouth and grinned.

"That good, huh?" With a shrug, Coop sampled one himself. The kid, Coop decided after the first bite, knew his cookies. "You'd better get next door."

Keenan devoured another cookie, stalling. "I gotta wash out my thermos, 'cause if you don't, it smells."

"Right." Cooper sat at the table to read through the lease while the boy dragged a stool in front of the sink.

Keenan squirted dishwashing liquid in the thermos, and then, when he noticed Coop wasn't paying any attention, he squirted some more. And more. He turned the water up high and giggled when soap began to bubble and spew. With his tongue caught between his teeth, he jiggled the stopper into the sink and began to play dishwasher.

Coop forgot about him, reading quickly. The lease seemed standard enough, he decided. Zoe had already signed both copies. He dashed his signature across from hers, folded his copy, then set the check he'd already written on the table. He'd picked up the keys and rose to tuck his copy in his pocket when he spotted Keenan.

"Oh, God."

The boy was drenched, head to foot. Soap bubbles dotted his face and hair. A good-sized puddle was forming on the tile at the base of the stool.

"What are you doing?"

Keenan looked over his shoulder, smiled innocently. "Nothing."

"Look, you've got water everywhere." Coop looked around for a towel.

"Everywhere," Keenan agreed, and, testing the opposition, he slapped his hands in the sink. Water and suds geysered.

"Cut it out! Jeez! Aren't you supposed to be somewhere else?" He grabbed a dish towel and advanced, only to be slapped in the face by the next geyser. His eyes narrowed. "Look, kid—"

He heard the front door slam. Like mother, like son, he thought.

"Keenan?" Zoe called out. "I hope you haven't been into those cookies."

Coop looked at the crumbs on the table, on the floor, floating in the soapy water.

"Oh, hell," he muttered.

"Oh, hell," Keenan echoed, beaming at him. He giggled and danced on his stool. "Hi, Mom."

Zoe, her arms full of day-old irises, took in the scene with one glance. Her son was as wet as a drowned dog, her kitchen looked as though a small hurricane had blown through. Hurricane Keenan, she thought. And her new tenant looked damp, frazzled, and charmingly sheepish.

Like a boy caught with his hand in the cookie jar, she noted, glancing at the telltale crumbs.

"Been playing dishwasher again?" With a calm that baffled Coop, she set the flowers down. "I'm just not sure it's the right career choice, Keen-man."

Keenan fluttered his long, wet lashes. "He wanted cookies."

Coop started to defend himself, then simply scowled at the boy.

"I'm sure he did. Go on into the laundry room and get out of those wet clothes."

"Okay." He jumped from the stool, splashing more water before he zoomed away. He stopped only long enough to give his mother a wet kiss before he disappeared into an adjoining room.

"Sorry I'm late," Zoe said easily, yanking the stopper out of the sink then walking to a cupboard to get a vase.

Coop opened his mouth. He started to explain what had gone on in the past ten minutes, but realized he wasn't at all sure. "I signed the lease."

"I see that. Would you mind putting some water in this?" She held out the vase. "I need to get a mop."

"Sure."

She was probably going to wallop the kid with it, Coop thought, and felt a quick tug of regret and guilt. But the sounds from the laundry room where she'd disappeared weren't those he associated with corporal punishment. They were a young boy's giggles, a woman's lusty laugh. Coop stood, a vase of water in his hands, and wondered at it.

"You're standing in a puddle," Zoe commented when she came back with a mop and pail.

"Oh, right." Coop glanced down at his wet high-tops, shifted. "Here's your vase."

"Thanks." She tended to her flowers first. "You met Mrs. Finkleman, I hear."

"News travels fast."

"Around here it does." When she handed him a dishcloth to dry his face with, he caught her scent—much more potent, much more colorful, than the flowers. She was wearing jeans and a baggy T-shirt with Floral Bouquet across the chest. Her hair, he noted, was some elusive shade between brown and blond. She wore it tied back in a jaunty ponytail.

When she lifted her brows, he realized he'd been staring. "Sorry. I mean—I'm sorry about the mess."

"Were you playing dishwasher, too?"

"Not exactly." It was impossible not to smile back, to ignore the quick pull of attraction.

It wouldn't be so bad, he mused, having a pretty landlady, sharing the house with her, maybe an occasional meal. Or an occasional—

"Mama!" Keenan stood in the doorway, wearing nothing but skin. "I can't find my pants."

"In the basket by the washing machine," she told him, without taking her eyes from Coop's.

He'd forgotten about the kid, let himself fantasize a little before remembering she didn't come as a single. He took a long mental step backward and jingled the keys to his new apartment.

"I've got some boxes out in the car," he told her. "I'm going to move some things in this afternoon."

"That's fine." It was silly to feel disappointed, Zoe thought. Foolish to have felt that fast feminine flutter when she recognized interest in his eyes. More foolish to feel let down because the interest had blanked out when her child called her. "Do you need any help?"

"No, I can handle it. I've got a game to cover tonight, so I'm going to move the rest in tomorrow." He backed toward the door. "Thanks."

"Welcome aboard, Mr. McKinnon."

"Coop," he said as he stepped outside. "It's Coop."

Coop, she thought, leaning on the mop handle. It had seemed like such a good idea to make use of the apartment upstairs. The extra income would take some of the pressure off, and maybe add a few bonuses. Like that trip to Disney World that Keenan wanted so badly.

It had been a risk to buy the house, but she'd wanted her son to grow up in a nice neighborhood, with a yard, maybe a dog when he was a little older. The rental income would take away some of the risk.

But she hadn't realized it could add another, more personal risk. She hadn't realized how awkward it might be to have a tenant who was male, single, and absolutely gorgeous.

She laughed at herself. Dream on, Zoe, she thought. J. Cooper McKinnon was just like the rest, who ran like a hound when they heard the patter of little feet.

Something crashed in the laundry room. She just shook her head.

"Come on, sailor," she called to Keenan. "It's time to swab the deck."

Chapter Three

"Pretty good digs, Coop. Really, pretty good." Ben Robbins, a staff reporter for the *Dispatch,* sipped a cold one while surveying Coop's apartment. "I didn't think much of it when we hauled all your junk up here, but it ain't half-bad."

It was a lot better than not half-bad, and Coop knew it. He had everything exactly where he wanted it. The living room was dominated by his long, low-slung sofa of burgundy leather and his big-screen television, so perfect for viewing games. A couple of brass lamps, a nicely worn coffee table scuffed from the heels of the dozens of shoes that had rested on it and a single generous chair completed the formal section of the room.

There was an indoor basketball hoop, small-scaled, for practice—and because shooting a little round ball helped him think. A used pinball machine called Home Run, a stand that held two baseball bats, his tennis racket and a hockey stick, a pair of old boxing gloves hanging on the wall and a scarred Fooz Ball table made up the recreation area.

Coop wouldn't have called them toys. They were tools.

He'd chosen blinds, rather than curtains, for the windows. Blinds, he thought, that would close out the light if a man decided to treat himself to an afternoon nap.

The bedroom held little other than his bed, a night-stand and another TV. The room was for sleeping—or, if he got lucky, another type of sport.

But it was his office that pleased him most. He could already imagine himself spending hours there at his computer, a game playing on his desktop TV. He'd outfitted it with a big swivel chair, a desk that had just the right number of scars and burns, a fax, a dual-line phone and a VCR—to play back those controversial calls or heart-stopping plays.

With all the plaques and photos and sports memorabilia scattered about, it was home.

His home.

"Looks like the neighborhood bar," Ben said, and stretched out his short, hairy legs. "Where the jocks hang out."

Coop considered that the highest of compliments. "It suits me."

"To the ground," Ben agreed, and toasted Coop with his bottle of beer. "A place where a man can relax, be himself. You know, since I started living with Sheila, I've got little china things all over, and underwear hanging in the bathroom. The other day she comes home with a new bedspread. It's got *flowers* all over. Pink flowers." He winced as he drank. "It's like sleeping in a meadow."

"Hey." With all the smug righteousness of the unencumbered, Coop propped his feet on the coffee table. "Your choice, pal."

"Yeah, yeah. Too bad I'm nuts about her. And her an Oakland fan, too."

"Takes all kinds. Talk is the A's are trading Remirez."

Ben snorted. "Yeah, yeah, pull the other one, champ."

"That's the buzz." Coop shrugged, took a pull on his own beer. "Sending him to K.C. for Dunbar, and that rookie fielder, Jackson."

"They got to be crazy. Remirez hit .280 last season."

".285," Coop told him. "With twenty-four baggers. Led the team in errors, too."

"Yeah, but with a bat like that . . . And Dunbar, what's he? Maybe he hit .220?"

"It was .218, but he's like a vacuum cleaner at second. Nothing gets by him. And the kid's got potential. Big, strapping farm boy with an arm like a bullet. They need new blood. Most of the starting lineup's over thirty."

They argued baseball and finished their beers in complete male harmony.

"I've got a game to cover."

"Tonight? I thought the O's were in Chicago until tomorrow."

"They are." Coop pocketed his tape recorder, his pad, a pencil. "I'm covering the college game. There's a hot third baseman who's got the scouts drooling. Thought I'd take a look, cop an interview.''

"What a job." Ben hauled himself to his feet. "Going to games, hanging around locker rooms."

"Yeah, it's a rough life." He slung an arm over Ben's shoulders as they headed out. "So, how's the story on neutering pets going?"

"Stuff it, Coop."

"Hey, some of us hang around the pound, some of us hang around the ballpark."

And a hell of a day it was for it, too, Coop thought. Balmy and clear-skied. He could almost smell roasting peanuts and hot dogs.

"While you're hanging around a bunch of sweaty college boys in jockstraps, I'll be snuggled up with a woman."

"Under a flowered bedspread."

"Yeah, but she says flowers make her feel sexy. And I'm here to tell you— My, oh, my..."

When Ben's small, square face went lax, Coop turned. He felt his own jaw drop. And, if he wasn't mistaken, his tongue landed on his shoes.

She was wearing what had to be the shortest skirt ever devised by man. Beneath it were a pair of endless legs that were molded into black fishnet hose. She swayed when she walked. How could she help it, when she stood in black skyscraper heels?

A tiny white bustier exposed a delicious amount of cleavage. Around her neck was a shiny black bow tie that, for reasons utterly inexplicable to Coop, made every male cell in his body sizzle.

Her hair was down, falling straight as a pin to her shoulders in a melding of tones that made him think of wild deer leaping through a sunlit forest.

She stopped, smiled, said something, but his mind had checked out the moment his eyes landed on her legs.

"...if you've settled in okay."

"Ah..." He blinked like a man coming out of a coma. "What?"

"I said I haven't had a chance to check and see if you've settled in okay."

"Fine." He folded his tongue back in his mouth and got a grip on himself. "Just fine."

"Good. Keenan came down with a cold, so things have been hectic. I caught a glimpse of you hauling things up the steps a couple of days ago."

"Hauling," he repeated. "Yeah. Ben," he said when his friend jabbed him. "This is Ben. He's been giving me a hand moving."

"Hi, Ben. I'm Zoe."

"Hi, Zoe," Ben said stupidly. "I'm Ben."

She just smiled. It was the outfit, she knew. As much as she hated it, she couldn't help but be amused by how it affected certain members of the species. "Do you work at the paper, too?"

"Yeah, I'm, ah, doing a story on neutering pets."

"Really?" She almost felt sorry for him, the way his Adam's apple was bobbing. "I'll be sure to look for it. I'm glad you're settling in okay. I've got to get to work."

"You're going out?" Coop said. "In that?"

Her lips twitched. "Well, this is my usual outfit when I'm carpooling, but I thought I'd wear it to work tonight. At Shadows? I'm a waitress. Nice meeting you, Ben."

She walked to her car. No, Coop thought, swayed to it, in those long, lazy strides. They were both still staring when she pulled out of the drive and cruised down the street.

"Your landlady," Ben said in a reverential whisper. "That was your landlady."

"I think it was." She hadn't looked like that when he signed the lease. Beautiful, yes—she'd been beautiful, but in a wholesome, unthreatening sort of way. She hadn't looked so...so.... Words failed him. She was a mother, for God's sake, he reminded himself. She wasn't supposed to look like that. "She's got a kid."

"Yeah? What kind?"

"Human, I think."

"Come on."

"A boy," Coop said absently. "This high." He held a hand, palm down, about three feet from the ground.

"She may have a kid, but she's also got legs. This high." Ben waved a hand in front of his own throat. "You got a charmed life, Coop. My landlord's got arms like cinder blocks, and a tattoo of a lizard. You got one who looks like a centerfold."

"She's a mother," Coop said under his breath.

"Well, I wouldn't mind coming home to her for milk and cookies. See you at the sweatshop."

"Sure." Coop stood where he was, frowning at the quiet street. Mothers weren't supposed to look like that, he thought again. They were supposed to look...motherly. Safe. Comfortable. He blew out a breath, willed away the knot in his stomach.

She wasn't *his* mother, he reminded himself.

By midnight, Zoe's feet were screaming. Her back ached, and her arms felt as though she'd been hauling boulders rather than drink trays. She'd deflected six propositions, two of them good-hearted enough to amuse, one of them insulting enough to earn the gentleman in question a bruised instep, courtesy of one of her stiletto heels. The others had been the usual, and easily ignored.

It went with the territory, and it didn't bother her overmuch.

The lounge earned its name from the shadowy effect of neon and all the dim corners. The decor was fifties tacky, and the waitresses were dolled up like old-fashioned mindless floozies to match.

But the tips were excellent, and the clientele, for the most part, harmless.

"Two house wines, white, a Black Russian and a coffee, light." After calling out her order to the bartender, Zoe took a moment to roll her shoulders.

She hoped Beth had gotten Keenan to bed without any fuss. He'd been cranky all day—which meant he was nearly over his sniffles. He'd put up quite a fuss that morning, Zoe remembered, when she'd nixed the idea of him going to school.

Didn't get that from me, she thought. She'd never fussed about not going to school. Now, at twenty-five, she deeply regretted letting her education slide. If she'd applied herself, tried for college, she could have developed a skill, had a career.

Instead, she had a high school diploma she'd barely earned, and was qualified for little more than serving drinks to men whose eyes tried to crawl down her cleavage.

But she wasn't one for regrets. She'd done what she'd done, and she had the greatest prize of all. Keenan. In a couple of years, she figured, she'd have saved enough that she could turn in her bustier and take a night course. Once she had a few business courses under her belt, she could open her own flower shop. And she wouldn't have to leave Keenan with sitters at night.

She served her drinks, took an order from another table and thanked God her break was coming up in five minutes.

When she saw Coop walk in, her first thought was Keenan. But the sick alarm passed almost as quickly as it had come. Coop was relaxed, obviously scoping the place out. When his eyes met hers, he nodded easily and made his way through the scattered tables.

"I thought I'd stop in for a drink."

"This is the place for it. Do you want to sit at the bar, or do you want a table?"

"A table. Got a minute?"

"At quarter after I've got fifteen of them. Why?"

"I'd like to talk to you."

"Okay. What can I get you?"

"Coffee, black."

"Coffee, black. Have a seat."

He watched her head toward the bar and tried not to dwell on how attractive she looked walking away. He hadn't come in because he wanted a drink, but because she seemed like a nice woman in a tight skirt—spot, he corrected. A tight spot.

Get hold of yourself, Coop, he warned himself. He knew better than to let a pair of long legs cloud his judgment. He'd only come in to ask a few questions, get the full story. That was what he did, and he was good at it. Just as he was good at dissecting a game, any game, and finding those small triumphs and small mistakes that influenced the outcome.

"We've been busy tonight." Zoe set two coffees on the table before sliding onto a chair across from Coop. She let out a long, heartfelt sigh, then smiled. "This is the first time I've been off my feet in four hours."

"I thought you worked in a flower shop."

"I do, three days a week." She slid her cramped feet out of her shoes. "Around Mother's Day, Christmas, Easter—you know, the big flower days, I can squeeze in more." She sipped the coffee she'd loaded with sugar and let it pump into her system. "It's just a small shop, and Fred—that's the owner—only keeps on a couple of part-timers. That way he doesn't have to pay any of the bennies, like hospitalization, sick leave."

"That's lousy."

"Hey, it's a job. I like it. It's just Fred and Martha—she's his wife. They've taught me a lot about flowers and plants."

Someone pumped quarters into the juke. The room heated up with music. Coop leaned over the table so that she could hear him. For a moment he lost the thread somewhere in her big brown eyes.

"Have I met you somewhere before?" he asked her.

"In the apartment."

"No, I mean..." He shook his head, let it go. "Uh, why here?"

"Why here what?"

"Why do you work here?"

She blinked, those long lashes fluttering down, then up. "For a paycheck."

"It doesn't seem like you should be working in a bar."

"Excuse me?" Zoe wasn't sure if she should be amused or insulted. She chose the former simply because it was her nature. "Do you have a problem with cocktail waitresses?"

"No, no. It's just that, you're a mother."

"Yes, I am. I have a son to prove it." She laughed and leaned her chin on her fist. "Are you thinking it would be more appropriate for me to be home baking cookies or knitting a scarf?"

"No." Though it embarrassed him that he did. "It's that outfit," he blurted out. "And the way all these men look at you."

"If a woman's going to wear something like this, men are going to look. Looking's all they do," she added. "If it makes you feel better, I don't dress like this for PTA meetings."

He was feeling more ridiculous every second. "Look, it's none of my business. I just have a habit of asking questions. Seems to me you could do better than this. I mean, you've got the flower job, and the rent—"

"And I have a mortgage, a son who seems to outgrow his clothes and shoes every other week, a car payment, grocery bills, doctor bills."

"Doctor? Is the kid sick?"

Zoe rolled her eyes. Just when she was starting to get irritated, he deflated her. "No. Kids Keenan's age are always bringing some germ or other home from school. He needs regular checkups with his pediatrician, with the dentist. Those things aren't free."

"No, but there are programs. Assistance." He stopped, because those big brown eyes had turned fierce.

"I'm perfectly capable of earning a living, and of taking care of my child."

"I didn't mean—"

"Maybe I don't have a college degree or any fancy skills, but I can pay my own way, and my son doesn't lack for anything." She jammed her feet into the backbreaking heels and stood. "We've been doing just fine on our own, and I don't need some nosy jock reporter coming in here and telling me how to be a mother. Coffee's on the house, you jerk."

He winced as she stormed away from the table, then let out a long breath. Handled that one *real* well, Coop.

He wondered if there would be an eviction notice on his door in the morning.

Chapter Four

She didn't kick him out. She had thought of it, but had decided the satisfaction she'd gain didn't quite equal the rental income. Besides, she'd heard it all before.

One of the reasons she'd moved from New York was that she'd grown impossibly weary of friends and family telling her how to run her life. How to raise her son.

Baltimore had been a clean slate.

She'd had enough money put aside to afford a nice two-bedroom apartment and invest the rest. And because she was willing to work at any job, and work hard, she'd rarely been unemployed. It had been difficult for her to put Keenan in day-care. But he'd thrived. He had his mother's knack for making friends.

Now, two years after the move, she had a house, and a yard, in the kind of neighborhood she wanted for her son. And she'd paid for every bit of it on her own.

Too many people had told her she was crazy, that she was too young, that she was throwing her life and her chances away. With a grunt, Zoe shoved the lawn mower around and began to cut another strip of grass. *Her* grass, she thought with clenched teeth.

She'd proved them wrong. She'd had her baby, kept her baby, and she was making a decent life for him. She and Keenan weren't statistics. They were a family.

They didn't need anyone to feel sorry for them, or to offer handouts. She was taking care of everything, one step at a time. And she had plans. Good, solid plans.

The tap on her shoulder made her jump. When she whipped her head around and looked at Coop, her hands tightened on the mower. "What?"

"I want to apologize," he shouted. When she only continued to glare at him, he reached down and shut off the engine. "I want to apologize," he repeated. "I was out of line last night."

"Really?"

"I'm sort of addicted to poking into other people's business."

"Maybe you should go cold turkey." She reached down to grab the pull cord. His hand closed over hers. She stared at it a moment. He had big hands, rough-palmed. She remembered the impression she'd gotten of strength and energy. Now the hand was gentle and hard to resist.

She hadn't felt a man's hands—hadn't wanted to feel a man's hands—in a very long time.

"Sometimes I push the wrong buttons," Coop continued. He was staring at their hands, as well, thinking how small hers felt under his. How soft. "It's

earned me a fist in the face a time or two.'' He tried a
smile when her gaze slid up to his.

"That doesn't surprise me."

She didn't smile back, but he sensed a softening.
The roar of the mower had awakened him. When he'd
looked out and seen her marching along behind it in
baggy shorts, a T-shirt and a ridiculous straw hat, he'd
wanted to go back to bed. But he'd been compelled to
seek her out.

It was only a flag of truce, he told himself. After all,
he had to live with her. More or less.

"I didn't mean to be critical. I was curious about
you. And the kid," he added quickly. "And maybe
seeing you in that outfit last night pushed a few of my
buttons."

She lifted a brow. That was honest enough, she
thought. "All right. No permanent damage."

It had been easier than he'd expected. Coop decided to press his luck. "Listen, I've got to cover the
game this afternoon. Maybe you'd like to come along.
It's a nice day for baseball."

She supposed it was. It was warm and sunny, with
a nice, freshening breeze. There were worse ways to
spend the day than in a ballpark with an attractive
man who was doing his best to pry his foot out of his
mouth.

"It sounds like fun—if I didn't have to work. But
Keenan would love it." She watched his jaw drop, and
smothered a smile.

"Keenan? You want me to take him?"

"I can't think of anything he'd rather do. Some of the kids play in their yards, and they let him chase the ball. But he's never seen the real thing, except on TV." She smiled now, guilelessly, and held back a hoot of laughter. She could all but see Coop's mind working.

"I don't know too much about kids," he said, backpedaling cautiously.

"But you know about sports. It'll be great for Keenan to experience his first real game with an expert. When are you leaving?"

"Ah . . . a couple of hours."

"I'll make sure he's ready. This is awfully nice of you." While he stood staring, she leaned over and kissed his cheek. After one hard tug, she had the mower roaring again.

Coop stood planted like a tree when she strolled away. What the hell was he supposed to do with a kid all afternoon?

He bought popcorn, hot dogs and enormous cups of soft drinks. Coop figured food would keep the kid quiet. Keenan had bounced on the seat of the car throughout the drive to Camden Yards, and since they had arrived he'd goggled at everything.

Coop had heard "What's that?" and "How come?" too many times to count. Nervous as a cat, he settled into the press box with his laptop.

"You can watch through the window here," he instructed Keenan. "And you can't bother anybody, because they're working."

"Okay." Almost bursting with excitement, Keenan clutched his hot dog.

There were lots of people in the press box, some with neat computers, like Coop, others with headphones. A few of them had smiled at him, and all of them had said hello to Coop. Keenan knew Coop was important. As his mother had instructed, he kept close and didn't ask for any presents. Even though there had been really neat stuff at the stands. His mother had given him five whole dollars and told him he could buy a souvenir. But there'd been so many he didn't know which to pick. And Coop had walked so fast he'd hardly been able to look.

But it didn't matter, because he was at a real ball game.

Wide-eyed, he stared down at the field. It was bigger than anything he'd imagined. He knew where the pitcher would stand, and he recognized home plate, but he wasn't sure of anything else.

The big scoreboard exploded with pictures, and words he couldn't read. Circling it all were the stands, filled with more people than he'd ever seen.

When they announced the lineup, he looked down at the players with naked admiration. The national anthem began, and, recognizing it, Keenan stood up, as he'd been taught.

Coop glanced over, saw the boy standing, with a hot dog in one hand and a big, dazzling grin on his face. Suddenly he remembered his first time at a ballpark. His eager hand gripping his father's, his eyes trying to see everything at once, and his heart so full of the excitement, of the game, of just being a boy.

As the players took the field, Coop reached over and tugged on Keenan's bright hair. "Pretty cool, huh?"

"It's the best ever. Those are our guys, right?"

"Those are our guys. They're gonna kick butt."

Keenan giggled and leaned closer to the glass to watch the first pitch. "Kick butt," he said with relish.

He didn't, as Coop had expected, fidget, whine or make a general nuisance of himself. Because he was accustomed to working under noisy and confusing conditions, Keenan's constant questions didn't annoy him overmuch. At least, he thought, the kid had the good sense to ask.

Between innings, Keenan peered over Coop's shoulder and sounded out the words that were popping up on the computer screen, and he did transfer some mustard from his hands onto Coop's sleeve. But it wasn't the disaster Coop had envisioned.

Coop even felt a quick tug of pride when the play-by-play announcer called Keenan over and let the boy sit in his lap for an inning.

Most kids would've been running around the booth begging for more candy. But this one, Coop thought, had come for the game.

"How come he didn't run all the way? How come he didn't?" Keenan shifted from foot to foot. His bladder was past full, but he couldn't bear to miss a minute.

"The throw went to second, so he was forced out," Coop explained. "See, the second baseman caught the ball and stepped on the bag to retire the side."

"Retire the side," Keenan repeated reverently. "But we're still winning?"

"The O's are up by one going into the top of the ninth. Looking at the batting order, I'd say they'll put in a southpaw."

"Southpaw," Keenan repeated, as if it were gospel.

"A left-handed reliever. Probably Scully." He glanced over and noted that Keenan was holding his crotch. "Uh, got a problem?"

"Nuh-uh."

"Let's hit the john—the bathroom." He took Keenan's hand and hoped it wasn't too late. As they passed through the door, Scully was announced as the relief.

"Just like you said." Keenan looked up at Coop with dazzling admiration. "You're smarter than anybody."

Coop felt a grin break out over his face. "Let's just say I know the game."

When they arrived home, Keenan was wearing a new Orioles jersey and carrying an autographed baseball in a pint-size baseball glove. He waved a pennant in his other hand as he scrambled up the steps.

"Look! Look what Coop got me!" He barreled into his mother who'd barely walked in the door herself. "We went into the locker room with the real Orioles, and they signed the baseball for me. To keep."

"Let's see." She took the ball and examined it. "This is really special, Keenan."

"I'm gonna keep it forever. And I got this shirt, too, like they wear. And a glove. It even fits."

Emotion backed up in her throat. "It certainly does. Looks like you're all ready to play ball."

"I'm gonna play third base, 'cause it's the...the..."

"Hot corner," Coop supplied.

"Yeah. Can I go show Mr. Finkleman? Can I show him my baseball?"

"Sure."

"He's gonna be surprised." He turned and threw his arms around Coop's legs. "Thanks, thanks for taking me. I liked it best of anything. Can we go again, and take Mama?"

"Uh, yeah, I guess. Sure." Feeling awkward again, he patted Keenan's head.

"Okay!" Giving Coop one last squeeze, Keenan raced out the door to show off his treasures.

"You didn't have to buy him all that stuff," Zoe began. "Taking him was enough."

"No big deal. He didn't ask for it, or anything." Coop stuck his hands in his pockets. "He got such a charge out of meeting the players, and one thing kind of led to another."

"I know. I hear our team won."

"Yeah. Clipped them by one. I had to stop by the paper and file the story, or we'd have been here sooner."

"I just got in myself." On impulse, she walked over, wrapped her arms around him and hugged. Coop's hands stayed paralyzed in his pockets. "I owe you. You gave him a great day. He won't forget it." She drew back. "Neither will I."

"It's no big deal. He just hung out in the press box."

"It's a very big deal, especially since I trapped you into it." She laughed and tossed back her hair. "You were so transparent this morning, Coop. The idea of having a four-year-old tagging along terrified you. But you did good, real good. Anyway— Sorry," she said when the phone rang. "Hello? Oh, hi, Stan. Tonight? I'm not scheduled." Letting out a breath, she sat on the arm of a chair. "I'll have to let you know. No, Stan, I can't tell you now. I have to see if I can find a sitter. An hour, then. Yes, I understand you're in a jam. I'll call you back."

"Problem?"

"Hmmm... Two of the waitresses called in sick for tonight. They're short-staffed." She was already dialing the phone. "Hi, Mrs. Finkleman. Yeah, I know. He had a great time. Mm-hmm..." Zoe's gaze flicked up to Coop as Mrs. Finkleman told her how important it was for a boy to have a man in his life. "I'm sure you're right. I was wondering if you're busy tonight. Oh. That's right, I forgot. No, it's nothing. Have a good time."

Zoe hung up and pursed her lips. "It's their bingo night," she told Coop. "Beth's got a date. Maybe Alice." She reached for the phone again, shook her head. "No, she's having her in-laws over for dinner." Her eyes lit on Coop and narrowed in speculation. "You didn't have any problem with Keenan today."

"No," Coop said slowly, wary of another trap. "He was cool."

"Stan doesn't need me in until nine. Keenan goes to bed at eight, so you wouldn't have to do anything but hang around, watch television or whatever."

"Hang around here, while you work?" He took a step back. "Just me and the kid—like a baby-sitter? Listen . . ."

"I'll pay you. Beth gets two an hour, but I can up the ante."

"I don't want your money, Zoe."

"That's so sweet." She smiled, took his hand and squeezed. "Really, so sweet of you. If you could come down about eight-thirty."

"I never said—"

"You can help yourself to anything in the kitchen. I'll make some brownies, if I have time. I'd better call Stan back before he pulls out what's left of his hair." She picked up the phone, beamed at Coop. "Now I owe you two."

"Yeah, right." He hurried out before she could find some way to owe him three.

Chapter Five

For the next couple of hours, Coop immersed himself in "All in the Game," his weekly syndicated column. The kid had given him the hook, he thought. The first visit to a ball game, the passing on of tradition, and the bond that was forged over the cheers, the crack of the bat, the peanut shells.

It was a good piece, Coop decided, and wrote easily. He supposed since he owed the idea to Keenan the least he could do was hang around downstairs and eat brownies while the kid slept.

He wandered back down just as Zoe came through the kitchen door.

She hadn't been sure he'd come. She knew she'd hustled him, and after she'd finished being amused by it, she felt guilty. But here he was, right on time, standing at the foot of the steps.

"I pushed you into a corner...." she began.

"Yeah, you did." She looked so somber, he had to smile. "You've got a real talent for it."

She shrugged her shoulders and smiled back at him. "Sometimes being pushy's the only way to get things done, but I always feel bad about it after. I did bake brownies."

"I could smell them all the way upstairs." When she didn't move, he tilted his head. Funny, though she was wearing that sexy waitress rig again, she didn't seem so outrageous. Except for that bow tie, he thought. Something about that black tie around that slim white throat shot straight to his libido.

"You going to let me in, or do you want me to stand out here?"

"I have this guilt thing," she explained, "whenever I have to ask anyone for a favor. And it was so sweet of you to take Keenan to the game, especially when . . ."

"When I'd been asking you out?"

She shrugged her shoulders again, let them fall. He was looking at her that way again, and something in her body was reacting helplessly. Better, she thought, to set the rules quickly. "I don't go out with men. I should have told you straight out."

He had to force himself not to lift a hand to that neat little bow and tug. "At all?"

"It's just easier not to. They're not interested in Keenan, or they pretend they are so they can talk me into bed." When he rocked back on his heels and cleared his throat, she laughed. "What they don't know is that they're clear as cellophane. You see, Keenan and I are a team. As a sportswriter, you should know what that means."

"Sure. I get it."

"Anyway, you gave him a really wonderful day, and I feel like I'm twisting your arm about tonight."

He decided, after a moment, that she wasn't doing it on purpose. There was just too much sincerity in that glorious face for a con. And if there was a twinge of guilt because he had given considerable thought to talking her into bed, that was his problem.

"Look, he's asleep, right?"

"Yes. All the excitement wore him out."

"So, I'll eat your brownies and watch your TV. No big deal."

Her smile came easily now, beautifully, and made his mouth water. "I left the number of the club by the phone, just in case. The Finklemans should be home by eleven. She'd come over and relieve you if you want."

"We'll play it by ear."

"Thanks, really." She stepped back into the kitchen to let him in. "My shift ends at two, at closing."

"Long day for you."

"I've got tomorrow off." After grabbing her purse, she took a quick look around. "Make yourself at home, okay?"

"I will. See you."

She hurried out, those incredibly sexy heels clicking across the tile. Coop let out a long breath and told himself to settle down. The lady had just set the ground rules. Fun and games were out.

She had the face of a siren, the body of a goddess, and legs designed to make a strong man whimper—but deep in her heart she was Betty Crocker.

Coop took a deep sniff and decided to content himself with a plate of double fudge brownies.

* * *

The storm rolled in just before midnight. Coop had taken Zoe at her word and made himself at home. He was stretched out on her couch, sunk deep in the cushions, with his feet propped comfortably on her coffee table. He was dozing in front of an old war movie, his only regret being that he hadn't thought to bring a couple of beers down with him.

Zoe's selection ran to milk, juice and some unidentified green liquid.

He'd poked around a little—it was simply in his nature. The clutter ran throughout the house, but he began to see a pattern to it. Obviously she wasn't a detail person, but the general lack of order made the house comfortable, even cozy. Coop wasn't sure if the result was by design or simply because she was a woman who worked two jobs and had a kid to raise.

And from the library books he'd found stacked here and there, it seemed she spent most of her free time reading up on flowers, car repair, tax laws and time management.

He couldn't help but think it was a waste of a perfectly stunning woman, this voluntary burial of self in books and nowhere part-time jobs.

But it wasn't his problem.

The crash of thunder from outside harmonized nicely with the artillery barrage on the TV screen. Coop had just decided that this baby-sitting racket was a snap.

Then he heard the wailing.

Marines didn't wail, he thought fuzzily, especially when they were battling Nazi scum. He yawned, circled his neck until it cracked, then spotted Keenan.

The boy stood at the base of the stairs in Batman pajamas, a battered stuffed dog clutched in one arm and tears pouring down his face.

"Mama!" His voice sharpened like an ice pick, then hitched. "Where's my mama?"

"She's at work." Coop straightened on the sofa and stared helplessly. "Something wrong?"

A flash of lightning lit the room. By the time the thunder rolled in answer, Keenan screamed like a banshee and launched himself into Coop's lap.

"I'm scared. There's monsters outside. They're coming to get me."

"Hey…" Coop gave the head buried in his chest an inadequate pat. "Hey, it's just a thunderstorm."

"Monsters," Keenan sobbed. "I want Mama."

"Well, she's—" He started to swear, caught himself. The poor kid was shaking. With an instinct he didn't recognize, Coop cuddled Keenan in his lap. "You don't like storms, huh?" All Keenan could do was shake his head and burrow deeper. "They're just like fireworks. You know, on the Fourth of July, or after your team wins the pennant? They probably just had a big game up there. They're celebrating."

"Monsters," Keenan repeated, but he'd calmed enough to lift his head and look at Coop. "Big black monsters with sharp teeth." He jolted at the next clap of thunder. Fresh tears started to roll. "They want to eat me."

"Nah." Experimentally, Coop tested Keenan's bicep. "You're too tough."

"I am?"

"You bet. Any monsters who looked in here would see you and run for their lives. They'd never take on Coop and the Keen-man."

Keenan sniffled, rubbed a fist over his eyes. "Really?"

"Absolutely." Coop saw Keenan's lower lip tremble when thunder grumbled. "Home run," he said, and Keenan's trembling mouth curved in a hesitant smile.

"Can I stay out here with you?"

"Sure. I guess."

Keenan, an expert in such matters, settled himself comfortably in Coop's lap, laid his head against Coop's heart and sighed.

Zoe was swaying with fatigue by the time she let herself in. It was nearly 3:00 a.m., and she'd been up and doing for twenty hours straight. All she wanted was to fall facedown on her bed and sleep.

She saw them in the gray light of the snowy television screen. They were curled together on the couch, the boy snuggled deep against the man. Something shifted inside her at the sight of them, both sleeping deeply, Keenan's tousled golden hair beneath Coop's broad, tanned hand.

She set her purse and her keys aside without taking her eyes off them.

How small her son looked, and how safe.

She slipped out of her shoes and walked to them on stockinged feet. In a natural gesture, she brushed a hand over Coop's hair before gently lifting her son. Keenan stirred, then settled against her.

"Mama."

"Yes, baby," she murmured. She nuzzled him as she carried him away, caught the scent of man mixed with boy.

"The monsters came, but we scared them away."

"Of course you did."

"Coop said the thunder's just fireworks. I like fireworks."

"I know." She laid him in his bed, smoothing the sheets, his hair, kissing his soft cheeks. "Go back to sleep now."

But he already had. She watched him a moment longer in the faint glow of his night-light, then turned and went back downstairs to Coop.

He was sitting up now, his head in his hands, the heels rubbing against his eyes. She switched off the buzzing television set, then sat on the arm of the couch. Any man who could sleep so comfortably with a child, to her mind, had unlimited potential.

She wondered, just for an instant, what it would feel like to curl up beside him.

"The storm woke him?"

"Yeah." His voice was rusty. He cleared it. "He was pretty spooked."

"He said you chased the monsters away."

"Seemed like the right thing to do." He turned his head to look at her. Those big brown eyes were sleepy and smiling. The quick hitch in his heartbeat warned him to be on his way. But he lingered. "He's okay now?"

"He's fine. You'd make a good daddy."

"Oh, well . . ." That had him moving. He stood, working out the kinks. "That's not my line. But it was no big deal."

"It was to me." She'd embarrassed him, she noted, and she hadn't meant to. "Why don't I fix you breakfast tomorrow?"

"Huh?"

"Pay you back with pancakes. Mrs. Finkleman tells me you bring in a lot of pizza and Chinese, so I don't imagine you cook. Do you like pancakes?"

"Who doesn't?"

"Then let me know when you're up and around. I'll flip some for you." She lifted a hand, brushed the hair from his brow. "Thanks for helping me out."

"No problem." He took a step away, swore under his breath and turned back. "Listen, I've just got to do this, okay?"

Before she could respond, he took her face in his hands and closed his mouth over hers.

The kiss was quick, and it was light, and it sent sparks snapping down her nerve ends.

When she didn't move a muscle, he lifted his head, looked at her. She was staring at him, her eyes heavy and dark. He thought he saw the same stunned reaction in them that was curling somewhere in his gut. She opened her mouth as if to speak, but he shook his head and kissed her again. Longer, deeper, until he felt her bones begin to melt. Until he heard the small whimper of pleasure purr in her throat.

Her hands slid up his arms, gripped, then moved up to tangle in his hair. They stood there, locked against each other.

One of them quivered, perhaps both. It didn't seem to matter as the warm taste of her seeped into his mouth, into his blood. It was like a dream that he hadn't yet shaken off, one that tempted him to sink back in, to forget reality.

She'd forgotten it. All she knew for one glorious moment was that she was being held in strong arms, that her mouth was being savored wonderfully, and that needs, so long dormant, were swimming to the surface and breaking into life.

Touch me. She wondered if she said it, or if the words simply whirled hazily in her head. But his hand, hard and sure, ran once down her body, kindling fires.

She remembered what it was to burn, and what it was like when the flames died out and left you alone.

"Coop." Oh, she wanted, so badly, just to let it happen. But she wasn't a young, reckless girl this time. And she had more to think of than herself. "Coop. No."

His mouth clung to hers for another moment, his teeth nipping. But he drew back. He was, he realized, as breathless as a man who'd slid headfirst into home plate.

"Now I'm supposed to say I'm sorry."

She shook her head. "No, you're not. I'm not."

"Good." The hands that were resting on her shoulders kneaded once, then slipped away into his pockets. "Me neither. I've been thinking about doing that since I first saw your feet."

Her brows rose. Surely she'd heard him wrong. "My what?"

"Your feet. You were standing on the ladder, painting. You weren't wearing any shoes. You've got tremendously sexy feet."

"Really?" It amazed her that he could tie her into helpless knots one minute, then make her laugh the next. "Thanks. I think."

"I guess I'd better go."

"Yeah, you'd better."

He nodded, started out. This time, when he stopped, she braced, and she yearned. But he simply turned and looked at her. "I'm not going to try to talk you into bed. But I want you there. I figured I should let you know."

"I appreciate it," she said in a shaky voice.

When the door closed behind him, she let her weak legs fold and sat down on the couch. What, she asked herself, was she supposed to do now?

Chapter Six

When Coop dragged himself out of bed, it was nearly noon. He stumbled into the shower and nearly drowned himself before both of his eyes opened. Wet and out of sorts, he rubbed himself down, gave a moment's thought to shaving, then dismissed the idea.

He tugged on gym shorts and a T-shirt before heading directly to the coffeemaker. While it brewed, he opened his front door and let the full power of the sun shock him the rest of the way awake.

They were in the yard, Zoe and Keenan, laughing as mother tried to help son hit fungoes with a plastic bat. The kid wasn't having much luck, Coop noted. But he was sure having fun. He started to step back inside before either of them spotted him. But the jock in him had him kibitzing.

"He'll never hit anything standing that way," Coop called out, and had two pair of big brown eyes looking up in his direction.

"Hi, Coop. Hi. I'm playing baseball." Thrilled to have an audience, Keenan waved his bat and nearly caught his mother on the chin.

"Watch it, champ," she said, and shifted out of range. "Good morning," she called out. "Want your breakfast?"

"Yeah, maybe."

Keenan took another pathetic swing and had Coop muttering under his breath. Swung like a girl. Somebody had to show the kid how to hold a bat, didn't they? he asked himself as he started down.

"You're choking it too much."

Zoe's brows drew together. "The book I got said—"

"Book." He cursed automatically. Keenan echoed him. "Sorry," he muttered when Zoe gave him a narrow-eyed look. "Now listen, you learn how to add and subtract from books. You don't learn baseball. Just like a girl." He crouched down and adjusted Keenan's hands.

Zoe had been ready to concede to the expert, but the last statement stopped her. "Excuse me? Are you implying that females can't play sports?"

"Not what I said. Swing from the shoulders," he told Keenan. Coop might have been grouchy, but he wasn't stupid. "There are plenty of terrific female athletes. Keep your eye on the ball, kid." He kept one hand around Keenan's and lightly tossed the ball up in the air with the other. The bat connected with a hollow thud.

"I hit it! I hit it really, really hard!"

"Major league stuff." Coop slid his eyes back up to Zoe's. "I thought you were making pancakes."

"I was— I am." She blew out a breath. "I guess you're taking over."

"Well, I don't know diddly about pancakes, and you don't know squat about baseball. Why don't we both do what we know?"

"Like it's a big deal to hit a stupid ball with a stupid bat," she muttered as she strode to the back door.

"You can't do it."

She stopped dead in her tracks, eyes narrowed, turned. "I certainly can."

"Yeah, right. Okay, Keenan, let's try it again."

"I believe it's my turn." Challenge in her every movement, Zoe slipped the bat from her son's hands.

"Are you going to hit it, Mama? Are you?"

"You bet I am." She held out a hand for the ball Coop was holding. She tossed it up, swung, and batted the ball to the chain-link fence bordering the side yard. Keenan let out a cheer and raced to retrieve it.

Coop sniffed, smiled. "Not bad, for a girl. But anybody can hit a fungo."

"Keenan's too young for anything but a plastic ball."

"No, a fungo's when you toss it up yourself and hit it."

"Oh."

"I'm gonna throw it, Coop. You catch."

"Sure, zip it in here."

It took Keenan three tries, running in closer each time, to send the ball anywhere near Coop.

"I suppose you don't think I could hit it if you threw it at me...." Zoe began.

"Pitch it to you," Coop said patiently. "I would pitch it to you."

"All right, pitch it to me, then." She raised the bat.

"Fine, but you might want to turn a little more to the side. That's it," he said, backing away. "Zoe, you're holding the bat like you're going to use it to hammer a nail. Okay, here it comes."

He tossed the ball soft and underhand, but she still had to grit her teeth to keep herself from jerking away. Because her pride and her son's respect for women were at stake, she swung hard. No one was more stunned than Zoe when she connected. Coop snatched the ball an instant before it could smash his nose.

"Well." Zoe handed the bat back to a wide-eyed Keenan, dusted her hands. "I'll go see about those pancakes."

"She hit it really hard," Keenan said admiringly.

"Yeah." Coop watched the back door swing shut behind her. "Your mother's really...something, kid."

"Will you pitch to me, Coop? Will you?"

"Sure. But let's work on that stance, huh? You gotta look like a ballplayer."

When Zoe finished flipping the last pancake on the stack, she looked out the window and saw her son swing the bat. The ball didn't go far, but Coop made a pretense of a diving catch, missing, while Keenan danced gleefully in place.

"Too hot to handle," Coop claimed, and Keenan jumped on top of him. "Hey, there's no tackling in baseball. Football's out of season." He scooped the

wriggling boy up and held him upside down. Somewhere along the line, his sour mood had vanished.

It became a habit to spend time with the boy. Nothing planned, just playing a little catch in the yard or
showing Keenan how to dunk baskets in the apartment. It wasn't as though he were attached to the kid,
Coop assured himself. But when he had some free time
and the boy wanted to hang around, what was the
harm? Maybe it was sort of nice to see those big eyes
all full of hero worship. And maybe it wasn't so much
of a hardship to listen to that rollicking belly laugh
Keenan burst into when something struck his fancy.

If the boy sometimes came along with the bonus of
his mother, it wasn't exactly a hardship.

The fact was, he had seen a great deal more of
Keenan than Zoe since the night of the thunderstorm.
She was friendly enough, but she'd been careful—or
so it seemed to Coop—not to be alone with him.

That was something he was going to fix, he decided
as he shut down his computer.

He grabbed a couple of miniature race cars, some
of the flotsam and jetsam of boyhood that Keenan had
left in his apartment. If Coop knew Zoe as he thought
he was beginning to, the toys would be an easier entry
than a bouquet of long-stemmed roses.

Jiggling the cars in his hand, he strode down the
steps to knock on her kitchen door.

In the laundry room, Zoe slammed down the lid on
the washer. "Who is it?"

"It's Coop."

She hesitated, started the machine. "Come on in. I'll be right out." She hefted a basket of clean laundry, as much out of defense as out of necessity, and went into the kitchen.

God, he looked good. She had really, really tried not to dwell on how good the man looked. So damn male, she thought, the rangy, athletic body, the muscles, the dark, untidy hair, and those wonderful pale green eyes. She wished her heart wouldn't always stutter when he aimed one of his cocky grins in her direction.

"Hi." She plopped the basket on the kitchen table and immediately began busying her hands folding socks.

"Hi." The kitchen was cluttered, as always. She really needed someone to help her organize, he thought. God, she smelled fantastic. "Keenan left these upstairs." Coop set the cars on the table. "I thought he might be looking for them."

"Thanks."

"So where is he?"

"In school."

"Oh, right." Coop knew Keenan's schedule as well as he knew yesterday's box scores. "You just get in from the flower shop?"

"Mmm-hmm . . . Business is picking up. We've got a couple of weddings. Actually, I could work full-time for the next three weeks, but it just doesn't fit Keenan's schedule."

"What do you mean?" Idly he plucked a shirt from the basket.

"Well, the spring weddings. The arrangements take a lot of extra hands, so Fred asked if I could put in full days for a while."

"So, that's good, right?"

"The school Keenan goes to is really more of a pre-school than day-care. It doesn't stay open after three. And I have the car pool next week, anyway. Plus, I promised to take him and some of the other kids swimming at the community center on Friday. He's really looking forward to it."

"Yeah, he mentioned it." About twenty times, Coop recalled.

"I don't want to let him down."

"So, I'll do it."

She looked back up, socks dangling from her hands. "What?"

He couldn't believe he'd said that. He stared at her for another moment, then shrugged. "I said I'd do it. It's no big deal. He can hang with me when he gets home from school."

She tilted her head. "Don't you have a job?"

"That's what I call it, since they pay me." He smiled, finding the idea went down easily. "I do most of my writing here, and he could tag along when I go in to the paper or on an interview. He'd probably get a kick out of it."

"I'm sure he would." She narrowed her eyes. Why couldn't she get a handle on J. Cooper McKinnon? "But why would you?"

He wasn't sure he had the answer to that, so he punted. "Why not? He's not that much of a pest."

With a laugh, she went back to her laundry. "Maybe he's not, but you forgot the car pool."

"I can drive. What's the big deal about hauling a bunch of kids to school and back?"

"I can't begin to tell you," she murmured. It was, perhaps, something every adult should experience for himself. "And the swimming."

"I was captain of the swim team in college. All-state."

She glanced up at that. "I thought you played baseball. Uh, Keenan mentioned it."

"Yeah, I did. Two hundred and twelve RBIs my last season. I played basketball, too, averaged forty-two points a game." He was bragging, Coop realized. Like some gawky teenager trying to impress the head cheerleader. He frowned down at the little cars, began to slide one over the table.

"Keenan says you make great engine noises."

"Yeah, it's a talent."

He'd embarrassed himself, Zoe realized, and she wanted to hug him. "Tell you what. Why don't we take it a day at a time? If you decide you can't handle it—"

His eyes flashed up at that. "I think I can handle one scrawny kid and a few of his pals."

"Okay. If you decide you don't *want* to handle it, no hard feelings."

"Fine. When do you want to start?"

"Tomorrow would be great."

"Okay." That was settled. Now, he thought, it was on to other business. "How about dinner?"

Her eyes widened in surprise. "Um...sure. We're just going to have chicken. I'll probably fry it."

"No." He stepped closer. She stepped back. "I mean, why don't we have dinner? Out. You and me."

"Oh, well..." Good answer, she thought foolishly. Very succinct. She took another step in retreat. "I have to work tonight."

"Tomorrow."

"I don't really go out."

"I've noticed. What are you backing away from, Zoe?"

"You." Annoyed with herself, she held up a hand. And found it pressed against his chest. "I don't want to date anyone. Start anything. I have very good reasons."

"You'll have to tell me about them sometime." He reached up, combed a hand through her hair and loosened the band that held it back.

"You're not going to kiss me again."

"Sure I am." He touched his lips to hers to prove it. His eyes remained open as he drew her lower lip into his mouth, as he used his tongue, his teeth, to tease and seduce. "You've got an incredible mouth."

She couldn't get her breath. Even as she gasped for it, her vision dimmed. It was all she wanted. It seemed her life depended on keeping her lips against his. This wasn't fair, she thought dimly as she began to sink into the glory of sensation. Too long, she told herself. Surely she was reacting this way only because it had been so terribly long since she'd allowed herself to feel only as a woman.

She was melting against him like wax. He hadn't known how painfully erotic it would be to feel that long, lean body go fluid. He'd only meant to kiss her, to test them both, but his hands were already reaching, stroking, exploring.

His touch, those hard, callused hands against her bare skin, all but brought her to her knees.

"I have to think."

"Think later." He pressed his mouth to her throat.

Oh, it was glorious, glorious to ache again. But she knew too well what came from soothing that ache. "Coop, we can't do this."

"Yes, we can. I'll show you."

With a laugh that came out half moan, she turned her head away. "My head's spinning. You have to stop. God, do you have any idea what you're doing to me?"

"I haven't even started. Come upstairs, come upstairs with me, Zoe. I want to feel you under me. I want to feel myself inside you."

"I want to." She trembled, the needs exploding inside her like firebombs. "Coop, I need to think first.

I have to think. I haven't been with anyone in five years."

His mouth stopped its desperate journey over her throat. Slowly he drew back to look at her. Her eyes were clouded, and her mouth was swollen and ripe. "No one?"

"No." She swallowed and prayed for her system to level before she gave in to the urge to rip off his clothes and cut loose. "Since before Keenan was born. I feel like all those needs dried up—like old leaves. You've set a match to them, and I don't know how to handle it."

"The kid's father," Coop said carefully. "You're still in love with him."

"No." She might have laughed at that, if she weren't so shaken. "He has nothing to do with it. Well, of course he does, but . . . I have to sit down." She walked unsteadily to a chair. "I knew this was going to happen. I think I knew it the first time I saw you. There's been no one, because I didn't want anyone. Because Keenan was all that mattered to me. I have plans." That came out as an accusation, and her eyes darkened. "Damn it, I have plans. I want to go back to school. I want to have my own flower shop one day." Her voice began to catch, alarming him.

"Zoe—"

But she barreled right over him. "And everything was going along fine. I got the house. I wanted him to have a house, and a yard, and neighbors. Everyone said I was crazy, that I'd never be able to do it, that I'd be sorry I'd given everything up to raise a child on my own. But I'm not sorry. He's the best thing that ever happened to me. And I've done a good job. Keenan's happy, and he's bright and funny and wonderful. We have a good life, and I know I can make it even better. I haven't needed anyone. And... Oh, God, I'm in love with you."

The hand he'd lifted awkwardly to pat her head froze. "What?"

"Oh, what a mess. What a mess." She plucked a tiny sock out of the laundry basket and wiped her eyes. "Maybe it's just hormones. It could be, you know. But I walked in and you were sleeping with him on the couch. It was so sweet. Then you were kissing me and everything went crazy. Then you're out in the yard looking so smug and male, showing Keenan how to hit that silly ball. And you're eating pancakes and looking at me. I can hardly breathe when you're looking at me."

Somewhere along the line, his mind had gone blank. "I think I missed a step."

"No, you didn't." She sniffled and struggled to get herself under control. "I've just taken too many. It's my fault. You've been nice to Keenan, and you've been honest with me." She sighed, dropped the damp sock in her lap. "Believe me, I know my emotions are my responsibility." Because he was still staring at her, like a man who'd just had the friendly family dog lunge for his throat, she smiled. "I'm sorry, Coop. I shouldn't have dumped all that on you. I didn't even know it was all bottled up."

This time he took a step back. "Zoe, I like the kid. Who wouldn't? And I'm attracted to you. But—"

"There's no need to explain." Steady now, she rose. "Really, there isn't. I don't expect anything from you, and I'm sorry if I made you uncomfortable. But I feel a lot better." And, oddly enough, she did. "When I go to bed with you, we'll understand each other."

"When you—"

"I think we both know that's going to happen," she said calmly. "We both want it to, and it's smarter to face that than to live with all this tension. Keenan's been wanting to spend the night with a friend of his. I'll arrange it." She laughed a little at Coop's expression. "It's a little hard to be spontaneous with a four-year-old around. I hope you don't mind planning out a night together."

"No, I mean, I don't— God, Zoe."

"If you'd rather not, or if you want some time to decide, that's all right."

He studied her face, felt that same greedy tug, and a flare of something entirely different. Entirely new. "No, I want you. Whenever."

"How about Monday night?"

"I've got a twilight doubleheader on Monday." He couldn't believe he was standing here planning out a wild night of love like a dentist's appointment.

"Ah . . . Wednesday?"

He nodded. "Wednesday's good for me. Do you want to go out somewhere?"

It was sweet, she thought, really sweet of him to ask. "It's not necessary." She laid a hand on his cheek. "I don't need flowers and candlelight. I'll come upstairs after Keenan's settled."

"Good. Fine. I . . . better get back to work."

"Do you still want to have Keenan tomorrow?"

"Yeah, no problem. Tell him to come on up." Coop backed toward the door as Zoe began folding laundry again. "I guess I'll see you."

She listened to him walk up the steps. He was certainly a mistake, she told herself. But she'd made others. Life got too mundane when you avoided all the wrong turns.

Chapter Seven

"He shoots, he scores!" Coop made appropriate crowd noises as Keenan dunked the basket.

"I can do it again! I can, okay?" From his perch on Coop's shoulders, Keenan swung his sneakered feet.

"Okay, you've drawn the foul." Coop scooped the palm-sized ball up and passed it into Keenan's eager hands. "It's game point, kid, ten seconds to play. This free throw is all-or-nothing. Got it?"

"Got it!"

"A hush falls over the crowd as Fleming steps up to the line. He's played the game of his life tonight, but it all comes down to this one shot. He eyes the basket. You eyeing the basket?"

"Eyeing it," Keenan said, with his tongue caught between his teeth.

"He sets...and shoots." Coop winced as the little rubber ball circled the rim, then watched through squinted eyes as it tipped in and dropped through the net.

"And the crowd goes wild!" Coop danced around the sofa while Keenan hooted and clapped on his shoulders. When he dumped the boy on the cushions of the sofa, Keenan let go with one of the rolling belly laughs that always made Coop grin. "You're a natural."

"You shoot it, Coop! You!"

Obliging, Coop executed a quick turnaround jump shot. This wasn't such a bad way to spend a rainy afternoon, he decided. And it helped keep his mind off how he was going to spend the rainy night ahead.

It was Wednesday.

"Okay, time out. I've got to finish up my piece on the track meet."

"Are we going to go to the paper again? It's neat there."

"Not today. I'm going to fax it in when it's done. You watch some tube." Coop hit the remote, then handed it over.

"Can I get a drink?"

"Yeah, there's some of that juice your mom sent up for you. Stay out of trouble, right?"

"Right."

When Coop headed into his office, Keenan scrambled up from the couch. He liked it best when he got to stay with Coop after school. They always got to do something neat, and Coop never asked if he'd washed his hands or said too many cookies would spoil his appetite.

Best of all, he liked when Coop picked him up. It was different than when his mother did. He liked when she held him, nuzzled him after his bath or rocked him when he had a bad dream. But Coop smelled different, and felt different.

He knew why, Keenan thought as he wandered into the kitchen. It was because Coop was a daddy instead of a mom.

He liked to pretend Coop was his daddy, and figured that maybe if he didn't do anything bad, Coop wouldn't go away.

After a couple of tugs, Keenan had the refrigerator open. He was proud that Coop had hung the pictures he had drawn for him on the door. He peered inside, saw the jug of juice his mother had bought for him. And the green bottles Coop liked.

"*B-E-E-R,*" Keenan said to himself. He remembered that he'd asked Coop if he could have a taste from the bottle, and that Coop had told him he couldn't until he was big. After Coop had let him sniff the beer, Keenan had been glad he wasn't big yet.

There was a new bottle in the fridge today, and Keenan knit his brow and tried to recognize the letters. *C-H-A-R-D-O-N—* There were too many letters to read, so he lost interest.

He took out the jug, gripping it manfully and setting it on the floor. Humming to himself, he dragged a chair over to get cups from the cabinet. One day he'd be as tall as Coop and wouldn't need to stand on a chair. He leaned forward on his toes.

The crash and the howl had Coop leaping up, rapping his knee hard against the desk. Papers scattered as he raced out of the office and into the kitchen.

Keenan was still howling. A chair was overturned, juice was glugging cheerfully onto the floor, and the refrigerator was wide open. Coop splashed through the puddle and scooped Keenan up.

"Are you hurt? What'd you do?" When his only answer was another sob, he stood Keenan on the kitchen table and searched for blood. He imagined gaping wounds, broken bones.

"I fell down." Keenan wriggled back into Coop's arms.

"Okay, it's okay. Did you hit your head?"

"Nuh-uh." With a sniffle, Keenan waited for the kisses he expected after a hurt. "I fell on my bottom." Keenan's lip poked out. "Kiss it."

"You want me to kiss your— Come on, kid, you're joking."

The lip trembled, another tear fell. "You gotta kiss where it hurts. You gotta, or it won't get better."

"Oh, man." Flummoxed, Coop dragged a hand through his hair. He was desperately relieved that no blood had been spilled, but if anyone, anyone, found out what he was about to do, he'd never live it down. He turned Keenan around and gave the little rump a quick kiss. "Does that do it?"

"Uh-huh." Keenan knuckled his eyes, then held out his arms. "Will you pick me up?"

"Yeah." He didn't feel as ridiculous as he'd expected when the boy's arms went around his neck. "Okay now?"

With his head resting on Coop's shoulder, he nodded. "I didn't mean to do it. I spilled all the juice."

"No big deal." Hardly realizing he did so, Coop turned his head to brush his lips over Keenan's hair. Something was shifting inside him, creaking open.

"You aren't mad at me? You won't go away?"

"No." What the hell was going on? Coop wondered as unexplored and unexpected emotions swirled inside him. "No, I'm not going anywhere."

"I love you," Keenan said, with the simple ease of a child.

Coop closed his eyes and wondered how a grown man was supposed to handle falling for a four-year-old boy.

Well, here she was, Zoe thought as she stood at the bottom of the steps leading to Coop's apartment. All she had to do was go upstairs, open the door and start an affair. Her stomach clenched.

Silly to be nervous, she told herself, and climbed the first step. She was a normal woman with normal needs. If her emotions were too close to the surface, she would deal with it. It was much more difficult to be hurt when you had no expectations.

She'd had expectations once, but she knew better now.

This was simply a physical attraction between two single, healthy people. She'd nearly backed down a step before she forced herself to move forward. All the practical details had been seen to. Her son was safely tucked away for the night at his sleep-over. She'd arranged for birth control—that wasn't an oversight she would make again.

No regrets, she promised herself as she lifted a hand to knock. She knew how useless they were.

He answered so quickly, she nearly jumped. Then they stood and stared at each other.

She'd worn a dress, one of those thin, breezy sundresses designed to make a man give thanks for the end of winter. Her hair was loose, falling over thin raspberry-colored straps and bare, peach-toned shoulders. There were nerves in her eyes.

"Hi." He glanced down to the cordless phone she held. "Expecting a call?"

"What? Oh." She laughed, miserably self-conscious. "No, I just don't like to be out of touch when Keenan's not home."

"He's all settled at his pal's?"

"Yeah." She stepped inside, set the phone on the counter. "He was so excited, he—" She broke off when her sandal stuck to the floor.

Coop grimaced. "I guess I missed some of it. We had a spill."

"Oh?"

"The kid took a tumble, sheared off ten years of my life. No blood lost, though. Just a half gallon of orange juice." When she only smiled, he stepped to the refrigerator. Why in hell was he babbling? "Want some wine?"

"That would be nice." *Why, he's as nervous as I am,* she realized, and she loved him for it. "Keenan's having a wonderful time staying with you. I have to study the sports pages now just to keep up with what he's talking about."

"He catches on fast."

"So do I. Go ahead," she said as he handed her a glass of wine, "Ask me about stats. I know all about RBIs and ERAs." She took a sip, then gestured with her glass. "I think the Orioles would have taken the second game of that doubleheader the other night if they'd put in a relief pitcher in the second inning."

His lips twitched. "Do you?"

"Well, the starter had lost his stuff, obviously. The guy who was announcing—"

"The play-by-play man."

"Yes, he said so himself."

"So, you watched the game."

"I watch 'Sesame Street,' too. I like to keep up with Keenan's interests." She trailed off when Coop reached out to twine a lock of her hair around his finger.

"He's got a thing for dinosaurs, too."

"I know, I've checked a half dozen books out of the library. We've—" The fingers trailed over her shoulder. "We've been down to the natural history museum twice."

She set the glass aside and fell into his arms.

He kissed her as though he'd been starved for her taste. The impact was fast, deep, desperate. The little purring sounds that vibrated in her throat had his muscles turning into bundles of taut wire.

"I wasn't sure you'd come."

"Neither was I. I—"

"Can't think of anything but you," he said as he swept her off her feet. "I thought we'd take this slow."

"Let's not," she murmured, pressing her lips to his throat as he carried her into the bedroom.

She had a quick impression of Spartan neatness and simple masculine colors and lines before they tumbled onto the bed.

Neither of them was looking for patience. They rolled together, a tangle of limbs grasping, groping, glorying. The sheer physicality of it, flesh to flesh, mouth to mouth, had Zoe's head reeling. Oh, she wanted to be touched like this, to feel so desperately like a woman, with a man's hand streaking over her, with his lips savoring every thud of her pulse.

So she lost herself. No more nerves, no more fears. And if she loved, it only made the joy of mating more lovely.

She was every man's fantasy. Stunningly responsive, breathlessly aggressive. And so beautiful, he thought. Undraped, the exquisite body was so slim, so perfect, he couldn't believe it had ever carried a child. In the gilded light of dusk, her face was elegant, heartstopping. Whenever he touched, wherever he touched, he could see the bold echo of her pleasure reflected in her eyes.

He watched those eyes glaze over, felt her body tense, heard her strangled cry of release. Swamped with the power of it, he drove her upward again until they were both panting for air, until she reared up from the bed and wrapped herself around him.

Damp skin slid over damp skin, hungry mouth sought hungry mouth. They rolled over the bed again, moaning, quivering. Then his hands gripped hers, and his mouth crushed her mouth. And he thrust inside her, hard and deep.

She felt the sensation as if it were a lance through her system, painful, glorious. For an instant, neither of them moved, they just stayed tensed and shuddering on the edge.

Then it was all movement, all speed, a wild race that ended with them both plunging deliriously over the finish line.

It wasn't exactly the way he'd imagined, Coop thought. They were sprawled across his bed, Zoe curled against him. The light was nearly gone, and the room was full of shadows.

He'd imagined they would progress to the bedroom by stages. They were both adults and had known that was the ultimate goal, but he'd thought they would move slowly.

Then she'd been standing there smiling, the nerves shining in her eyes . . . He'd never wanted anything or anyone more in his life.

Still, he thought she deserved more than a quick tussle, however rewarding. But the night was young.

He flexed his arm to bring her head a little closer, brushed his lips over her temple. "Okay?"

"Mmm... At the very least." Her body felt golden. She was surprised her skin didn't glow in the dark.

"I rushed you a little."

"No, perfect timing."

He began to trail a finger up and down her arm. He wanted her again. Good God, his system was already churning to life. A little control, Coop, he ordered himself. "You're going to stay?"

She opened her eyes, looking into his. "Yes."

"I'm going to go get the wine."

"That's good." She sighed as he left the bed. She'd forgotten how to deal with the after, she realized. Or with the before and during, for that matter, she thought with a wry smile. Though she thought she'd done pretty well so far.

She hadn't known how much had been bottled up inside her. Or just how much she'd needed to feel like a woman again. But then, she hadn't known she could love again.

She shifted, slipping under the tangled sheets, automatically lifting them to her breasts when Coop came back with the wine and glasses.

The sight of her in his bed shot to his loins, with a quick detour through the heart. He said nothing, pouring wine, offering her a fresh glass and settling beside her.

"Why haven't you been with anyone?" The moment the question was out, he wished for a rusty knife to hack off his tongue. "Sorry, none of my business."

"It's all right." Because I haven't fallen in love with anyone before you, she thought. But that wasn't what he wanted to hear, she knew. Nor was it really what he'd asked.

"You want to know about Keenan's father."

"None of my business," he repeated. "Sorry, it's the reporter in me."

"It was a long time ago—a lifetime ago. I don't mind telling you. I grew up in New York. I think I mentioned that my mother's an actress. I was the result of a second marriage. She's had five. So far."

"Five?"

Zoe chuckled into her wine, sipped. "Clarice falls in love and changes husbands the way some women change hairstyles. My father lasted about four years before they parted amicably. Clarice always has friendly divorces. I didn't see much of him, because he moved to Hollywood. He does commercials and voice-overs mostly. Anyway, I think she was on husband number four when I was in high school. He had some pull with the Towers Modeling Agency. They're pretty big."

"I've heard of them."

"Well, he got me in. I started doing some shoots. And I caught on."

"That's it," Coop said, interrupting her. "I knew I'd seen your face before."

She moved her shoulders. "Five, six years ago, it was hard to avoid it. I did twenty covers in one month, the year after I graduated school."

"Cover of *In Sports,* swimsuit edition."

She smiled. "You've got a good memory. That was six years ago."

He remembered the long, sand-dusted legs, the lush wet red excuse for a bathing suit, the laughing, seductive face. He gulped down wine. "It was a hell of a shot."

"And a long, grueling shoot. Anyway, I was making a lot of money, getting a lot of press, going to lots of parties. I met Roberto at one of them."

"Roberto." Coop grimaced at the sound of the name.

"Lorenzi. Tennis player. You might have heard of him."

"Lorenzi? Sure—took the French Open three years ago in straight sets, then blew Wimbledon in the semis. He's got a bad attitude and likes to race cars and chase women on the side. Hasn't been seeded above twenty-fifth in the last two years. Got some bad press this spring when he tipped back too many vinos and punched out a photographer." Coop started to drink, stopped. "Lorenzi? He's Keenan's father? But he's—"

"A womanizer?" Zoe supplied. "A creep, a rich, spoiled egotist? I know—now. What I saw then was a gorgeous, charming man who sent me roses and jetted me off to Monte Carlo for intimate dinners. I was dazzled. He told me he loved me, that he adored me, worshiped me, he couldn't live without me. I believed him, and we became lovers. I thought, since he was my first, he'd be my only. Anyway, I didn't realize he was already getting tired of me when I found out I was pregnant. When I told him, he was angry, then he was very calm, very reasonable. He assumed I'd want an abortion and agreed to pay all the expenses, even to make the arrangements.''

"A real prince."

"It was a logical assumption," Zoe said calmly. "I had a career on fast forward, in a field that wouldn't wait while I put on weight and suffered from morning sickness. He, of course, had no intention of marrying me, and thought, rightly enough, that I knew the rules of the game. I did know them," she said quietly. "But something had changed when the doctor confirmed the pregnancy. After the disbelief, the panic, even the anger, I felt good. I felt right. I wanted the baby, so I quit my job, moved away from New York and read everything I could get my hands on about parenting."

"Just like that?"

"Well, there were some scenes, some dire predictions, and a lot of anger, but that's how it worked. Roberto and I parted less than amicably, but with the agreement that he would stay out of my life and I would stay out of his."

"What have you told Keenan?"

"It's tough." And it never failed to make her feel guilty. "So far I've just told him his father had to go away, that he wasn't going to come back. He's happy, so he doesn't ask a lot of questions."

"Are you? Happy?"

"Yes." She smiled and touched his cheek. "I am. All my life I wanted a home, a family, something solid and settled. I didn't even know it until Keenan. He changed my life."

"No urge to go back and smile for the camera?"

"Oh, no. Not even a twinge."

He cupped a hand behind her neck, studying her. "It's such a face," he murmured. Right now he liked the idea of having it all to himself.

Chapter Eight

The concept of car pools obviously had been devised by someone with a foul and vicious sense of humor. Having lived most of his life in cities where public transportation or a quick jog would get a man from his home to his office, Coop had never experienced the adult version.

But he'd heard rumors.

Arguments, petty feuds, crowded conditions, spilled coffee.

After a week as designated driver, Coop had no doubt the kiddie version was worse. Infinitely worse.

"He's pinching me again, Mr. McKinnon. Brad's pinching me."

"Cut it out, Brad."

"Carly's looking at me. I told her to stop looking at me."

"Carly, don't look at Brad."

"I'm going to be sick. Mr. McKinnon, I'm going to be sick right now."

"No, you're not."

Though Matthew Finney made gagging noises that had the other kids screeching, Coop gritted his teeth and kept driving. Matt threatened to be sick twice a day unless he rode in the front seat. After five miserable days Coop had his number. But that did very little to soothe his nerves.

Keenan, who had waited all week for his turn in the front, swiveled in his seat to make monster faces at Matt. This incited a small riot of elbow jabs, howls, screaming giggles and shoves.

"Keenan, turn around!" Coop snapped. "You guys straighten up back there. Cut it out! If I have to stop this car..." He trailed off, shuddered. He'd sounded like his own mother. Now Coop was afraid *he* would be sick. "Okay, first stop. Matt, scram."

Fifteen minutes later, his back seat thankfully empty, Coop pulled into the drive and rested his throbbing head on the steering wheel. "I need a drink."

"We got lemonade," Keenan told him.

"Great." He reached over to unbuckle Keenan's seat belt. All he needed was a pint of vodka to go with it.

"Can we go swimming again soon?"

The idea of taking a herd of screaming kids back to the community pool anytime within the next century had a stone lodging in Coop's heart. "Ask your mother."

Coop started to look in the back seat and realized he couldn't face it. Earlier in the week he'd made that mistake, and discovered wads of chewing gum on the rug, cookie crumbs everywhere, and a mysterious green substance smeared on the seat.

In his weakened state, even a candy wrapper was likely to tip the balance.

"Yoo-hoo!" Mrs. Finkleman stripped off her flowered garden gloves and headed across the lawn in a flowing tent dress and electric-blue sandals. "How was your swim, little man?"

"We had races, and Brad dunked Carly and made her cry even though Coop told him not to, and I can hold my breath underwater for twelve seconds."

"My goodness." She laughed and ruffled Keenan's hair. "You'll be in the Olympics next." Her shrewd eyes took in Coop's haggard face. "You look a little frazzled, Coop. Keenan, why don't you run in and tell Mr. Finkleman you want a piece of that cherry cobbler he baked today?"

"Okay!" He tugged on Coop's hand. "Do you want some? Do you wanna come?"

"I'll pass. You go ahead."

Mrs. Finkleman chuckled as Keenan darted away and scrambled up the steps. "Little angel. We'll keep him entertained for a couple of hours—or he'll keep us entertained. You look like you could use a few minutes in a quiet room."

"Padded room," Coop muttered. "How does anyone survive kids?"

"It's easier if you go through the stages with them. Once you've walked the floor all night with a colicky baby, nothing much fazes you." She sighed. "Except science projects. Science projects always took me to the edge. And that first driving lesson." She shook her head at the memory. "That can bring you to your knees." She beamed and patted his arm. "But there's years yet to worry about that. And you've been doing a fine job. Why, Harry and I were just saying how nice it is that Zoe and Keenan have a man in their lives. Not that Zoe hasn't been handling everything. Raising that sweet-natured boy all alone, and working two jobs and tending the house. But it does my heart good to see you and that little angel playing ball in the yard, or the way Zoe lights up when you're around. You make a lovely little family. Now, you go and take a nice nap. We'll keep an eye on your boy."

"I'm not— He's not—" But even as Coop stammered, she was drifting away.

Family? he thought as a ball of ice formed in his stomach. They weren't a family. Oh, no, he promised himself as he walked around the house to his steps. He hadn't taken that on.

He liked the kid, sure. What wasn't to like? And he was damn near nuts about the mother. But that didn't make them a family. That didn't make things permanent. Maybe he'd volunteered to spend time with the kid, taught him a few things about ball, pitched him a few, but that didn't make him Daddy.

He headed straight for the refrigerator, popped the top off a beer and took a long pull.

Sure, maybe he enjoyed having the kid around, and Lord knows he enjoyed being with Zoe. He'd even been sort of pleased when a woman at the pool mistook Keenan for his and commented on what a handsome son he had. But that didn't mean he was going to start thinking about family health insurance or college funds.

He was single. He liked being single. It meant coming and going as he pleased, planning all-night poker games, spending all day with the sports channel blaring.

He liked working in his own space—that was why he did the bulk of his writing at home, rather than at the paper. He didn't like people messing with his things or structuring his time or planning outings.

Family life—as he remembered from his childhood—was lousy with outings.

No way was he changing his nice comfortable existence to accommodate a family.

So he'd made a mistake, Coop decided, and stretched out on the couch with his beer. He'd given Zoe and the kid a little too much of his time, a little too much of his attention. It hadn't been anything he didn't want to give, but he could see now that the gesture could be misconstrued. Particularly since Zoe had once brought up the *L* word. Only once, he reminded himself, and he'd like to think that had just been a woman thing.

Still, if he didn't back off, they might start to depend on him. He shifted uncomfortably as the idea flitted through his mind that he might also come to depend on them.

It was time to reestablish himself as the tenant upstairs.

* * *

Keenan raced out of the house next door the minute his mother pulled her car in the drive.

"Hi, Mama, hi! I held my breath for twelve seconds underwater!"

Zoe caught him on the fly and swung him twice. "You must be hiding gills in there," she said, tickling his ribs. "Hi, Mrs. Finkleman."

"Hi yourself. We've had ourselves a fine hour. I sent Coop up for a nap when they got home. He looked like he'd had a rough day."

"Thanks." She kissed Keenan's waiting lips, then smacked her own. "Mmm... Cherries."

"Mr. Finkleman baked them, and they were good."

"I bet. Did you say thank you?"

"Uh-huh. Matt almost throwed up in Coop's car."

"Threw up," Zoe said as she carried Keenan inside.

"Uh-huh. 'Cause it was my turn to ride in the front. I had the best time, and Coop helped me to swim without my bubbles. He said I was a champ."

"That's just what you are." She collapsed with him on a chair. The idea of fixing dinner, changing into her uniform and serving drinks for six hours loomed heavily. "Give me a hug," she demanded, then soothed herself with some nuzzling. "Definitely a champion hugger. Why don't you come in the kitchen and tell me what else you did today while I fix dinner?"

A half hour later, as Zoe was draining pasta and Keenan was entertaining himself with crayons and paper on the kitchen floor, she heard the sound of Coop's feet on the stairs. Her heart sped up. The normal, healthy reaction made her smile. Imagine, she thought, believing herself immune to men.

She left the pasta draining in the sink and went to the back door just as he came to the foot of the steps.

"Hi."

"How's it going?" Coop jingled the keys in his pocket. Did she look all lit up? he wondered. She was smiling, and despite the shadows of fatigue under them, her eyes did have the prettiest lights in them.

"I was just going to call upstairs. I thought you'd like some dinner after a hard day at the pool." She opened the screen door and leaned out to kiss him. The smile dimmed a bit when he eased back. "It's just chicken and pasta."

It smelled nearly as good as she did. He glanced inside—the homey scene, cluttered counters, fresh flowers, steam rising from a pan on the stove, the child sprawled on the floor, the pretty woman offering him food and kisses.

A definite trap.

"Thanks, but I'm on my way out."

"Oh. I thought you had a couple hours before game time." She laughed at his arched brow. "I guess I've been paying more attention to the sports scene. Baltimore versus Toronto, game one of three."

"Yeah." When she starts to take an interest in *your* interests, she's really shutting the cage door. "I've got some stuff to do."

"Can I go with you?" Keenan dashed to the door to tug on Coop's slacks. "Can I go to the game? I like watching them with you best."

Coop could almost hear the locks clicking into place. "I've got too much to do," he said, with an edge to his voice that had Keenan's lips quivering. "Look, it's not just a game, it's my job."

"You said I was good luck."

"Keenan." Zoe put her hand on her son's shoulder to draw him back, but her eyes stayed on Coop's. "Did you forget Beth was coming over to stay with you tonight? She'll be here soon, and you're going to watch a tape of your favorite movie."

"But I wanna—"

"Now go wash your hands for dinner."

"But—"

"Go on now."

The way Keenan's face crumpled would have softened an ogre's heart. Dragging his feet, he headed out of the kitchen.

"I can't take him with me everywhere...." Coop began defensively.

"Of course not. He's just overtired. I couldn't have let him go, in any case." She hesitated, wishing she could ignore her instincts. "Is everything all right?"

"Everything's fine." He didn't know why he shouted it. He didn't know why he felt like something slimy stuck to the bottom of a shoe. "I have a life, you know. I don't need kids climbing up my back or you fixing me dinner. And I don't have to explain myself."

Her eyes turned very cool, her face very composed. "You certainly don't. I appreciate you helping me out the past couple of weeks. Let me know if I can return the favor."

"Look, Zoe—"

"I've got to get dinner on the table, or I'll be late for work." She let the screen door slam between them. "Enjoy the game."

She knew exactly how long he continued to stand there while she worked at the stove. Knew exactly when he turned and walked away.

It wasn't unexpected, she reminded herself. This backing away was typical, even understandable. Perhaps it had taken Coop a few weeks to completely comprehend that she didn't come as a single. She was part of a pair, a ready-made family, with its share of responsibilities and problems and routines.

And he was opting out.

He might not even know it yet, she thought, but he was in the first stages of a full retreat.

Her eyes blurred, her chest heaved. Resolutely she choked the tears back. She would indulge herself with a nice long cry later, she promised. But for now she had a little boy to soothe.

When he came back in, she crouched down until they were eye-to-eye.

"You had a good time with Coop today, didn't you?"

Keenan sniffled, nodded.

"And he's taken you a lot of places. You've had fun, and done a lot of new things."

"I know."

"You should be grateful for that, baby, instead of pouting because you can't have more."

She straightened again and hoped she could take her own advice.

Chapter Nine

"You're spending a lot of time around here." Ben edged a hip onto the corner of Coop's desk. All around Coop's cubicle phones rang, keyboards clattered.

"So?" Without taking his eyes from the computer screen, Coop hammered out the draft of his weekly column.

"I just figured you had it made in that apartment of yours. I mean, great location." He thought of Zoe. "Great view. You didn't spend as much time in here when you lived downtown."

"I needed a change of scene."

"Yeah." Ben snorted and picked up a baseball from Coop's desk. "Trouble in paradise?"

"I don't know what you're talking about. And I've got a column to write."

"Pretty obvious the last few weeks that you've been stuck on the landlady." He tossed the ball from one hand to the other. "I mean, when a man hauls a kid around, buys little baseball jerseys, it follows that he's hooking a line into Mom."

Coop's eyes flashed up. "I like the kid, okay? I don't have to use a four-year-old to get a woman. The kid's cool."

"Hey, I got nothing against rug rats. Might even have a few of my own one day. The thing is, when a woman's got one, a man has to play Daddy if he wants the inside track."

"Who says I have to play at anything to get a woman?"

"Not me. But it was you who couldn't shoot hoop last week because you were taking the family to the aquarium." Ben winked, set the ball down. "Still, I bet you scored better than I did." Ben jerked back as Coop lunged for his throat.

"It's not like that," Coop said between his teeth.

"Hey, hey. Just yanking your chain. I wouldn't have made any cracks if I'd known you were serious about her."

Coop's grip loosened. "I didn't say I was serious. I said it wasn't like that."

"Whatever you say."

Disgusted with himself, Coop dropped back in his chair. He and Ben had been riding each other about women for better than five years. No reason to over-react, he thought. Or to make a fool of himself. "Sorry. I've got a lot on my mind."

"Forget it. What you need's a distraction. You coming to the poker game tonight?"

"Yeah."

"Good. Losing money should put you back on track."

Something had to, Coop thought as he sat back alone in his cubicle to stare at his screen. For the past three days he'd slept little, eaten less, and gone around in a constant state of flux.

Because he was avoiding the issue, he decided. Opting to bunt, when he should be swinging away. The only solution to getting his life back in order was to face the problem head-on.

He flicked off his terminal.

The beautiful thing about an afternoon off, Zoe thought, was the solitude. No customers to talk to, no orders to fill. It meant she didn't have to be sales-clerk, or waitress, or Mom, or anything but Zoe.

Sitting on the back stoop, she struggled to under-stand the assembly instructions for the new barbecue grill she'd bought. She was going to surprise Keenan with hamburgers.

She liked the quiet—her kind of quiet, which meant there was music throbbing from the kitchen radio. She liked the loneliness—her kind of loneliness, which meant Keenan would dash toward her shortly with open arms and chattering voice.

She knew the upstairs apartment was empty, and she tried not to think about that. Tried not to think about the fact that Coop had been away more than he'd been home in the last few days.

Foolish of her to have thought he was different. He'd wanted her, he'd had her, and now he'd lost in-terest. Well, she had wanted him, so they were even there. If her heart was suffering it would pass. It had passed before. She and Keenan could get along fine on their own. Just like always.

Her screwdriver slipped, scraped her knuckles, had her swearing.

"What the hell are you doing?"

Eyes hot, she looked up at Coop. "Baking a cake. What does it look like I'm doing?"

"You can't put something together if you're going to spread parts all over the damn place." Automatically he bent down to organize. She rapped his hand away with the rubber grip of the screwdriver.

"I don't need you to put things together for me. I'm not some poor helpless female who needs a man to pick up the slack. I managed just fine before you came along."

Stung, he rammed his hands in his pockets. "Fine. Do it yourself."

"I am doing it myself. I like doing it myself."

"Terrific. And when the thing topples over, you won't have anyone else to blame."

"That's right." She blew her hair out of her eyes. "I accept when something's my fault." She picked up a wrench and locked a bolt in place. "Do you plan to hover over me all afternoon?"

"I want to talk to you."

"So talk."

He had it well planned. He was a writer, after all. "I realize the way I've been hanging around with you and the kid—"

"His name is Keenan," Zoe said between her teeth.

"I know what his name is. The way I've been hanging around the last few weeks might give the wrong impression."

"Oh, really?" She looked up again, tapping the wrench against her palm.

"He's a great kid, he kind of grows on you. I've gotten a kick out of spending time with him."

Though she hated herself for it, Zoe softened. She understood that he was genuinely fond of Keenan. That only made it all the more difficult. "He likes spending time with you. It's been good for him."

"Well, yeah, on the one hand. On the other, I started thinking that he—that you—that both of you might get the wrong idea. I mean, tossing a ball around or taking him to a game, that's cool. I just don't want him thinking it's like—permanent."

"I see." She was calm now, frigidly so. It would help keep the hurt in check. "You're afraid he might begin to see you as a father figure."

"Well, yeah. Kind of."

"That's natural enough. But then, he spends a lot of time with Mr. Finkleman, too, and with Billy Bowers down the street."

"Finkleman's old enough to be his grandfather, and the Bowers kid is eighteen." Coop backed off, realizing there was a touch of jealousy in the defense. "And they don't have the same sort of thing going with you."

She arched both brows. "Thing?"

"Relationship," he said tightly. "Whatever the hell you want to call it. Damn it, we only slept together once."

"I'm aware of that." Carefully she set the wrench aside. It would give her only momentary pleasure to heave it at his head.

"That came out wrong," he said, furious with himself. "It sounded like it didn't mean anything. It did, Zoe." A great deal, he was afraid. A very great deal. "It's just that . . ."

"Now you're terrified that Keenan and I will trap you into a family. That you'll wake up one morning and be Daddy, with a wife and a mortgage and a small boy who needs attention."

"Yes. No. Something like that." He was burying himself, he realized, and he suddenly didn't know why. "I just want to make myself clear."

"Oh, I think you have. Perfectly." She rubbed her hands on her knees as she studied him. "You needn't worry, Coop. I advertised for a tenant, not a father for my child, or a husband for myself. I slept with you because I wanted to, not because I thought I could lure you to the altar."

"I didn't mean it like that." Frustrated, he dragged a hand through his hair. However well he'd planned this little scene, it was going all wrong. "I wanted you. I still do. But I know how badly you were let down before. I don't want to hurt you, Zoe. Or the kid. I just don't want you thinking I'd slide into the gap."

The anger came back, one swift wave of it that reddened her vision. She was on her feet before either of them realized she'd moved. "Keenan and I don't have a gap. We're a family, as real and as complete and as full a family as any could be." She jabbed the wrench at his chest. "Just because Daddy doesn't make three doesn't mean we're less of a unit."

"I didn't mean—"

"I'll tell you what you mean. You see a woman and a small boy and you think they're just pining away for some big strong man to come along and fulfill them. Well, that's bull. If I needed a man, I'd have one. And if I thought Keenan needed a father to make him happy, I'd find him one. And," she continued, advancing and giving him another jab, "if you think you're at the head of some fictional list, you're wrong. Maybe I'm in love with you, but that's not enough. It's not just me, and it's not just you. Keenan comes first. When and if I want a father for Keenan, he'll be someone with compassion and patience, someone willing to adjust his life to make room for my son. So relax, Cooper. You're in the clear."

"I didn't come here to fight with you."

"Good, because I'm finished."

He grabbed her arm before she could turn away. "I haven't. I'm trying to be straight with you, Zoe. I care about you, okay? About both of you. I just don't want it to get out of hand."

"Out of whose hands?" she retorted. "Yours? Then that's no problem, is it? Because you know how to hold on to everything inside, really tight. Just keep holding on to it, Coop. Don't worry about me or about Keenan. We'll be fine." She jerked her arm free and sat again. Picking up the instruction sheet, she gave it her full attention.

Now why, he wondered, did he feel as though he'd just been rejected? Shaking his head, Coop took a step in retreat. "As long as we're clear."

"We are."

"I've, ah, got a little time, if you want me to help you put that grill together."

"No thanks. I can do it." She slanted him a look. "I'm going to grill burgers later. You're welcome to join us. Unless you're afraid it will lead to a commitment."

She shoots, he thought wryly, she scores. "Thanks anyway. I've got plans. Maybe I could take a rain check."

"Fine. You know where to find us."

He got drunk. Not sloppily, but thoroughly. When Coop poured himself out of the cab and staggered toward the house, he already knew he'd hate himself in the morning. But it was tonight he had to deal with.

He leaned heavily against Zoe's front door and waited for the porch to settle down under his feet. She might think they'd finished, he told himself blearily, but she was wrong. Dead wrong.

He'd thought of a dozen things he had to say to her.

There was no time like the present.

Lifting a fist, he pounded on the door. "Come on, Zoe." He pounded again. "I know you're in there." He saw a light flick on inside and kept on pounding. "Come on, come on. Open up."

"Coop?" From the other side of the door, Zoe belted her hastily donned robe. She'd been home from the lounge for barely twenty minutes, and in bed for less than five. "It's after two o'clock in the morning. What do you want?"

"I want to talk to you. Let me in."

"We'll talk in the morning."

"You just said it was morning."

When he pounded again, she flicked off the locks. "Stop that—you'll wake Keenan." Furious, she yanked open the door and had the surprise of a hundred-and-seventy-pound male tumbling against her. "Are you hurt? What happened?" The alarm signals that had screamed on shifted when she caught the scent of beer. "You're drunk."

"Mostly." He started to straighten, then lost himself in the smell of her. "God, you feel good. What d'you wash this in?" He nuzzled her hair. "Smells like moonbeams."

"Really drunk," she said with a sigh. "Sit down. I'll get you some coffee."

"Don't want coffee. Doesn't sober you up, only wakes you up. And I'm awake, and I have something to say to you." He drew away then, and discovered he wasn't as steady as he'd hoped. "But I'll sit down." He did, heavily. "Hate getting drunk. Haven't done it like this since I played minor league. Did I tell you I played minor league ball? Triple A.''

"No." Baffled, she stood her ground and watched him.

"Right out of high school. Two years. Thought I'd make it to the show. The majors. But I didn't, so I went to college, and now I write about people who did."

"I'm sorry."

"No." He waved that away. "I like writing. Always did. Like watching the games and seeing all the little dramas. If I'd've played, I'd be nearly washed up now. I'm almost thirty-three. Old man for the game." He focused on her, smiled. "You're the most beautiful woman I've ever seen in my life. You know, the kid looks just like you. Look at him, see you. It's spooky. I see you all the time. Minding my own business, and pop! There's your face in my head. What d'ya make of that?"

"I don't know." She wanted to be angry with him, really she did. But he was so foolishly drunk. "Why don't I take you upstairs, Coop? Put you to bed."

"I want you in my bed, Zoe. I want to make love with you. I want to touch you again."

She wanted that, too. Very much. But new lines had been drawn. "You said you wanted to talk to me."

"Do you know what your skin feels like? I can't describe it, it's all soft and smooth and warm. I started thinking about your skin when I was playing poker and getting drunk tonight. I won, too. Took a big pot with a pair of sixes. Pulled in over two hundred and fifty dollars.''

"Congratulations."

"But I kept thinking about you. You have this little dimple right here." He nearly poked himself in the eye, then dragged a finger down his cheek to the corner of his mouth. "I kept thinking about that little dimple, and your skin, and those big eyes and killer legs. And I kept thinking how I like to watch you with the kid, like I do sometimes from upstairs, when you don't know. Didn't know that, did you?"

"No," she said quietly. "I didn't."

"Well, see…" He gestured wildly. "You've got this way of running your hand over his hair. It gets to me." He shook his head. "It really gets to me. Keenan loves me, you know. He told me he did. So did you."

"I know."

"And I meant everything I said this afternoon."

"I know." Sighing, she walked over to undo his shoelaces.

"Every word, Zoe. I've got my life set, just like I want it."

"Okay." She pried off his shoes, hefted his legs onto the couch.

"So you can stop popping into my head, 'cause it's not changing anything."

"I'll keep that in mind."

He was asleep before she bent over and kissed his cheek.

Chapter Ten

As hangovers went, Coop knew, this would be a champ. He didn't have to open his eyes, he didn't have to move, not when his head was already beating like the army drum corps.

He wasn't sure how he'd managed to get home and into bed, but the blur of the evening wasn't comforting. Still, he thought it best to wait to tax his brain.

Cautious, close to fearful, he opened his eyes. The little face directly above him had him jerking back, then moaning at the pain.

"Good morning," Keenan said cheerfully. "Did you sleep over?"

"I don't know." Coop lifted a hand to his head. "Where's your mother?"

"She's making my lunch. She said I could come in and look at you if I didn't wake you up. I didn't wake you up, did I? I was really quiet."

"No." Coop closed his eyes again and prayed for oblivion.

"Are you sick? Do you have a tempature?" Keenan laid a small, light hand on Coop's aching forehead. "Mama can make it better. She always makes it better." Very gently, Keenan replaced his hand with a kiss. "Does that help?"

Oh, hell, Coop thought. Even a hangover didn't have a chance against this kid. "Yeah, thanks. What time is it?"

"The big hand's on the ten and the little hand's on the eight. You can sleep in my bed until you're better, and play with my toys."

"Thanks." Coop made the supreme effort and sat up. When his head rolled, he did his best to catch it in his hands. "Keenan, be a pal and ask your mom for some aspirin."

"Okay." He raced off, and the sound of his sneakers pounding the floor had Coop shuddering.

"Headache?" Zoe asked a moment later.

Coop lifted his head. She was still in her robe. The robe he remembered from the night before. He was beginning to remember quite a bit from the night before. "If you're going to yell at me, could you do it later?"

In answer, she held out aspirin and a glass filled with reddish liquid.

"What is it?"

"A remedy from Joe the bartender. He guarantees it'll take the edge off."

"Thanks."

There was a blast of a horn from outside that cut through Coop's skull like a dulled knife. While he was dealing with the shock of that, Keenan came racing back.

"Bye, Mama, bye!" He gave her a smacking kiss, then turned to hug Coop. "Bye."

As the door slammed behind him, Coop gulped down Joe's remedy.

"Do you want coffee?" Zoe ran her tongue around her teeth and tried not to smile. "Some breakfast?"

"You're not going to yell at me?"

"For barging in here, drunk, in the middle of the night? And for passing out on my sofa?" She paused just long enough to make her point. "No, I'm not going to yell at you. I figure you're suffering enough."

"I am, I promise you." He got up to follow her into the kitchen. "Not just physically. I feel like a total jerk."

"You *were* a total jerk." She poured a mug of coffee, set it on the table for him. "My mother's third husband had a fondness for bourbon. He swore eggs the morning after were the cure. How do you want them?"

"Scrambled would be good." He sat gingerly at the table. "I'm sorry, Zoe."

She kept her back to him. "For?"

"For being a jackass yesterday afternoon, and a bigger jackass last night."

"Oh, that." With the bacon frying, she chose a small bowl to scramble eggs in. "I don't imagine it's the first or the last time you'll be one."

"You didn't..." He shifted miserably. "Ah, you didn't tell Keenan I was..."

"Drunk and disorderly?" A half smile on her face, she glanced over her shoulder. "I told him you weren't feeling well and went to sleep on the couch. Which was close enough."

"Thanks. I wouldn't want him to think...you know. I don't make a habit out of it."

"So you said last night." She turned the bacon, whipped the eggs.

He watched her, gradually getting past the astonishment that she wasn't going to rub his nose in the mess he'd made of things. Remembering the afternoon before, when she'd stood up to him with all that pride and fury shining in her eyes. And the other night, when he'd fallen asleep on her couch—the way she'd looked when she slipped the boy from his arms into hers and carried him into bed.

A dozen other pictures, captured in so short a time, flitted through his head, until they were whittled down to one. This one. Zoe standing at the stove, with the morning sun streaming over her tousled hair, her robe flowing down, breakfast smells warming the room.

How could he have thought he didn't want this? Just this. And what did he do now that he knew the truth?

"Food should help." She set the plate in front of him. "I've got to get ready for work."

"Can you— Have you got a minute?"

"I suppose." She poured herself another cup of coffee. "I don't have to be in until ten."

He began to eat while thoughts scrambled in his brain. "This is good. Thanks."

"You're welcome." She leaned back against the counter. "Did you want something else?"

"Yeah." He ate more, hoping eggs equaled courage. Then he put his fork down. It was the ninth inning, he thought, and there were already two outs. "You. I want you."

She smiled a little. "Coop, I doubt you're in any shape for that, and I really have to go to work, so—"

"No, I don't mean that. I mean I do, but not—" He broke off, took a long, deep breath. "I want you to marry me."

"I beg your pardon?"

"I think you should marry me. It's a good idea." Somewhere in the back of his mind, he realized, he'd been working on this all along. He had it figured. "You can quit your night job and go back to school if you want. Or open that flower shop. Whatever. I think that's what we should do."

"Really." Because her hand was unsteady, she set her coffee down. "Well that's very generous of you, Coop, but I don't have to get married to do any of those things. So thanks just the same."

He stared. "No? You're saying no? But you love me. You said it. Twice you said it."

"We can make it three," she said evenly. "Yes, I love you. No, I won't marry you. Now I really have to get ready for work."

"Just a damn minute." Hangover forgotten, he pushed back from the table and rose. "What kind of game is this? You love me, your kid's crazy about me, we're terrific in bed, I even know how to drive a damn car pool, but you won't marry me."

"You're such an idiot. You're such a fool. Do you think because I didn't put up a struggle before I fell into your bed that you can have everything your own way? When you want it, how you want it? Well, you're wrong. And you *are* a jackass."

He winced as she stormed from the room. Strike one, he thought. And he hadn't even seen the pitch.

But the game wasn't over, he thought grimly, until the fat lady sang.

Zoe was still steaming when she came home from work. Of all the arrogant, interfering, self-absorbed idiots she'd ever known, J. Cooper McKinnon took the gold medal. Imagine him telling her that marrying him was a good idea, then ticking off all the advantages she'd gain.

Oh, he thought he was a prize.

One day he's telling her to get any ideas of sneaking him into a relationship out of her head. As if she'd been baiting traps for him. The next he's taking pity on her and offering her a big male helping hand.

She should have bitten it off.

Not once, not once had he said what she would bring to him, what he felt for her, what he wanted. Not once had he brought up the fact that he could or would accept another man's child as his own.

She jerked open the front door, slammed it. He could take his half-baked proposal and sit on it.

"Mama! Hey, Mama!" Keenan zipped into the living room and grabbed her hand. "Come on, come on. We've got a surprise."

"What surprise? What are you doing home, Keenan? You're supposed to be at the Finklemans'."

"Coop's here." He tugged manfully on her hand. "We have a surprise. And we have a secret. And you have to come *now!*"

"All right, I'm coming." She braced herself and let Keenan drag her into the kitchen.

There were flowers, banks of them, vases and baskets overflowing on the counters, on the floor, on the windowsills. There was music, some soft, dreamy classical sonata, on the radio. The table was set, crystal she'd never seen before glinting in the sunlight, a bottle of champagne chilling in a silver bucket. And Coop was standing there, in a neatly pressed shirt and slacks.

"It's a surprise," Keenan announced gleefully. "We made everything look nice so you'd like it. And Mrs. Finkleman said we could use the glasses and the plates. And Mr. Finkleman made his special chicken 'cause it's resistible."

"Irresistible," Coop said, his eyes on Zoe. "You, ah, said you didn't need flowers and candlelight, but

I've never taken you out on a date. I thought this was the next-best thing."

"Do you like it, Mama? Do you?"

"Yes, it's very nice." She bent down to kiss Keenan. "Thank you."

"I get to go to the Finklemans' so you can have romance."

"Ah, come on, kid." Coop scooped Keenan up. "Let's get you started. You were supposed to keep quiet about it," he muttered when he carried the boy outside.

"What's romance?"

"I'll tell you later."

Satisfied with that, Keenan draped his arm around Coop's neck. "Are you gonna tell Mama the secret about us all getting married?"

"That's the plan."

"And you'll live with us and you can be my Daddy and that'll be okay?"

"That'll be great. It'll be perfect." He stopped by the fence to press a kiss to Keenan's mouth. "I love you, Keenan."

"Okay." He squeezed his arms hard around Coop's neck. "Bye."

"Bye."

"Yoo-hoo!" Mrs. Finkleman stood at the back door. She sent Coop a wink and an exaggerated thumbs-up sign before whisking Keenan inside.

She was standing pretty much where Coop had left her when he came back. He wasn't sure whether or not that was a good sign.

"So, ready for some champagne?"

"Coop, this is very nice of you, but—"

"Like the flowers?" Nervous as a cat, he popped the cork.

"Yes, they're wonderful, but—"

"I couldn't get them where you work, or I'd have spoiled the surprise. Keenan really gave me a hand setting things up." He handed her the glass, and when she was distracted, he leaned in for a slow, warm kiss. "Hi."

"Coop." She had to wait for her heart to finish its lazy somersault. "I know you must have gone to a lot of trouble—"

"I should have gone to it before. I didn't know I wanted to."

"Oh, Lord." She turned away and struggled to get her emotions under control. "I've given you the wrong impression this time. I don't need the trappings. I don't have to have romantic evenings and—" she waved toward the tapers on the table, waiting to be lit "—candlelight."

"Sure you do. So do I, when they're with you."

"You're trying to charm me," she said unsteadily. "That's new."

"You know what I am. The way this house is set up, we've practically been living together for the past month or so. People get to know each other quicker that way than just by socializing. So you know what I am, and you fell for me anyway."

She took a drink. "You're awfully smug about it. I told you my feelings are my responsibility, and that holds true. A romantic dinner doesn't change it."

It looked like strike two, but Coop knew that if he was going to go down, he'd go down swinging. "So I want to give you a nice evening. Is something wrong with that? I want to do better than propose over scrambled eggs when I've got a hangover." His voice had risen, and he bit down on it. "Damn it, this is my first time, have a little tolerance. No, don't say anything, let me finish this. You don't need me." He took another long breath. "Not for taking care of things, for you or the kid, I mean, for mowing the grass or putting stupid barbecue grills together. What about what I need, Zoe?"

She blinked at him. "Well, that's just it. Don't you see? You made it clear that you don't need or want ties. I come with ties, Coop."

"I made it clear," he muttered. "I didn't make anything clear, because I didn't know. Didn't want to know. I was scared. There. You feel better knowing that?" He glared at her. "I was scared, because I need you. Because I need to see your face and hear your voice and smell your hair. I just need you to be there. And I need to help you mow the grass and put the grill together. I need you to need me back."

"Oh." She shut her eyes. "I like hearing that."

"Then tell me you will." He took her arms until she opened her eyes again. "It's my last swing, Zoe. Marry me."

"I—" Yes. She wanted to say yes. "It's not just me, Coop."

"You think I don't want the kid? God, open your eyes. I'm crazy about him. I fell for him before I fell for you. I want to marry both of you, then maybe have another kid or two so I can start out on the ground floor. We already worked that out."

"You— Who did what?"

He swore, stepped back, shrugged. "I kind of ran it by the kid. I figured I should smooth the way a little, and find out where he stood." When she just stared, he jammed his hands in his pockets. "It didn't seem fair not to bring him into it, since he'd be mine."

"Yours," she murmured, staring blindly into her wine.

"Since you two are a team, it would be sort of like an expansion. Anyway, he's for it. So it's two against one."

"I see."

"Maybe I don't know a lot about the daddy stuff, but I love him. That's a good start."

She looked at him again, looked into his eyes. Her heart opened, flooded. "It's a good one, all right."

"I love you." His hands relaxed in his pockets. "That's the first time I've said that to a woman—except my mother. I love you, Zoe. So why don't you marry me and give me and the kid a break?''

"It looks like I'm outvoted." She lifted a hand to his cheek.

"Is that a yes?''

"That's definitely a yes." She laughed as he swung her into his arms. "Daddy.''

"I like the sound of that." He crushed his lips down on hers. "I like it a lot.''

* * * * *

Nora Roberts

is one of Silhouette Books's most popular and prolific authors, as well as a *New York Times* bestseller. She has contributed to most Silhouette lines and several short-story collections. Demand for early titles has been so great they are being brought back as part of a special "Language of Love" collection.

Nora was the first author inducted into the Romance Writers of America's Hall of Fame and has received awards for her fiction, her creativity, her sales and her contribution to the genre. She has received lifetime achievement awards from the Romance Writers of America, Waldenbooks and *Romantic Times* magazine, bestselling title and series awards from B. Dalton, Waldenbooks and Bookrack, and numerous awards from booksellers, readers and peers for individual titles.

Nora Roberts is a consummate storyteller. Her generous spirit, humor, creativity, willingness to take chances and commitment to her characters, her writing and, most especially, her readers, have earned her fame worldwide.

The Baby Machine

Ann Major

A Note from Ann Major

Because I was deeply in love with my husband when he asked me to marry him, I said yes in the next breath.

Then he said he wanted five children, and I said, "I don't want any."

Not that I didn't like babies. I just felt too young and immature to assume such responsibility.

After we'd been married a year, Ted pressured me to get on with producing the longed-for brood. To convince me that having a baby was easy, he insisted that I watch one of his patients in the delivery room. Since the woman had already had eight children, he figured the delivery would be a snap.

What men don't know about women could fill volumes of romance novels. The poor woman couldn't have screamed louder if you'd thrown her naked to a starving group of grizzly bears. Needless to say, another year passed before I would even allow him to whisper the word *pregnancy*.

When I finally did give birth to our first son, I felt as proud as a queen who'd produced a long-awaited, royal heir. I instantly felt committed to Ted in a new and profound way.

Romance for me has never had much to do with candle-lit dinners and champagne, but everything to do with the connection of two people on emotional, spiritual and physical planes. So, for me, watching a football game with my husband can be a very romantic kind of thing. Just driving up to the high school to pick up one of our kids—together—seems sexy and romantic. Thus, I don't feel our children have interfered with our romance as much as they have enhanced it because of the deeper emotional texture they have brought to our relationship.

Of course, as a young mother I always insisted that my children take naps every afternoon from two until five. Not that they always slept, mind you, but the little dears did dutifully stay in their rooms and were silent—even Kimberly, even when she was a terrible two.

Everyone thought I selfishly wanted that time to write, and I did . . . weekday afternoons.

But on the weekends when Ted was home . . . Guess again.

Ann Major

Chapter One

Anger and grief burned through Jim Keith Jones like acid as he set the chain saw down and picked up the ax. In six days, that rich vulture, Kate Karlington, would repossess what to her was probably just another motley collection of real estate, but what to him was a lifetime of dreams and hard work.

He'd built his little empire from scratch—vacant lot by lot, house by house, building by building. He'd painted and hammered and mowed and hauled trash—there hadn't been a job he'd been too good to do to keep his properties up for his tenants.

Next Friday, Karlington would smilingly pick his bones clean and leave him for dead. Only, he wouldn't be dead; he'd be groveling in the gutter where he'd started, alive with the bitter reality that he had failed again.

Karlington wasn't the only reason his mood was so foul. It was May, a month that could be oppressive in Houston because so many days were as white and humid and smotheringly hot as this one. But today was especially dreadful because three years ago to the day he'd buried Mary on a muggy afternoon like this.

Jim Keith's filthy sleeveless sweatshirt was drenched with perspiration. His curly black hair was glued to his tanned brow. His dark eyes were bloodshot from the ravages of the binge he'd gone on the night before. His damp ragged jeans clung so tightly to his hard thighs, the navy denim looked as if it was painted on.

Slowly, carefully, his powerful brown arms lifted the ax and then sank it into the rotten trunk with all the savage vengeance his lean muscular body was capable of. When the blade crunched into soft wood, his perfectly sculpted mouth grimaced as if razor-edged steel had sliced through his skull. No wonder. He had a six-star hangover. He had celebrated the anniversary of Mary's funeral by tying one on.

He had gone home last night and drunk his dinner and watched home videos of Mary until he'd passed out. He did that every time her birthday and their wedding anniversary rolled around, too.

This morning he'd awakened to a fuzzy white television screen, crawled to his refrigerator, drunk a single beer, brewed a pot of black coffee and scrambled a mountain of eggs. Then he'd showered and driven to his sister Maggie's house and dutifully picked up his nine-year-old son, Bobby Lee, who had tearfully begged him to let him sleep in or watch cartoons instead of taking him to some apartment complex to work. Not that Bobby Lee ever did much.

Father and son were now hard at work cleaning up Jim Keith's worst apartment project, which was located just off the Eastex Freeway in a crime-ridden neighborhood populated with low-income families. Or rather, Jim Keith was working. Bobby Lee never really did much.

But even after a morning of mowing and chopping and weed pulling, Jim Keith still felt like death warmed over.

On her deathbed, Mary had begged him to be strong.

Dear God he'd tried.

He swung the ax again, and wood chips flew as the blade bit into the trunk. For three long years he'd tried. But every night when he finished work, the demons of loneliness and dark grief still haunted him. It was all he could do to get through the days and nights, all he could do to go through the motions of being a father, of being a businessman.

Of being a human.

But he was losing it.

In those last months before her death, he hadn't cared about anything except saving Mary. He hadn't thought of his future or his son's, and because he hadn't, he'd borrowed money and taken Mary to Germany in the hopes of finding a miracle cure that his insurance wouldn't pay for. That was why he was badly overextended. That was why, despite his economizing over the past three years, despite his working seven days a week, come Friday he was really going to lose everything, even the roof over his head, to Karlington.

While oil revenues, property values, and job opportunities had plummeted, utility bills and property taxes had soared. Thus, the Houston real estate situation had deteriorated dramatically. Entire office buildings were fenced off and vacant. Thousands of apartment buildings had been bulldozed and the land sold for next to nothing. Entire neighborhoods of foreclosed houses sat empty. Banks had failed. Things were turning around now, but it was too late for him.

The economic situation would have been precarious for any man, but it had proved too much for a heavily indebted man devastated by the death of his beautiful young wife. Karlington had swooped down like a scavenger and bought his notes at a humiliatingly low, deeply discounted price. Nothing could save him from her—nothing short of a miracle.

And he'd lost faith in miracles when Mary died.

He wouldn't have bothered to clean up the project today, since it was as good as Karlington's, except wielding the ax was therapy.

The blade sliced one final time into the soggy trunk, and the rotten pecan tree groaned, toppling with a violent thud to the spongy, overgrown lawn.

He pitched the ax into the weed-choked flower bed beside his wheelbarrow and scanned the empty grounds for Bobby Lee. Jim Keith frowned when he saw the abandoned trash can and the door to number 20 sagging open. He'd ordered Bobby Lee to pick up everything inside and out of that apartment two hours ago. It was a thirty-minute job at best even for Bobby Lee, who moved as slow as molasses, but it looked as if Bobby Lee hadn't even spent five doing it.

Since Bobby Lee liked cars, Jim Keith headed toward the parking lot. Jim Keith's frown deepened as he considered Bobby Lee's laziness. The kid took after the Whits, Mary's easygoing bunch, most of whom were lazy as hell and hadn't amounted to much. Not that they cared. They got through life on charm. Maybe he shouldn't worry. When they found life too tough, most of them married well.

Mary herself had been no fireball. But she'd more than made up for it by being so pretty and sweet and fun-loving—and so damned good in the sack. She'd loved him since they'd been kids. His friends had teased him about the way she'd chased after him down the halls in high school.

"Oh, hi there, Jimmy," she'd purred from behind him, acting as if she was surprised to see him even though she was breathless from her breakneck run. When he'd turned around, she'd tossed her nose in the air so that her gold straight hair danced on her shoulders. Then she'd casually smiled up at him as if she wasn't especially anxious to see him after all. So then, of course, he'd had to prove himself and chase her. She'd known how to set the hook, let him nibble just a bite or two to get a delicious taste, before she snapped the line good and tight.

They'd been petting one night, and he'd wanted her so badly he couldn't wait. And she'd said, "Jimmy, you can't have me unless you marry me."

"Is that a proposal, baby?"

She'd giggled. "Now that you mention it—"

He'd started the car and driven hell-bent for Mexico. The old car had died at the border. They'd had to walk across the bridge and look for an official to marry them. Neither of them was even eighteen. They'd sold the car for scrap and hitchhiked back to

Houston. He'd paid the first month's rent with the money from the car and dropped out of high school and started working harder than he'd ever worked.

Mary had always praised everything he'd done. Somehow he hadn't cared that she was so disorganized and never got much done. He'd loved her. God, how he'd loved her. They'd had tough times, but they'd made it. Until she'd gotten sick. Until he'd failed to save her.

Never again would he let himself fall in love. Because bright as the years with her had been even when they'd been poor as dirt, her illness and death had taught him about the dark and terrible price of love.

He scowled when he reached the parking lot and saw it was empty. Now where the hell was Bobby Lee?

Jim Keith was about to turn around when he saw the gleaming perfection of a dark green Jaguar gliding smoothly beneath the towering pine trees.

Then he stopped dead in his tracks when he recognized the woman behind the wheel—Kate Karlington.

Not that she'd recognize a lowlife like him. But he knew what she looked like, from seeing the society columns in the newspaper.

Fighting the murderous rage building inside him, he shrank behind the wall of his building as she stealthily parked her car under a towering cottonwood. High on her own success—her inherited success—she thought she knew everything and was always writing columns in the Houston papers about how to succeed in a recession. If she was so smart, how come she drove a car like that to this neighborhood and risked it being stolen or stripped?

She had her nerve, too. He'd had her served with a peace bond to stop her from snooping around his projects and harassing his managers. If he called the cops now, they'd haul her to jail. The thought of the elegant know-it-all Kate Karlington handcuffed and on her way to the clinker brought out the wicked white grin that had captured Mary's heart.

When the regal-looking young woman coolly unfolded her long, slim body from the car, holding a briefcase, his wolfish grin deepened. Then his eyes skimmed over her angrily—top to bottom.

Why did she have to be so damned beautiful?

His heart began to pound like a sledgehammer, and no longer solely from anger. The hot day seemed to press in on him harder than ever. It wasn't even noon, but he felt an odd, unwanted hunger.

Which only made him hate her all the more.

Black-and-white pictures didn't do her justice.

Mary had been soft and gentle and golden. This witch's beauty was so strong and bold and opulently charismatic, it struck him like a body blow even at this great distance. Her hair was shiny coils of vivid flame caught in a green silk scarf at her nape. She had the kind of figure a man who didn't despise her would die to get his hands on—lush breasts, a narrow waist, curving hips and long legs. She had a brisk walk that told him she was a woman of immense energy.

In the bedroom he imagined she would be volcanic.

Why the hell had his mind wandered to the bed-room?

Kate wore a green silk blouse and green linen slacks. He noticed the crisp, starched look of those slacks. They had obviously been ironed within seconds of being put on. Precisely applied and dramatic makeup darkened her eyes and made her lips brighter.

He found he couldn't take his eyes off her till she disappeared around the back of his building. But that was only because the sneaky bitch was his enemy.

No way was he calling the cops.

No way would he forgo the pleasure of teasing and torturing her himself.

Chapter Two

Kate Karlington, who was reputed to have inherited her father's cold but very shrewd business mind, was fastidious to a fault. Above all she appeared *in control*. Her curly red hair was tightly pulled back; her linen slacks crisply pressed. Every business document in her briefcase was tidily filed by subject and date. Every square in her calendar was carefully marked with her plans for that day.

Her teachers and her strict father had severely punished her for inefficiency, sloppiness and neglect, and she had learned their lessons well. Thus, when she stumbled in one of Jones's potholes in his poorly paved parking lot and got a run in one of her expensive stockings, she frowned impatiently. She paused to study the ruinous neglect of Jones's forlorn-looking buildings. Pink bricks were blackened from mildew. Several broken windows were taped.

Neglect ate into profits. She deplored greedy, shortsighted landlords like Keith Jones who milked their properties for all they were worth, thereby depriving tenants of the basic amenities they were paying their good money for. Did Jones realize how foolish he'd been? Dissatisfied tenants always moved. Couldn't he see that his neglect had lowered his rents and caused his high vacancy rate?

Fools like him deserved to go bankrupt. Not that they ever blamed themselves. No doubt Jones saw her as the villain in this foreclosure.

Her heart hardened as she viewed the sagging gutters at the roofline and the many huge potholes in the asphalt parking lot. Paint peeled from wooden facings. This project was in even worse shape than his other properties. She wished Jones hadn't fallen behind on his notes, so she wouldn't have to foreclose next week and sink her good money after his bad or, worse, bulldoze the buildings. Not that his properties weren't prime locations.

How she pitied poor people who had to live in buildings like these. Her green eyes narrowed on a crack that ran from the top of one building, all the way down to a scraggly bush and to—

To two filthy, unlaced athletic shoes sticking out from the dense foliage. The toes were glued together in a raptly tense, pigeon-toed position. The ragged cuffs of a pair of equally filthy jeans were all that was visible of the slim little boy.

Kate softened inwardly. She wanted people to believe she was a cool, controlled, brilliant businesswoman who gloried in her independence and glamorous single life, who gloried in the local fame she had achieved through her weekly column. She wanted them to think that she was just like her controlled, highly disciplined father who had never loved another human being in his life, that her sole passion was enlarging the Karlington empire, just as his had been. In truth, she wished she *was* like that. She wanted to be as invulnerable to hurt as he had been, but there had always been in her that secret weakness, that craven, instinctive yearning for any scrap of tenderness and love.

When she was growing up, her father had never allowed her to have a pet or friends. Later, after she'd run away to her aunt Mathilde's, he'd coldly refused to take Kate back. Instead, he'd sent her to schools as far away as possible, rarely allowing her to come home for holidays. So she had grown up lonely. Feeling isolated and rejected even after she'd obtained several degrees, she had fallen for the first man who had pretended he loved her. Not that the illusion had lasted long, for her father had ruthlessly exposed all of Edwin's failings and his true motivations in marrying her. Edwin had had other women all along. He had married her for the Karlington money; he had never loved her.

After he'd left her, she'd discovered she was pregnant. When she told him, he'd been coldly indifferent. During those brief first months of her pregnancy, she'd imagined that at last she would have someone she could love and who would love her. Then, at the end of her fifth month, she had miscarried.

The baby's memorial service had seemed the end of everything. It had taken her a long time to recover. Outwardly she seemed fine. Inwardly the wounds sometimes felt as raw as ever.

Her failed marriage had made Kate wary of men, but even though the loss of her baby had hurt far more, even though she didn't trust herself with men,

she secretly longed to try to have another child. And
it seemed that the closer she got to her thirtieth birthday, the stronger the instinctive urge to be a mother
became. She couldn't walk through Neiman's or Saks
without staring at the children's clothes in frustration
and wishing she had a little girl or a little boy of her
own to buy something cute for. She would remember
the months of joy when she had planned for the birth
of her baby, and all the darling things she had bought.
Only to have to pack them away.

*Was she really doomed to spend her whole life
alone?*

The ragtag boy was so quiet and still, for a second
she was terrified he'd been hit by a car and crawled out
of the street to die. Then she heard a page flip and an
awestruck exclamation.

"Golly-damn-bongo!"

She sank down beside him, sighing in relief and in
shock at his language, for never having had them, she
idealized children. "Hello there," she said softly.

He started guiltily, scrambling out from under the
bush, intending to run.

Until she grabbed him gently but firmly by the collar.

Despite his filthy T-shirt and ragged jeans, he was
beautiful. He had dark curly hair and dark flashing
eyes. "I didn't mean to scare you," she said, again in
her gentlest tone.

"I wasn't scared. I ain't some sissy," he said in a
rough, put-on, big-boy voice.

"*Am not,*" she corrected. "Of course you're not. But what were you doing under there?"

He thrust back his chin and glued his dark rebellious eyes to a distant spot behind her. "Just readin'," he mumbled, reddening.

"Must be good. Can I see—"

"No!"

Her brows arched.

"I mean it's nothing you'd be interested in—ma'am," he said more politely.

When she reached down for the magazine, he lunged to grab it.

Then the wind caught the sexy centerfold, and it fluttered like a flag. The boy cried out in acute dismay, springing for the slick, greasily thumbed thing.

But she was quicker.

"Oh, my," she gasped, shocked as she got an eyeful of bulging bosom and pink fanny.

The little scamp would have run, but she clung to his collar.

The young woman who adorned the centerfold was amazingly proportioned. *Golly-damn-bongo is right,* Kate thought with a smile, and then was horrified that she could be amused. Boy and woman blushed as they studied the centerfold with equal fascination until she remembered herself and snapped it out of his line of vision.

Kate found the picture deeply degrading to all women on principle. No wonder little boys grew into men seeing women as nothing more than sex objects. No wonder rich men thought women could be bought.

Not just rich men. She remembered the way Edwin had used the Karlington money to attract younger women.

"Where did you get this, young man?"

"Found it."

"Where?"

"Dunno."

"You do, too!" She shook him slightly.

"Under a bed. I was cleaning out an apartment for my father... picking up trash...."

"Where is your mother?"

"Dead."

The word wrenched her because of her own lonely, motherless childhood and her hard, rejecting father.

"She died three years ago when I was only six." He lowered his head.

Kate had been about the same age when her own mother died. If this beautiful child were hers, Kate would never have set him to clean some trashy apartment.

"Where's your father?"

"Doing the yard."

Kate frowned. So his father was the yardman. It surprised her that Jones, who was so close with his money when it came to paint, lumber and asphalt, would spend a cent on grass. She guessed that even he had some standards—low as they were.

"Don't tell on me," the boy pleaded in a pitiful voice. "Dad's not feeling too good and he gets mad when I slack off."

She'd always been terrified of her father, too. "Is he sick?"

"Hung over."

Kate's eyes narrowed. There was ice suddenly, on her forehead, icy indignant rage spreading from the nape of her neck down her spine. Why had this wonderful little angel been given to some alcoholic brutish laborer who would neglect him, a man who was obviously lousy at his job... when she—

"I won't let him hurt you," she said protectively as she led the child into the courtyard.

She saw the ax and the chain saw first; and then the wheelbarrow and the mower and the tangled mountain of clippings the dark giant had piled beside him.

When she walked briskly up to him, he ignored her and continued to rip weeds from the flower bed.

He wasn't lazy.

Kate admired energy in people, especially when they applied it to something constructive. She didn't have a single employee who worked so ferociously as this brute.

She saw him well for the first time.

Rivulets of steamy sweat raced down the man's neck and his arms. She licked her lips. Just for a second before she caught herself, she felt a funny feeling start in the pit of her stomach at the sight of so much hard male muscle. She, who had schooled herself never to look at men, couldn't be fascinated by this man's flexing, bronze biceps.

She tried to swallow but couldn't. She looked away instead. "Hello," she said, intending her firmest, no-

nonsense tone, only to be furious when her voice sounded vulnerable and shaky—almost sexy.

She didn't want to like him.

Her experiences with men had taught her they came in two categories. Rich men of her own class were too often like her father—selfish to the core. When they wanted to get rid of a child, they paid someone to take care of it. When they wanted a woman's body, they found her price. Such men didn't have to give emotionally of themselves. All her father had ever given her were things. When she was a teenager and had asked him to take her places, he'd had a fancy convertible delivered to her school.

Poorer men worshiped money as ardently as rich ones because they believed it was magic. She had learned that from Edwin, her ex-husband, who had pretended he'd loved her when all he'd ever wanted was her money.

"I—I said hello," Kate repeated, forcing herself to look at the man again. Dear God. Her voice came out even huskier than before.

He went still, as if the raspy sound had electrified him.

Her gaze fixed on his rigid brown arms. She felt her own muscles go as tense as his. It was as if she were in tune with this scowling brute. Which was ridiculous.

Slowly he brushed the dirt from his fingers and rose angrily to his full height.

Clearly he didn't want to be interrupted.

He was very, very tall. Well over six feet.

She liked tall.

No, she didn't!

He was a sleek-muscled, black-haired, deplorably handsome Adonis, who was so disgustingly male and virile that her womb ached with sudden awareness of the profound loneliness of her life. Despite the differences she imagined between herself and him—class, education, ambition, the zillion cultural refinements she possessed and he could not possibly—his hot, faintly insolent gaze lit that spark of deep feminine yearning.

He was as set on disliking her as she was on him. But for an infinitesimal moment as his smoldering black eyes slid from her face down her body, she knew that on some primitive level she wanted to devour him in the same hideous, stripping way his gaze was so hatefully devouring her.

No... She—she, cool, collected Kate Karlington, who had schooled herself to turn up her nose at the advances of far more eligible bachelors, wouldn't allow herself to have the hots for this sulky, musclebound Neanderthal.

Her blood burned through her like fire anyway. Suddenly she felt so dizzy, she was afraid she might actually faint.

"What's the matter?" he demanded in a harsh baritone that was absolutely beautiful.

"I—I'm fine...."

"You're shaking like a leaf."

"Allergies," she lied.

"Right," he muttered in that velvety, deeply unsettling tone.

He was smarter than she'd thought. She had to make her point and escape him. "I—I found your son in the parking lot—reading...."

The brute's dazzling smile made her whole body tighten. Why did his rugged masculine face have to be carved in such appealingly tough lines? He had a strong jaw, a straight nose. Spiked black lashes set off his bold angry eyes. She noticed the tiny lines at the corners of those dark eyes that seemed so intelligent—silent testimony that when he wasn't sulking, he had a sense of humor.

"Bobby Lee reading?" His wicked smile broadened. "That's a new one."

She caught the smell of his beery breath, and some stronger, sweaty male scent that was not altogether displeasing as he ruffled his son's black hair with brutish pride. When the beast's gaze raked her with scathing intent, she took a hesitant step backward before she reminded herself of her mission.

"Don't you even care what he was reading?" she demanded.

Her high-and-mighty tone brought a swift scowl.

"I care," he said with soft menace. "Show me."

"Here!" She thrust the magazine forward.

Roughly he yanked it from her and studied the nude centerfold with an embarrassing avidity.

Kate colored when his black eyes flicked back from the lush splendor of the naked girl to trail down her own body.

As if to compare her to—

His look shamed her to the core.

She wanted to run, to die.

He rolled the magazine up and stuffed it into the back pocket of his jeans. Then he knelt to his son's level and said, "We'll take this up again tonight when we're alone...and have a man-to-man talk. For now, get back to number 20 and clean it up—on the double. Or I'll give you an extra hour of pulling weeds."

The kid bolted like a streak of lightning.

"The threat of weed pulling always gets him going," the Neanderthal muttered with a grim smile, his gaze following the running child and his flapping shoestrings.

She was furious. "Is that all you intend to do?" She curled her long nails into her palms. "What kind of father are you? You find your son reading filth, and...and you don't even care."

The man's eyes returned to her slowly. "He's my kid—not yours! And I'm a helluva lot more concerned about his habit of shirking work than the fact that he has a boy's natural interest in sex."

"A boy's natural interest? Is that what you call it? Why am I surprised that someone like you would be more concerned with driving a child, too young to work, to do your job than with his morals? You probably don't even know what morals are. You probably don't care that he cusses, either."

The man's hard features went tighter. "Hey— you're way out of line, lady. Who the hell do you think you are, coming here, criticizing the way I raise my child? All boys do some cussing and looking at pictures like that when they get the chance."

As he moved toward her, she shrank from him. To her horror, her shoulders hit cool pink bricks, and she realized he had her cornered against a cracked, mildewed wall. He leaned into her, his huge body cutting her off from freedom.

"Where were you raised—a convent?"

She whitened. He was closer to the truth than he knew.

"It's plain as day you have problems you can't deal with, lady. You're probably so damn rich, you never worked an honest day in your life. You just go out and buy what you want or use your money to take what you want. You probably think you're too good to get dirty and sweaty. Well, I started working younger than him. Work won't hurt him. Neither will that magazine."

"Why did I ever think I could talk to you?" She started to push past him, but he brought his arms up beside her, blocking her escape.

"And another thing, lady—the fact that I'm not horrified by Bobby Lee's interest in sex has nothing to do with my morals, which I probably have way more of than you do.

"I let you butt your long, uptight nose into my life just for the fun of it. But you got me all stirred up and curious. Why the hell is a beautiful woman like yourself so scared of sex when it's the best thing this life has to offer?"

"A man...like you...would think that."

"Most of the women I've known would agree."

"Only the worst kind of woman would consort with someone as low as you."

"I should break your snotty little neck for that."

"Violence . . . from a man like you wouldn't surprise me, either."

He took a deep calming breath. "I don't know why I give a damn what you think, but, for the record, I'm not some kind of savage where women are concerned. I married my high school sweetheart. And I would have been faithful to her till I died if she hadn't died first." His voice broke, and he looked away, his shattered face darker and angrier than ever as if he despised himself for revealing anything so personal to her.

She saw the wild grief in his ravaged eyes and forgot her terror of him.

There was a long awkward moment. She felt drawn to him because she instinctively knew that his grief and loneliness were every bit as terrible as her own.

On some crazy, overwrought impulse, she gently touched his arm, her soft fingertips sliding comfortingly along his hard, hot muscles. Flesh to flesh. Heart to heart. Woman to man.

The touch of him compelled her. For one long instant, she felt the most powerful, uncanny connection to him she had ever felt to anyone.

Then he jerked his arm away. "Don't touch me! Don't you ever put your lily-white hands on me again," he roared.

"I—I didn't mean to! I must have been crazy to! It . . . it was an accident!"

"Good!"

"Just get out of my way, and I'll go," she said primly.

"Not till you tell me what you're doing on Jones property. My, er, boss gave me instructions about a certain woman—Karlington. He told me to call the cops if she came around."

"I'm not her!"

"She's got red hair."

Her eyes widened, and he laughed at her fear.

"If you don't let me go, I'll scream."

"Would you really?"

She tried to nod, but the muscles in her neck felt frozen.

"I could stop you from that, you know."

But instead of pressing his physical advantage, he lifted his arms, and she moved away from the wall, away from him, only to trip over his wheelbarrow and cry out furiously.

When he started toward her, she held up her hands. "No— Don't come near me! I can get up by myself." She brushed frantically at the loose dirt and grass on her linen slacks.

"You didn't tell me what you're doing here," he demanded.

"I—I was looking for an apartment."

"Like hell." His words were harsh. "This isn't exactly your kind of neighborhood."

"N-not for myself," she improvised wildly. "For someone who...who works for me."

"Oh, right. Some lowlife like me. Lady Bountiful apartment hunting for her...her yardman, maybe? Why is that such a hard one to swallow?" He flashed that cynical smile of his again and dug in his pocket.

He knew she was lying, and for some idiotic reason she felt ashamed that he thought she was a snob.

While his fingers moved beneath the denim, her gaze flicked to his powerful body.

The bronzed muscular perfection of his lean frame drew her. For no reason at all, she thought of her big double bed and how empty and cold it felt every night.

She looked breathlessly away, but not before his dark gaze swung to her, and she felt the leap of some wild charge between them. He was as turned on by her as she was by him.

She shuddered, and he scowled. She realized a man like him might have taken her touching his arm as an invitation to do anything; he was so strong, she couldn't have stopped him. She was lucky he disliked her and had jerked away from her.

She didn't feel lucky. She felt lonely.

So lonely.

Dear God. She wanted to run, to forget Keith Jones and his deplorable properties and his even more deplorable employee.

But the brown hand had closed over the object it had been digging for. Carelessly, the yardman pulled his hand from his pocket and tossed her a shiny key.

His toss was on. But she was so upset, her catch was off. As she leaned down to pick it up, she was aware of his bold eyes on her.

"Number 15 is empty and ready to rent," he said casually in that harsh, but oh-so-compelling voice. "I cleaned it and repaired the appliances myself, and I could give you a personal tour. I'm good with my hands." He paused. Maybe to let that last sentence sink in and torment her. "Good at fixing things, I mean. There's a kitchen, a living room, a bath. And, of course, a bedroom." He drawled that last word ever so suggestively. "Or you can look it over yourself."

She gasped in relief. "I—I'll look it over on my own."

"Independent lady..."

"Bingo."

"You can leave the key in the door. I'll be here...if you need me.... For anything."

She felt hot and weak. He was horrible. He seemed to hate her, and yet he seemed to find some savage delight in tormenting her, too. Why did some terrible wanton weakness make her want to ask him to show her the apartment after all?

No....

When she whirled away from him, she thought she heard him chuckle darkly.

But when she turned back, he scowled at her obligingly.

Damn the man.

Chapter Three

Kate stood frozen in the doorway of number 15, wanting to leave but not wanting to risk more attention from the insolent yardman, who was now mowing the courtyard.

So she lingered in that shadowy entrance—trapped by her ridiculous fear of a man who was so far beneath her, she should never have noticed him in the first place. Nevertheless, she had to admit to a grudging admiration for him, at least for his work. Menial though some might believe it, he obviously took pride in it.

The apartment was immaculate. Not only did all the ancient appliances sparkle, they worked. Maybe his boss wasn't so bad after all. Maybe Jones did try to offer decent housing. Maybe he just couldn't afford to paint the outside.

Since her gaze was glued to the man's broad back, she saw the splash from the swimming pool only out of the corner of her eye. But she panicked when she realized that Bobby Lee, who had been playing by the pool only a few seconds before, had vanished.

As she raced for the pool, she had no way of knowing whether or not he could swim. Then she saw a sickening dark shape with flailing legs on the bottom of the deep end.

Rushing through the chain-link gate, she sprang toward the pool, but as she dove, the slim heel of her Italian sandal snagged in a crack in the cement. She pitched wildly off balance, her head striking the hard tile edge of the pool. Her body slid into the water just as the kid's curly black head broke the aqua surface.

When Kate woke up, her throat and nasal passages burned with every breath. She groaned as she felt large hands gently probing her damp hair. Then the brutal fingertips dug too deeply into the gash in her scalp, and her eyes snapped open.

"Ouch!"

For an instant she didn't recognize the swarthy hard face so close to hers. Then the dark eyes flashed, and the man smiled sardonically as if he didn't respect her much.

And she knew who he was.

Confused, she glanced wildly past him and saw scuffed black work boots tossed in a corner, a masculine tie looped carelessly over a doorknob and a denim work shirt draped over a dresser that was littered with magazines and newspapers and a tattered paperback copy of *The Fatal Skin* by Honoré de Balzac.

He wasn't neat. Which didn't surprise her.

But he read. Which did.

"Where am I?" she demanded even as she saw that the insolent brute had taken advantage of the situation and maneuvered her into his bedroom.

"My bed," he replied, his husky voice low and somehow dangerous.

She pushed his hands away furiously.

"As if I couldn't figure that out! I meant why am I here? How did I get here?" she squeaked shrilly, struggling to sit up.

"I wouldn't sit up if I were you," he advised. "Take it easy. You've had a blow to the head. Not that it seems to have improved your disposition. On the contrary—"

"It'll take more than a blow to my head to keep me in your bed!"

But as she spoke, the crisp cotton sheet and heavy blankets sliding downward against her cool skin almost exposed a bare breast. Blushing, she grabbed at the sheet, conscious of a new horror and an excellent reason for staying right where she was.

Beneath his sheets and blankets, she was stark naked.

She froze, her hands groping wildly over her body just to make sure while his gleaming dark eyes told her he was enjoying her discomfiture immensely.

"You...you stripped me," she whispered, yanking his sheet to her chin and holding it there primly.

His loathsome smile broadened. "Doctor's orders."

A dozen hot nerves were quivering in her temple. "I'll bet!" She was about to explode. Instead she stopped herself and sucked in her breath.

"You were soaking wet. Doc said the first thing to do was make sure you were dry and warm. You see, you hit your head on the pool edge and fell in—unconscious.''

"And you saved me?"

"You got it, baby. I'm your hero. I pulled you out of the pool and called a doctor. Which makes me your Sir Lance in shining armor."

He smiled as if he was loving every minute of this!

She felt a killing rage and an unendurable shame. "Not in a million lifetimes." Just the thought that he was gloating over having seen her without a stitch on made her cheeks burn.

"And where are my clothes?"

His black eyes went cold. "I bet Bobby Lee you'd act high and mighty and refuse to thank us."

She clamped her lips together in a stubborn line. Gratitude was the last thing she felt. Still, he did have her trapped . . . and in his bed. "Thank you—for saving me," she muttered grudgingly. "Now...if...if you would . . . please . . . please . . . just get my clothes, I'll dress and go."

"Relax." His avid attention focused on her hot face. "You're not leaving till the doctor gets here and says you can."

"I—I'm sure . . . I've caused you enough trouble."

"Don't worry about it," he murmured ruthlessly. "I knew you were trouble the minute I set eyes on you. Besides I've enjoyed...getting to know you better."

Inwardly she was seething—and he knew it. His gorgeous mouth was twitching, which meant he loved it. Outwardly she struggled to act calm and dignified. "Look, you may be used to situations like this—"

"Why do I have the feeling you're about to hurt my feelings by attacking my morals again?" he taunted softly.

"Well, a man like you probably has strange naked women in his bed all the time—"

"Right! A man like me.... So, we're back to me being a lowlife, are we? No one has been in my bed...since my wife died. And you, my holier-than-thou Karlington witch, are no stranger to me. If I did want a woman, you're the very last I'd choose—to have naked in my bed." He had drawled her name very softly, very nastily.

She bristled even as his frigid tone sent a chill down her spine. "How do you know my name?"

"When you were out cold, I told Bobby Lee to look in your purse for your driver's license."

He was lying. She could feel it.

"Bobby Lee's okay, then?" she asked weakly.

"He was diving for a toy car. He's fine."

"You should have been watching him."

The man's features were half in shadow, the hard angular planes revealing little. "Hey, you're the last person I'd let tell me what I should and shouldn't do. You're the fool who would have drowned if I hadn't saved you."

"Well, if you'll just get my clothes, I'll cause you no further trouble."

"No way do I believe that.... Not that I'll give you your clothes...."

Her pulse began to throb unevenly.

"Don't worry—I have no designs on your body, charming though it is," he said bluntly. "But you're staying till the doctor says you can go. You see, Miss Karlington, my boss told me you were repossessing everything he owns. He ordered me not to allow you to set foot on his property till you got title. He'll fire me for sure if he finds out I let you snoop around here and then you nearly drowned in his pool—because of my kid."

"I hope you do get fired. I hope you starve."

Low, harsh laughter came from his throat. "Because you've always been so rich, you've never had it tough," he murmured tightly. "You wouldn't mind Bobby Lee losing his home."

"I—I don't want to hurt Bobby Lee. Only you—because—"

"Because I didn't pussyfoot around someone as high and mighty as you think you are," he ground out. "Because I was afraid you'd go into shock and I had the audacity to undress you when you were shivering and unconscious. Honey, you were out cold, and your skin was like ice."

She was still stuck on the word *honey*, savoring it, hating him for saying it in that cynical and yet deeply caressing tone that made her feel very feminine and cherished even as it turned her blood to molten fire.

"If you get me fired, Bobby Lee'll pay, too. What happens to me, happens to him. The question is, are you as cold and ruthless as Jones says you are?"

"Oh, all right. I'll see your doctor," she snapped, not answering his question because for some reason she didn't want to admit she was probably worse than Jones said she was.

His eyebrows arched nastily.

"I'm staying for Bobby Lee's sake! Not yours. And I won't say a thing to Jones to get you in trouble even though you're insolent…and…arrogant. Even though you don't know your...your place."

"Which is light years socially beneath your brightly shining star?" he added shortly.

"You said it, buster. I'll even pay for the doctor. There's a fifty in my purse—"

"I'll pay," he growled.

"Oh, don't be so proud! You can't possibly afford—"

"Jones'll reimburse me. The last thing he'd want is *your* money."

"You make it sound as if he hates me." It irritated her that Jones went around running her down to her future employees.

"Yeah. Do you blame him?" Flushing darkly, the brute leaned closer, and a shiver of alarm darted through her. "But then, Jones hasn't had the pleasure of getting to know you personally—on the intimate level that I have."

Kate tried to tell herself that he was crude and uneducated and insolent, that she hated the idea of such a man's dark callused hands on her skin, of his bold eyes burning now with memories of her naked body. But as his gaze devoured her lips, and his mouth came nearer, a violent quiver went hotly through her, and without fully realizing what she did, she closed her eyes and pursed her lips almost expectantly.

If he'd been as tempted to kiss her as she'd been to let him, he mastered the impulse. Instead of his warm mouth on hers, she felt a draft of cool air and heard his raspy chuckle as the door swung open.

When her eyes flew open again, the Balzac novel was gone and a tanned hand was pulling the door shut.

Monday morning, Kate's temple still ached as she flicked on the lights of her darkened office and walked briskly to her desk with her heavy briefcase. She opened her crisp beige drapes, and hazy sunlight flooded her opulent, immaculate office.

She wore a starched white cotton blouse and a perfectly pressed denim skirt. Her hair was pulled straight back from her face and secured tightly in a big white clip.

For a long moment she stared out the ceiling-to-floor windows at the bustling city wrapped in smog. She felt strangely restless and lonelier than ever before, cut off from that world of ordinary people who had families and lovers and children.

Her father had warned her she would be alone at the top, that her money would set her apart, that she could trust in nothing and in no one except herself; that men would want her only for her power or for her fortune, that she would have to learn to make men her tools, her serfs, and not become theirs.

Own or be owned. Control or be controlled. Those were her father's rules. He said there was no such thing as a power vacuum. Either you were in charge or you were exploited.

Once she had not wanted to believe that, and she had been naively loving. But Edwin's cruel betrayal had taught her that her father was right. Never had she felt more exploited than when she'd lain in the hospital after her miscarriage and her father had coldly informed her by phone how much he'd paid in the divorce settlement to be rid of Edwin.

She had asked her father, "Did you tell him I lost the baby?"

"You little fool... Yes."

And when Edwin had not bothered to come to the baby's memorial service, her heart had hardened. Not only toward him, but toward all men.

Kate came back to the present.

She turned her back on the window and sat down, a tiny solitary figure dwarfed by her immense office. With a shaking hand she withdrew the thick, perfectly organized Jones file from her briefcase and thumbed through the neat pages.

Involuntarily her thoughts turned to her accident Saturday and to that humiliating encounter with Jones's insolent yardman and to his friend, the helpful Dr. Sager. When she took over the Jones properties, she would have that rude, impossible handyman fired. Then she remembered Bobby Lee and realized that much as she hated helping the father, she would have to arrange for one of her friends to hire him for the sake of his child. She had seen the man's work and could personally recommend him. Even though she knew that, professionally, she was an idiot to let go of someone so good, she was too afraid of seeing him again.

Because she had dreamed of him.

Because she had longed for him even though she knew he hated her, and she hated him.

She had puttered about her apartment Sunday, going through the motions of neatening and straightening drawers and closets that had already been perfect. She had felt edgy and restless and lonely, which she, independent Kate Karlington, resented because she believed she didn't need a man for anything.

Not true. Men had one use for which there was no good substitute. She thought of how warm the yardman's hard arm had felt beneath her fingers before he had jerked away from her.

Her thoughts strayed beyond sex. More than anything in the world, Kate wanted a child. She wanted someone to love, someone who would love her. But she was old enough to have come to terms with some other facts about herself and her beliefs. Her cruel experiences had taught her to distrust herself with men; she didn't want to risk another failed marriage.

She remembered how joyous, how filled with hope she'd felt when she'd been pregnant. The motherhood angle seemed a more enduring love bond.

There should be some sort of painless baby machine a mature woman such as herself could use to get pregnant.

A baby machine . . .

In spite of herself, Kate smiled faintly and closed her eyes, trying to imagine one. It should be a robot with steel arms and bright lights for eyes. The procedure to get pregnant would have to be painless and, of course, it wouldn't be fraught with emotional complications. But neither the vision nor the procedure would take shape in her mind. Instead she imagined an angry man whose powerful body seemed made of melted bronze, whose raven-black hair was glossily curled, whose cruel white smile made her shiver as he pulled her naked body beneath his onto a soft bed of tangled white sheets.

Softly she touched her breasts through her starched cotton shirt, and unbidden came the forbidden memory of the yardman's insolent black eyes moving lingeringly over her body, of the molten electricity that had raced through her every time he'd looked at her even when she'd known he disliked her. She remembered his breath, warm and beery smelling, and yet earthily pleasant; she remembered his desperate pain when he'd mentioned the death of his wife. And she remembered his dear, motherless little boy. For all their differences, she sensed the man was as lonely as she was. More than anything she wanted to see the man and his beautiful little boy again.

She tried to imagine the man, dressed in a three-piece suit, with an education as fancy as hers. Fortunately, Kate's ridiculous daydreams were shattered when her large polished mahogany door was pushed open by her secretary. Esther Ayers rushed in clutching her baby daughter, Hannah, in one arm and a bottle of juice and a stack of legal papers in the other.

"Sorry, Kate, but Mom had to go to the dentist, so I had to bring Hannah in for an hour or so. You see, yesterday we took Mother to a restaurant for Mothers' Day after church. Mother shattered a molar when she bit into an oyster."

Mother's Day—Kate ignored her own pain as she remembered going to her own mother's grave and then to the grave of her baby with a bouquet of daisies. She had never gotten to celebrate a single Mother's Day with her mother. She herself would probably never really be a mother.

She got up slowly and held out her arms to the golden two-year-old. With a giggle, Hannah sprang into them.

Esther set the papers on her desk. "These have to be signed so they can go out—today."

"You know I love for you to bring Hannah," Kate said softly. She touched her forehead to the child's and then caressed her golden ringlets. "Hello, there, my beautiful darling. Now how many piggies—"

"Fingas, Kate! Toes! Not piggies!" Hannah squealed, hiding her eyes bashfully.

"Your Mr. Jones has been calling all morning demanding to see you," Esther said.

"My lawyers have advised against such a meeting till the day of the foreclosure."

"You should try telling him that."

The phone rang again.

"That's probably him," Esther said.

Esther was about to pick up the phone, but Kate lifted the receiver herself, knowing Esther really wasn't tough enough to handle certain macho, overbearing types. Kate knelt so Hannah could get down to explore.

"Karlington Enterprises. Miss Karlington's office," Kate said smoothly, pretending to be her secretary.

"Honey, put the dragon lady through, and I swear I'll take you to the fanciest lunch Houston can offer."

Bribery. Kate frowned, even though she knew Esther was too loyal to ever go out with him.

"I'm so sorry. Miss Karlington has someone in her office at the moment, sir," Kate said frostily. Which wasn't exactly a lie.

"Good! She's there! I'll be right over."

"No, I don't want—! I mean *her* lawyers have advised her not to see—"

"Honey, the trouble with this damned country is the lawyers are running it."

"She's too busy to see you. Besides, you're the last man she wants to see."

"Then why did she come snooping around my property Saturday? You tell her that one of my people says she took off her clothes, hopped in his bed and sexually harassed him. Those are some pretty serious charges. I try to run a moral establishment."

"He what? I tell you Ms. Karlington did no such thing! He stripped her—"

Kate broke off, her skin flaming as Esther's curious gaze rose to hers.

"She tried to seduce him into kissing—"

Frantically Kate waved her curious secretary out of the room.

"She most certainly did not!"

"I'm surprised Miss Karlington would keep her secretary so well-informed about such activities—"

Kate's voice was steel. "This is Kate Karlington, Mr. Jones."

"I knew it all the time."

"And I don't want to see you."

"Oh, but you do," he said very softly. "Every bit as much as I want to see you. Women have chased me all my life. From my yardman's description of you, I doubt you'll be any exception. I'm looking forward to meeting you—in the flesh."

"You are as impossible as that horrible man who works for you."

"He and I have a great deal in common."

"I wouldn't brag about it if I were you."

"Funny, but he told me that under different circumstances, you two could have hit it off."

"He what?" she screamed.

When he didn't answer, she realized he'd hung up.

Dear God! He was probably on his way over.

Chapter Four

"I-cream! I-cream!" Hannah leaned forward and pointed to the giant poster of a pink cow licking the top of a huge double-dip parfait coated in chocolate syrup and peanuts. Then Hannah turned her attention back to the man behind the black-and-white-tiled counter who was digging in a huge ice-cream carton for a ball of vanilla.

"I want my *big* i-cream!"

"He's making it, Hannah darling. Just as fast as he can," Kate said soothingly.

"Zakly like the picture?"

"Exactly, precious."

As soon as Kate had hung up from speaking to Jim Keith Jones, Hannah had insisted on being taken downstairs to the ice-cream parlor, which was on the street level. Such trips had become ritual affairs whenever Esther brought her daughter to the office, and today Kate had been only too happy to leave Esther to deal with the troublesome Mr. Jones.

The glass door of the shop suddenly swung open, and a familiar-looking black-haired little boy burst inside and dashed to the counter. "Dad, can I have one of those—" He pointed to the same poster that had caught Hannah's attention.

Hannah put her thumb in her mouth and chewed on it, regarding the interloper curiously while the door was opened slowly and closed again.

"Sure, son. Whatever you want," came the deep velvet tones of an unforgettable, masculine baritone. Kate turned around wildly. The bold blaze of devil-black eyes stared holes through her.

Her heart began to hammer in a painful rush.

"Why, if it isn't the beautiful witch Karlington," came the smooth whisper of the yardman Kate would have given anything to avoid. He didn't look the least bit surprised to see her. Nor the least bit flustered.

Kate clutched the counter for support as the man behind it placed a cherry on top of Hannah's magnificent, double-dip parfait. "There you go, miss—"

"It's not as big as the picture," Hannah cried in dismay.

The yardman smiled grimly. "Most things men do don't live up to a woman's expectations. Not that I've had many complaints from women."

Kate ignored the plastic cup and the towering parfait in the outstretched hand and whirled angrily to stare at the tall man now striding toward her.

He had talked to his boss.

She was about to tell him he was the most conceited blabbermouth she had ever met, but she stopped short. He no longer looked at all like a yardman. Someone with impeccable taste had put him in an elegant black three-piece suit, and he looked even better in it than she'd imagined he would.

No longer did he seem such a lesser being—a ghetto-toughened, uneducated hunk fit only to do menial work. No, this man could fit as easily into her elegant world as he could a darker, more dangerous one. Despite his rough edges, there was the unmistakable aura of keen-minded power about him, as if he was as ruthlessly used to commanding others as she.

Why did the image of that tattered novel by Balzac flash in her mind?

"What a coincidence," he purred raspily, "our meeting again." He was smiling in that grim, bold way that so unnerved Kate because she sensed that their meeting here was no coincidence. He had deliberately hunted her down for some purpose of his own.

She flashed him a tight smile of dismissal and picked up Hannah's parfait.

"Thanks for telling your boss what happened! Did he send you over to do his dirty work?" she whispered.

"Oh, this was my brainchild," he replied while his son ordered a parfait.

"Why?"

"Would you believe I was worried about you and wanted to make sure you were okay?"

"No!"

"Right." His voice was both soft and deep, but he didn't smile. "And you probably intend to hold what happened Saturday against me forever."

"You and I are hardly going to have a forever."

"I'm truly glad you're better."

She couldn't believe it when he touched her injured temple very gently, smoothing her red hair away from her face. "We may be more involved than you think."

"I-cream! I-cream!" Hannah cried impatiently. "Melting!"

"Sorry, darling." Kate turned her back on the yardman and carried Hannah to the nearest booth, placing the mountain of ice cream in front of her, and sitting opposite the child so she could help her.

The yardman handed his son a five-dollar bill, and, without asking if he could join Kate, pulled up a tiny pink stool that was much too small for him and thrust his long legs on either side of it. Hannah had eaten only one bite, but ice cream was already dripping over the plastic sides of her cup and down her chin. Nevertheless, she smiled flirtatiously at the handsome man she took to be her new admirer.

The elegant yardman smiled back at her, picked up a napkin and wiped her small face with a fatherly, well-practiced expertise.

The ogre's roughly carved features were almost sweet as he dealt with Hannah.

"You have a beautiful little girl, Mrs. Karlington— underneath the chocolate syrup," he said.

"It's Miss—"

"Right. I think my boss read somewhere that your husband ran off with a younger woman."

"And I divorced him and took my maiden name back. And Hannah's—not my daughter, either."

The yardman's hard black eyes met Kate's, and she realized he'd caught the pain in her voice.

"But you wish she was," he said quietly.

"Yes," Kate admitted, unnerved that he seemed to understand her on a soul-deep level.

"Maybe you wouldn't like a kid any more than a husband if you were stuck cleaning up chocolate twenty-four hours a day."

"You're wrong. Very, very wrong." Kate frowned.

Bobby Lee joined them, sitting on a stool across from Hannah.

"Why did you really come here?" Kate asked the yardman.

"I told you—to make sure you're okay."

"I'm okay. So you can go. Unless you have some other reason—"

"As a matter of fact I do."

"I'm all ears."

"Since you're going to buy the Jones properties, and I...I work for Jones, I thought maybe I should ask what you intend to do about his people. I mean the little guys...like me."

"I intend to keep most of his people," she hedged, not wanting to admit that she had decided to terminate him.

"That's a relief."

She flushed guiltily.

His face grew hard. "And what about me? Are you going to toss me out into the cold?"

Again he seemed to have read her mind.

Something inside her froze. "Each case will be judged individually," she whispered, turning pale.

"I'm afraid I made a very bad impression."

"Yes."

"I did so deliberately."

"Why did you have to tell your boss everything that happened?"

"He and I are very close."

He took her hand, and the shock of his touch was electric. She tried to draw back, but he held on to her slim fingers tightly.

"W-what do you think you're doing?" she managed to ask.

"Now, this isn't an apology. It's an explanation. I don't like people who walk over other people. Who use their money to buy lawyers and steal legally. I see them as bullies." His hard voice softened. "Even when they are very beautiful."

The warmth in his eyes made her shiver. "I can see Jones has been talking to you out of hand. If your boss has problems, it has nothing to do with me. It's due to his own ineptness."

His fingers tightened on hers. His hard mouth thinned, but he did not defend his boss. "Has your own life gone perfectly? Have you never made a mistake that you deeply regret?"

She stared at him in silence, too aware of her small hand locked in his larger one. Too aware of his heat, his power, his charisma. His immense frame seemed to shrink the size of the booth, to overwhelm her.

"You can work for me—for double what Jones paid you," she said on a desperate note.

His mouth twisted. "You're more generous than you know. But I won't hold you to that."

Hannah looked up and declared proudly, "I'm tru." She lifted her golden head out of the ice-cream dish, her chin and nose dripping with chocolate syrup and vanilla ice cream.

And one glance at her brought the adult conversation to an abrupt end.

Ten minutes later, when Jim Keith strode into Kate's outer office and lavish waiting room, Hannah giggled flirtatiously at him. He smiled back at her on his way past Esther, who was talking on the phone at her desk.

"Wait for me here, Bobby Lee," Jim Keith commanded, pointing to a chair near Hannah.

Bobby Lee ran over to play with the little girl. Jim Keith was about to push open the massive mahogany door that led to Kate's office, when Esther called to him frantically.

"Sir? Sir, do you have an appointment?"

"Your boss is expecting me."

Esther studied her appointment book. "I don't see a ten forty-five."

Jim Keith moved swiftly to her desk, leaned down, and scribbled his name. When he finished, huge, bold black scrawl filled the entire page. "Now you do. We've talked on the phone."

"Jones?" Esther squeaked, deciphering the scribble. Then her big eyes traveled slowly from her book up the vast length of the man to his smiling face. When his masculine beauty struck her full force, her mouth sagged open.

"You're much better looking in person, too," he said with a gentle, arrogant smile. Then he moved away—toward Kate's door.

As he pushed it open, he heard Esther buzzing Kate frantically. "I'm sorry, Kate. I—I couldn't stop him! Keith Jones is on his way in."

"Call security," Kate ordered brusquely just as Jim Keith walked up to her desk, seized the phone, and replaced it in its cradle.

"Why, it's... it's you," she gasped, her horrified eyes trailing up the long length of him just as Esther's had. Kate turned purple. "You're... that awful yard-man."

He forced a smile. "Not awful—surely. Think of me as your gallant rescuer."

"You should have told me who you were Saturday!"

"It was more fun not to."

"I don't like being made a fool of. You'll pay for that little joke, Mr. Jones. Do you hear me?"

"With what? You're already set to take over everything I own," he countered pleasantly.

"A snake with your vile sense of humor deserves to go under."

"Just like a rich witch like yourself deserves to trample everyone in her path. You've taken a lot of other men's properties. Did they all deserve to go under, too?"

"Oooooo!"

"Baby, I learned a long time ago there's no justice in this world."

He leaned over and grabbed the file she had on him and his properties. When she got up, he waved her down and snapped the manila folder open and thumbed through it, quickly scanning the bleak numbers.

He whistled. "You damn sure have the goods on me!"

"I know everything about you, Mr. Jones."

"Everything about my financial predicament," he clarified. Looking up, his dark face was weary with defeat. "But not everything. Still, you're thorough," he admitted grimly.

For some reason she didn't feel like gloating. Her mouth felt too tight to smile. "I try to be businesslike, Mr. Jones."

"Ruthless! You certainly have me by the—"

"Which is right where I want you."

"Indeed?" His brazen gaze swept below his belt and then back to her with a derisive grin.

Her swift blush of humiliation was not nearly so satisfying as he'd anticipated. Instead he was moved by her wide vulnerable eyes. She was scared. Fortunately, before he said anything mushy or stupidly comforting, two burly security guards rushed in.

"Take him," Kate ordered coldly, recovering herself.

"I could have turned you over to the cops Saturday," Jim Keith whispered as the men moved toward him. "I knew who you were. Or I could have let you drown at the bottom of my pool. Instead I saved your life."

She didn't answer. She refused to look at him.

Her men grabbed his shoulders. "Let's go, mister."

Jim Keith shrugged them away. "Kate, for God's sake, you've won," he whispered. "I just came over here because I'd really like to talk to you."

She continued to stare down at her desk. She clenched her hands, and he saw that her knuckles were white. He was almost surprised when she uttered a strangled whisper to her two men. "You can go for now. I'll buzz you—if I need you."

When they were alone again, she got up and went to the window and, turning her back, stared down at the city. The sunlight backlighted the sexy shape of her body, and he remembered just how good she'd looked naked in his bed. His loins tightened.

Suddenly her vast office seemed airless. His suit felt like a straitjacket, and he was tugging at his tie.

"So—what could we possibly have to talk about?" she asked in a quiet, businesslike tone.

"I need more time," he rasped. "Six months."

"I am afraid not."

"You were born rich," he began.

She breathed deeply. Which made her breasts rise and fall. Which made him feel hotter. He yanked the knot of his tie loose.

"A harder fate than you can possibly imagine," she whispered. "My mother died, and my father... I ran away when I was five and lived with an older, childless aunt for a year. Then my father took me away from her and put me in boarding schools. I hardly saw him—until I was grown."

"The finest schools, I'm sure. And after that you languished at Harvard and Cornell."

Languished . . . "Yes. . . ." She nodded.

Jim Keith tried not to see the tears in her eyes. He forced a hard note into his voice. "Well, I was born poor, which might be a tougher fate than you could imagine, honey. I would have given anything to have the time or the money to get even one college degree—here locally. You have three eastern degrees."

"Lucky me." She caught herself. "Look—I thought you wanted to talk business. I've got more to do than listen to your poor-boy jealousies."

He got up slowly. "I'm not jealous of you, damn it. I wouldn't be you for anything in the world. Is your work only money, numbers . . ."

"What else should it be?"

"I spent years building up everything you're going to take Friday."

"I know."

He moved nearer. "But do you know how that feels? I know my stuff doesn't equal a fraction of your net worth, but I put myself into buying it. Into running it. I don't sit around in some fancy skyscraper with dozens of employees and handmaidens bringing me coffee. I know every tenant and every man who works for me. Every manager. I've overseen every repair. I've done a lot of them myself."

"Then you've spread yourself too thin. Mr. Jones, you borrowed a great deal of money three and a half years ago, and yet your properties are terribly neglected. What did you do, party it all away?"

"Party it away?" he asked, thunderstruck. He thought of Mary—sick and thin, dying even, and the money he'd borrowed to save her. Maybe he'd been a fool not to listen to the American doctors who'd warned him the German doctors would fail, but this witch's contempt made something explode inside him.

"You're in way over your head, too, honey," he growled. "What I did with the money is none of your business."

"If I could see where you'd spent a dime on your property—"

"You push. You want more, more, but nothing you get will ever be enough without—"

Later he would never know what drove him to do what he did. Later he would hate himself. But he didn't think. The rage inside him had been building for months, for years, from that first terrible moment when Mary had been diagnosed, and suddenly Kate was here—sexy Kate, his destroyer.

Kate, cruelly beautiful, magnificently beautiful with her healthily flushed cheeks and flaming hair; Kate, more wondrously beautiful and far more desirable even than his gentle Mary. Kate, who made his blood pulse with angry blazing needs he would have given anything to deny if only he hadn't been too furious and too aroused to think straight.

She looked so cool and imperious—untouched by the real world and real feelings, so untouched by the kind of unfair fate he had endured. Had she ever known the bitter taste of failure? He could not go down without making her suffer just a little, too.

So he grabbed her, his fingers sinking into her soft flesh with a crushing grip as he caught her to his hard body. Then his angry lips were devouring hers with more hunger than he'd ever felt. His tongue filled her mouth, tasting her, exploring her. Claiming her. His hands slid down her back and buttocks, arching her into his body.

And she felt good, so good that his hunger was suddenly stronger than his anger. Maybe she was hard and ruthless when it came to business, but in his arms, she became the softest and most pliant creature. She made not the slightest effort to resist him.

At first she went rigidly still, but when his mouth touched hers, she made a soft, endearing little moan that tugged at his heart. She opened her lips to his tongue. Her need seemed delicious and sweet. She seemed somehow so untouched and innocent. And suddenly he craved more of her.

Her trembling hands came around his neck, her fingers gently clutching at first and then raking through his inky hair as if she could no more deny her own feelings for him than he.

"I'm supposed to hate you," she whispered raggedly even as she clung, breathing hard, pressing her slim, trembling body into his.

"Likewise," he muttered as he lowered his mouth to hers again. This time her tongue came inside his lips, and her response aroused him to do more, to want more, until he felt himself swept near some fatal edge on a burning tide of desire.

She was his enemy, and surely God had the cruel-est, the most warped sense of humor to make Kate Karlington the one woman whose look and touch could make him want to get past his grief over Mary.

But he did. He wanted to strip her and devour her slim pale body. All day Sunday, visions of her naked loveliness had haunted him.

He wanted to plunge deep inside her and stay en-cased in her warm velvet flesh, joined—until he made her know that she could never belong to anyone but him.

He cursed God that she who thought him a fool for his failures was the one woman he wanted. Suddenly he knew how ridiculous she must find him. How she must despise him. This realization made her sweet-tasting, eager mouth and warm voluptuous body a torture.

He forced himself to let her go, and the instant he did, she slapped him.

Then she gasped at the livid white mark on his tanned cheek and stumbled backward. The intense emotion in her eyes was more desperately sad than angry. "Get out," she whispered. "Get out."

Her half-open, cotton blouse hung limp and wrin-kled. Her lovely face was tear-streaked and swollen from his kisses. Her eyes were ravaged and pain-filled. Her hair had come out of its clip and fell in wild tan-gles about her shoulders.

She looked young and vulnerable, more fragile than he could ever have imagined Kate Karlington being. But more than anything, she was desirable.

"I'm sorry," he whispered hoarsely. "I shouldn't have kissed you. I just wanted to make you know that I was more than just a bunch of debits and credits in one of your files. More than a failure. I'm a man. A human being. I guess I won't blame you for cutting me to ribbons now."

He expected her to lash back at him. Instead her face softened. Her vulnerable green eyes widened, and he felt uncomfortably aware of some powerful unwanted bond with her. Her hands shook as she tried to rebutton her blouse.

Maybe she wasn't an ice-cold witch after all. Maybe the fiery softness he'd sensed in her when she'd yielded to his kisses was real. Maybe she was as lonely and as deeply hurt by life as he.

"You're wrong about me," she said, pulling her hair back nervously into her clip. "And...I'm sorry I slapped you." She reached up to stroke his rough cheek where she'd hurt him.

Her fingers were unbearably cool and light against his burning skin.

His hand closed over her delicate wrist. When he felt her pulse racing beneath his thumb, his own heart began to pound. He wanted to take her in his arms, to kiss her again.

Was he crazy?

"Mr. Jones, I don't really want to take over your properties right now. I—I would have let you have the time, but the fact is, time won't help you."

Every nerve in his hard body tightened warily.

"You need capital, Mr. Jones, and you don't have it. I do." Her voice was sweet; she almost sounded as if she really cared.

He *was* crazy. *She was his enemy.*

He cast her slim hand aside and stepped back, rejecting the comfort of her touch and her voice because he wanted them too much. "Right. You're all heart," he ground out.

"Then I'll see you Friday," she whispered as he rushed past her toward the door. "Then we'll be done with each other once and for all."

"Till that happy day," he muttered bitterly, ignoring the shimmering pain in her eyes as he stalked out.

Chapter Five

Jim Keith signed away everything he owned with an angry flourish of scrawling black ink. Then he threw his pen down in disgust and rose from the desk to his full height.

Although he didn't look at Kate, he was too aware of her sleek, long-limbed body in that exquisitely tailored, navy linen suit, and the cool perfection of her professional presence somehow magnified his masculine feelings of failure. He had spent the past week alternately hating her and hungering for her and then despising himself for the insane war going on inside him.

He glanced toward her and was struck again by how pale and exhausted she appeared this morning, as if she, too, was suffering. There were dark circles beneath her lovely eyes. She looked thinner—hardly a worthy foe. The stark truth was he'd been bested by a spoiled woman who was so fragile, he could easily have torn her apart with his bare hands. Not that he had ever physically hurt a woman, not that he even wanted to hurt her—not in that way. No, what he wanted—

Just for a second his gaze slid from her white face to the prim starched collar of her creamy blouse, which she had buttoned all the way to the top as if to conceal as much flesh as possible. He remembered another blouse, a white cotton blouse—torn open nearly to her waist, the thick cotton wrinkled from his rough lovemaking. He remembered how wantonly beautiful she'd looked, flushed from his kisses—not so perfect but somehow so human—and he wanted to be alone with her. To loosen those buttons, to touch the skin beneath the creamy cotton, to show her that although she had taken everything he owned, he could conquer her just as easily.

He squared his broad shoulders in a gesture of denial. What he had to do was get away from her, to forget her. To start over.

He grabbed his bulging briefcase and was almost out the door when she called out to him, the honey of her phonily sweet voice making his stomach claw.

"Mr. Jones, before you go, I'd like to talk to you—alone."

Although gently spoken, it was a command.

His mouth tightened as he fought against the violence he felt. Somehow he managed an indifferent shrug. "What could you and I possibly have to talk about now?"

"I have a proposition that might interest you."

Her tone was softer, beguilingly softer—it tore him apart.

Jim Keith's black gaze swept from her blazing green eyes downward, noting her curves hungrily, and thinking that despite her pallor and her prim suit, despite her extreme nervousness, she had never looked more beautiful.

"Sorry, not interested," he muttered brutally, shoving the door open with his thick briefcase.

She went white, those huge eyes of hers flickering with pain at his insulting tone. He realized suddenly that she wasn't gloating, that she hadn't really wanted to hurt him—that this foreclosure was strictly business as far as she was concerned.

Too bad he couldn't write it off as just another business deal gone sour.

The craziest thing of all was that *he* actually felt an odd pang of remorse at having hurt her.

"I really would like to talk to you," she said, her voice tighter, but nicer than he deserved.

Nicer than he wanted.

"All right. But make it fast." He yanked the heavy chair away from the desk and sat down again while the others paraded dutifully out of the room.

"Does everyone always do what you want them to?" he spat contemptuously.

She paled at some unhappy memory, but she ignored Jim Keith's thrust. "Last week, you asked me what I intended to do about the people who worked for you. About you. And I said—"

"I remember what you said. Every damned word. You don't have to repeat it. I know you're as eager to be rid of me as I am to be rid of you. I won't hold you to what you said."

"I really would like to offer you a job."

"No way."

"You haven't even heard what I have in mind."

"Look, you've now got everything I ever owned. Isn't that enough? Are you determined to gobble me alive, too?"

"No—"

"Yes. You are. Look, I've been on my own since I was sixteen. Paper route. All sorts of things. I haven't worked for anyone in years. And never for a woman. Much less for the one woman who repossessed everything I once owned. I wouldn't know how to be one of your obedient lackeys."

"I wouldn't expect you to be," she said in that thick, velvety voice.

"How could I work for you—managing properties that were once mine?"

"Lots of people have done it."

"Not me. Besides, why would you want to hire a failure?"

"I don't see you that way."

Although her kind words warmed him, he laughed mirthlessly, more determined than ever that what he really wanted was to rid himself of her forever.

"Except for that one loan three and a half years ago, your management has been superb. I have taken on a lot of properties besides yours, and I'm overextended. I—I don't mean financially.... I really do need some managerial help." She wrote down a figure on a piece of paper and handed it to him. "This is the annual salary I'm prepared to offer you. I wish I could pay you more, but as you know, the real-estate market is precarious. I wouldn't want to make a promise I couldn't afford to keep."

He glared at the huge number and then at her, even more furious than before—because he needed the money so desperately, and she was being so generous.

No! She wasn't generous! When she wanted something, she bought it.

But the offer tempted him. So did the woman.

"Is there anything you've ever wanted and never been able to buy?" he demanded in a hard whisper.

"You might be surprised."

Working for himself, he'd never taken home nearly as much as she was offering him—which she knew. He'd plowed most of his profit back into the properties. "What makes you think I'd be worth that amount?"

"I'm sure you'll earn every penny."

He wondered what she wanted him to do to earn so much money. He sucked in a deep breath and decided it would be stupid to insult her by asking.

If he went to work for her, he'd be selling out.

If he didn't, he'd be a fool. He was dead broke. Hell, he needed the job. He would make enough so he could save, so he could eventually reinvest and begin again on his own. It wasn't as if she'd own him forever.

"I know you don't like me very much," she said softly, "but we won't have to see that much of each other."

"Is that a promise?"

"Yes." The pain in her voice tugged at some tender emotion in him he didn't want to acknowledge. "I'm sorry. About today. I—I really don't want you to hate me."

He wished he did hate her, but he remembered how cute he'd thought she was when she'd gamely taken him on about Bobby Lee's lurid reading material. He remembered her diving into that pool to save his kid. He remembered the wild terror he'd felt when he'd pulled her limp body from the pool, when he'd struggled to force air into her lungs. He remembered as well his thrill of joy when she'd spit out water and gasped that first tortured breath. Most of all he remembered how awed he'd been by the perfection of her naked body, how hungry he'd been for the taste of her mouth, how hungry he still was—and for so much more than kisses. Even though he wanted to hate her, he was powerfully drawn by her.

He wanted to work for her... and not just for the salary, and not just to find some way to exact revenge. He wanted to figure her out.

"How could I possibly like you?" he asked cruelly in response to her earlier statement. "You're a Karlington. You've bought me—like you've bought everything else you ever wanted."

"Must you always be so rude... and—and so insolent to me?"

"Why not? You have it coming. Besides, when you get to know me better, you'll find out I have a lot more flaws."

"When I get to know—"

"Yes. You see, I've decided I have no choice but to take the job. And whatever it is, I'll do my best to satisfy you, honey. At the price you've named, I am yours." As her shimmering green gaze fearfully met his, he could feel his own heart surging very hard and very fast. "And I promise you, Kate—you'll get a helluva lot more than your money's worth."

Kate Karlington had frequently remembered his promise in the three months that had followed, for never had any employee worked harder and made himself more invaluable to her than Keith, as she called him now. It was as if he was determined to prove his worth both to himself and to her.

Not that she saw much of him. He deliberately kept out of her way. And the fact that he did, only made her perversely crave to be near him. She sought him out on a thousand pretexts, and it hurt her that although he was unfailingly courteous, he remained tightly guarded around her, while with everyone else, he was genial and easygoing. With Esther he was almost flirtatious, and Kate could always tell when he was in her outer office by Esther's warm laughter. Occasionally he took Esther to lunch. And because he did, a tight, jealous coolness had come into her own relationship with her secretary.

Keith welcomed input from both tenants and managers and, to Kate's surprise, from her. He was not threatened by other people's good ideas. On those rare occasions when she chose to override him, he usually gave in gracefully. She'd known he'd be good, but not nearly as invaluable as he was. While she was steady, he was more innovative and more willing to take risks.

Although they didn't think alike, their talents balanced each other. They worked well together.

He was very protective of her and wouldn't allow her to go out to troubleshoot at the tougher projects, especially at night. He handled all the difficult clients and hostile tenants himself. Thus, she was working shorter hours while her properties were better run, better maintained, safer and more profitable than they'd ever been before. There was only one thing he could be awful about: he'd repeatedly and quite arrogantly refused to help her buy discounted notes or negotiate repossessions.

Once when she'd needed to go out of town and had asked for his help with a foreclosure, she'd lost her patience and pressed him too hard.

"No," he had thundered, his control breaking. "You may think you own me body and soul, but you don't, Kate. Not quite. I won't steal for you—no matter how much I need the damned money you pay me."

"You leave me no choice—"

"Why don't you fire me, then?" he asked, his eyes blazing as he strode toward her. He was so furious, he had forgotten what she suspected was his unwritten code—to keep to the opposite side of any room he was forced to share with her.

Kate glanced fearfully up at him. Physically he was so huge and powerfully built, he could have done anything to her.

Not that he raised either of his large, tightly clenched, brown fists. Still, she backed away just a little, licking her dry mouth.

"Why don't you put us both out of our misery? Fire me. Then we'll finally be rid of each other." His eyes met hers and then ran down her body burningly.

"D-don't look at me like that."

"Like what, honey?"

"Like you want to eat me alive."

His face tensed; so did his whole body, as he sought to curb his fierce emotion. "Maybe that's not so easy sometimes. Especially when I think you really want me to."

"I don't!" she denied swiftly.

"You're lying. We both know it."

"No—"

He laughed. "If you don't like it, go on then, fire me. Do it, honey, and I'm outta here."

She knew he would go; she'd never see him again. Some part of her wanted that as much as he did. And yet some other part only felt alive knowing he was near.

Kate glared at him. "I—I can't."

"Then do your own dirty work," he snarled softly. "But, honey, I'm available to you—personally—anytime after hours."

"What?"

"You bought me, remember? You can have my body. Just not my soul."

His insolent macho remark cracked like a bullet. Surely he didn't think her so, low, so desperate—

"Dear God," she whispered.

His feverish gaze made her all too aware that he had meant every chilling word. He smiled wolfishly as a telltale tide of hot color crept into her cheeks.

"You are awful," she gasped. "Simply awful."

He just smiled.

She was silent.

"If you change your mind, honey, you'll have to chase me. Because I damn sure don't intend to throw myself at you again and beg you for it," he taunted.

"You're crazy if you think I'd ever, ever do that!"

His black eyes cut her like impaling shards of razor-sharp glass. "Maybe..." His dazzling smile was equally ruthless. "But I think not."

"You coldhearted, conceited bast—"

She uttered a wild, strangled cry, but when he reached for her, she was too agitated to note that his hard face had softened with remorse and concern for her. Not wanting his pity, she pushed him away, and he stiffened as she ran blindly past him.

She had rushed home to pack and then canceled her business trip because she was too overwrought to go, and the next morning she had convinced herself that she really would have to fire him. But the first thing she saw when she walked into her office was a single red rose and a crisp white note covered in his bold black scrawl. *Forgive me. I was very angry and very rude. And I'm sorry.* That was all. There was no signature. But she sank down in her chair, clutching his note and the rose to her heart.

After that terrible confrontation, Keith was more careful than ever to avoid her. But when Keith's sister, Maggie, who often baby-sat Bobby Lee, brought the little boy to see his father at the office, Bobby Lee always left his aunt and father and rushed in to say hi to Kate. The boy seemed to sense the natural affinity she felt for children, and the two of them grew closer. The child was so open and friendly with Kate that she could easily bestow on him all the warmth and affection that his father would have coldly rejected. Maggie and she had become friends, too.

Once when Kate had been embracing Bobby Lee in a proud, motherly hug after he showed her a blue ribbon he'd won in a swim meet, she'd looked up to see Keith standing silently in the door. His expression had been dark, almost...almost jealous. No. She was wrong. The last thing Keith wanted was kindness or warmth for himself from her. He probably just resented his son developing a close attachment to her.

Something Maggie had said about Bobby Lee's mother had made Kate increasingly curious about Keith and about that ill-advised loan that had caused him to lose his holdings. Since Keith always cut her off every time she got near any subject that was remotely personal, Kate did what she'd always done—she bought the information she wanted by hiring a private investigator. And after she found out that he'd come from a big, poor but loving family, that he'd married his high school sweetheart whom he'd appar-

ently loved so deeply, he'd mortgaged himself to the
hilt to try to save her when she'd become ill, Kate had
burst into tears, regretting that she'd foreclosed on his
properties.

Kate remembered how he'd come to her and begged
her to extend his loans for six months. If she'd only
known why he'd borrowed the money, she might not
have been so tough, and now he might not be so determined to keep their relationship so cool and professional. She longed for a way to make amends, to
establish some middle ground that would lead to a
warmer, friendlier relationship, but he was so fiercely
proud and so determined to avoid her, she was baffled as to how to approach him. When Esther, who
had become his friend, told her he'd begun to date
again, Kate felt more desolate than ever.

She was losing him.

She had never had him. So, he was the father of the
most darling little boy, a child she could have easily
adopted for her own.

So, Keith had stripped her and teased her. So, he
had kissed her once and made her feel more wantonly
alive than she'd ever known she could feel. So, he was
fabulous at running her business. So, he was the most
handsome hunk she'd ever known and was right about
her wanting him—desperately.

To him she was merely the woman who'd foreclosed on him, and his boss, a woman he would brutally humiliate the first chance he got. She knew that
he was saving his money, planning for the day when he
could quit her.

Why did she care anyway? Hadn't she learned anything from Edwin? The wrong kind of relationship with Keith could prove far more devastating.

But Kate couldn't quit wanting him. One summer evening she was leaving her office late when she saw a ribbon of light beneath Keith's door. She was surprised since he usually stayed away from his office—to avoid her, she suspected. Then she remembered Esther gaily having told her he'd been forced to make a late appointment with Mr. Stewart, a difficult owner from out of town for whom they managed two thousand rental units and three strip shopping centers, all of which needed an infusion of cash.

She should have gone home; instead she knocked hesitantly on Keith's door.

He opened it himself, and as always, just the nearness of his darkly handsome face and his broad-shouldered frame in that crisp white shirt made her blood pressure rise.

"Kate," he drawled coolly, frowning, his black gaze meeting hers and darkening briefly before he forced a wary smile.

She hardly noticed Mr. Stewart's short, rotund figure rising clumsily from his chair. She was shivering from the feel of Keith's fingers at her slim back, guiding her inside, as if their relationship was an easy, harmonious one.

"I'm sorry to interrupt," she began.

"On the contrary, I'm glad you did," Mr. Stewart said.

Keith led her to the chair beside his own. "Since you're here, maybe you can convince Mr. Stewart he's going to continue to lose money if he doesn't put some real money into his properties."

Then she and Keith worked together, as though they were equal partners, smoothly presenting their arguments, backing each other up, and an hour and a half later Mr. Stewart handed Keith a large check and promised more.

Then Mr. Stewart was gone, and Kate was alone with Keith for the first time since that last terrible encounter.

"You were good," he said quietly, his dark eyes fastened on her face in that intense way that made her pulse race.

"So were you," she whispered, unused to praise from him and feeling too hot suddenly.

She wished she could forget that awful taunt of his, but it haunted her. *If you change your mind, honey, you'll have to chase me. Because I damn sure don't intend to throw myself at you again and beg you for it.*

Unaware of her thoughts, he stood up and pulled his suit jacket off the back of his chair. She got up, too, and went nervously to the window.

If you change your mind . . .

Behind her he snapped the chain on his desk lamp, and the tiny room melted into soft darkness. She became aware of the sparkling stars and the spread of city lights and of the brilliant silver moon. It was Friday night, a night lovers spent together. As usual, she was set to spend it alone.

Her stomach growled unromantically.

He laughed huskily, almost easily—something he hadn't ever done around her. "Sounds like someone besides me worked up an appetite."

"I *am* hungry," she admitted, shyly meeting his eyes again and feeling drawn to him as never before. He looked away.

If you change your mind, honey, you'll have to chase me....

Suddenly she realized she was starving, and not just for food. For companionship. For Keith's companionship. For much much more than that.

He rammed his hands deep into his pockets, spoiling the fit of his suit. "We'd better get the hell out of here."

"It's such a pretty night," she whispered, stalling, not following him as he headed toward the door.

"Hot and humid," he said a little impatiently as he thrust the door open.

"But pretty from here," she said, lingering still. "What do you do most Friday nights?"

"Not much," he said grimly.

"Do you have a date tonight?"

"Do you?"

"Not yet," she said.

"What's that supposed to mean?"

"I—I could buy you dinner?" *Was that chasing?*

"I don't think that's such a good idea," he countered.

Rejection. Her father had never wanted to spend time with her. She had never known how to make friends.

Why had she bothered to ask him? She felt hollow now. She should shut up and thereby salvage what was left of her wounded pride. She should leave and pretend she felt nothing. But she had no pride where he was concerned, and even to her ears, her low voice sounded too pleading.

"Look, I know you probably still resent what I did three months ago when I foreclosed—"

"Don't," he said almost sharply.

"But I'm sorry," she went on desperately in a rush. "I—I didn't know about your wife then."

"How did you find— The last thing I want to discuss with you is Mary." But his tone was softer, gentler, as if he sensed her pain.

"I—I don't blame you for hating me."

"Damn."

When she approached the door, she felt him tense as if her nearness bothered him, too, but he just stood there stiffly, waiting for her, holding the door, not looking at her.

"I know you didn't want to work for me, and still you've been wonderful—"

She walked on past him, passing so close to his body that her arm brushed his. Fleetingly she felt the warmth of him like a small electric shock.

She stopped. "Keith, you may not believe this, but I know what it feels like to lose...everything. To... fail."

"You're right. I don't believe it."

She heard his key click in the lock. She would have given anything to know what he was thinking, what he was feeling. She wondered if he had any idea how truly sorry she was.

She had always wanted love and affection and warmth, but she'd never known how to get it. Her shoulders hunched.

Then from behind her came his low voice, slower and warmer than she'd ever heard him speak to anyone. "Kate, how do you feel about barbecue?"

She whirled around, feeling a sudden overwhelming eagerness, her eyes shining. "What?"

He took her trembling hand in his and smiled. "It's yes to supper, if you'll come eat barbecue with me."

"I never do. You'll have to pick the restaurant."

"No problem. And another thing, Kate—tonight, I pay."

"You don't have to." She grinned impishly. *"I'm chasing you."*

His swift hot glance told her he knew exactly what she meant. "Are you sure?"

"Very."

For a moment he hesitated. Then his arm touched her back possessively, and he led her toward the elevator.

Chapter Six

Jim Keith was coldly furious with himself as he took a pull from his long neck and watched Kate across the crowded restaurant. She was saying hi to some tony acquaintances of hers, and from the way Kate's glamorous, blond girlfriends were eyeing him and Kate was blushing, he figured they must be teasing her about him. Since they looked like society types, they probably disapproved of her going out with a guy who wasn't part of their rich crowd. The beer was icy, which was good, because he suddenly felt so hot.

Why the hell had he let that vulnerable, pleading look of Kate's get to him and make him agree to come out with her? Why hadn't he made some excuse and said he planned to spend the evening with Bobby Lee? Why did sharing a simple dinner with Kate have to seem so dangerous?

Because she had said, "I'm chasing you," in that sweetly beguiling way that had made his flesh feel tight and wild. That made him know how much he wanted her.

Because just finding himself alone with her in the velvet darkness of his car had made him forget they came from two different worlds, made him forget that she was rich and he was a failure. More than anything, he had hungered fiercely to pull the car over and put his hands all over her.

Not that she had come on to him again during the short drive to the restaurant. She'd seemed as tense and shyly nervous as he—as if she'd regretted asking him.

He took another pull from the bottle as he remembered that drive. While he'd turned on the air-conditioning full blast, she'd flipped his radio to a booming rock station. But the jungle beat had only fired his blood. When he'd finally stopped at the restaurant, her fingers had been so shaky, she hadn't been able to unfasten her seat belt. She'd cried out in frustration, and he'd turned off the radio and helped her, saying hoarsely and yet gently, "Look, we can forget you said it. You can still back out—"

"So can you," she had whispered.

And maybe he would have if she hadn't reached across the darkness almost reluctantly and touched his rough cheek with those tender, trembling fingertips, if she hadn't then buried her face gently in the hollow of his neck for a long moment, drawing a deep, shaking breath. If he hadn't taken her in his arms and held her comfortingly. If she hadn't felt so small and warm, so utterly defenseless and yet so deliciously feminine—so damnably right.

Just when he'd figured she'd never have the guts, she'd picked up the gauntlet he'd so cruelly thrown down. If she'd capitulated earlier, she wouldn't have been half so dangerous. But now he no longer saw her as some cruel, avaricious vulture who'd mercilessly stripped him. Even if she was too rich and too elegant, too well educated and too hung up for someone of his more common background, he also saw that she was vulnerably human. He was beginning to see that her cold rejecting father had made her feel worthless and unlovable.

Keith had also grudgingly come to admire certain aspects of her character. Despite her money, she didn't behave condescendingly to him. She didn't shirk work, and she seemed to appreciate his. They both had high energy levels. She genuinely loved kids. Indeed, she was always so sweet to Hannah and Bobby Lee that at times Keith was almost jealous of his own son.

Nor could Jim Keith deny that she was the cause of his starting to get over Mary. Whenever Kate came within five feet of him, every muscle in his body got so tense and hard, it was all he could do not to seize her and show her how much he wanted her. That was why he'd been so awful to her and tried to force her to fire him when she'd pushed him about helping her with that repo. He hadn't known how he could go on working for her, wanting her and pretending he didn't.

But she hadn't fired him even when he'd hurt her. And he'd realized he would have been even more miserable if she had. So he'd played this waiting game, his pride demanding that she, who was so far above him socially and monetarily, she who was his boss, humble herself and come to him.

He didn't like her being richer and probably smarter than he was, but he had found more to like about her every day. He had always been confident about his appeal to women, but the opposite was true of her. She had no idea how attractive she was. He hadn't ever seen her flirt with another man. He felt sorry for her, and yet at the same time he was glad she lacked confidence with other men. That made the fact that she found him attractive and was brave enough to show it all the more special.

Thus, what he felt now was much more powerful than a mere physical attraction or that initial vengeful desire to get even. If she was confused, so was he. He knew she was afraid of him, afraid of all men, and yet hellishly compelled anyway. Just as he was.

He'd taken Esther to lunch to learn about Kate. Esther had described Kate's motherless childhood, her cold, rejecting father, the lonely boarding schools, and Edwin's marrying her for her money and then breaking her heart by leaving her, forcing her to deal with the unexpected pregnancy alone. But the thing that had hit him the hardest was what Esther had said about Kate's miscarriage.

"She was like a ghost when she came out of that hospital," Esther had said. "When Edwin didn't come to the memorial service, Kate wouldn't let anyone else comfort her. We were afraid that she might do something desperate, but slowly she got better."

Jim Keith's heart had gone out to Kate for her lonely life. Since he'd always had to work so hard for every dime, since she was rich and he was broke, she probably saw him as a money-grubbing bastard who could never be interested in her without ulterior motives. She'd probably think he was after her money or revenge. Then he'd played on her fears and made things worse by saying he'd sold her his body.

Damn—he regretted that.

From across the room, Kate smiled shyly at him again, and the vulnerable warmth in her eyes lit every part of him. A long shuddering wave of desire racked him as he studied the lush curve of her mouth and remembered her sweet taste. His hand froze on the long neck. Then slowly he raised the bottle to his lips and tried to quench his hot thirst for her with another icy swig.

But Kate couldn't seem to quit looking at him, and as he drained the bottle, he knew nothing but the taste of her lips could ever satisfy him. He set the empty bottle down and shoved it away, easing his long body slowly off the wooden bench.

As if in a dream, she moved toward him, too. Behind her the red-and-white-checkered tablecloths and blinking neon beer sign that hung on the wall blurred hazily.

They met halfway across that smoky, crowded room—on the edge of the dance floor, standing so close, they could have touched, and yet not touching as the silence between them grew as hot and taut as his nerves. Someone put a quarter in the jukebox, and the throbbing rhythm and the singer's melancholy crooning only magnified the tense longing he felt for her.

"Dance with me," she whispered.

His breath caught as she came into his arms. She stretched onto her tiptoes; one of her slender hands reached up and clutched his wide shoulder, and just that feather-light touch against his crisp cotton shirt brought a sudden flare of heat to every male cell in his body.

"Kate..." he said hoarsely, warningly.

Her light fingertips moved across his shoulder to his throat. "Please, Keith. Hold me."

When her warm breath whispered across his skin, he knew he was lost.

"Why the hell not?" he muttered thickly as his hard arms circled her closely.

When she pressed her slim body into his, his blood began to pound with a furious rush. He crushed her so tightly against his chest that he could feel her nipples grow erect beneath her thin silk blouse. Instinctively her slim body swayed so perfectly with his that it seemed they'd been dancing together all their lives. And yet, it wasn't that way at all. For she was thrillingly, wondrously new to him.

He lowered his dark head and saw that her inky lashes were trustingly closed against cheeks that were rapturously aglow. His hand stole slowly up and down her back, beneath the thick waves of her silky hair, molding her to him even more tightly until his every breath was hot and raspy. Until his heart thundered, until his blood coursed through his arteries like fire. Until the music and the beer and the soft perfumed essence of her voluptuous body worked together to destroy what was left of his iron control.

They were only halfway through the song when he felt too wretchedly turned on to take another step.

Sweat was beading his dark brow when he broke away from her abruptly.

In the dimly lit restaurant, she looked at him with wide, unafraid eyes, her red hair curling against her pale face. And he thought never had any woman seemed more beautiful.

"What's wrong?" she asked innocently.

"Either we get the hell out of here and I take you to bed—now, or we sit down and order," was all he could manage.

She almost sprinted to their table. He followed at a slower pace. They ordered ribs and sausage and more beer.

Maybe it was the beer that got him talking. Maybe it was just Kate—looking at him with those adoring green eyes as if she hung on his every word. Whatever it was, he forgot how rich and socially wrong she was for him and broke every damned rule he'd ever made about how he'd behave around her.

He'd sworn he'd never get personal. To his horror he found himself telling her about Mary, how he'd loved her, how happy they'd always been even when they'd been poor, how he'd wanted to die when she'd died, how he'd felt so guilty about failing to save her that he hadn't cared much about real estate for a long time, how he'd gone on living only because of Bobby Lee. But how lately he'd been glad he had—because of Kate.

Most women didn't want to hear about another woman, but Kate seemed so genuinely interested in him that he couldn't stop talking. At several points, her hand had closed over his, and it was as if he gave her his pain and she willingly took it.

He told her about his habit of drinking on Mary's birthday and on their anniversary, about how he'd been doing that the night before he'd met her and that was why he'd deliberately goaded her that first day. He told Kate that even when he'd thought he'd hated her, from the minute he'd seen her sneaking onto his property, he'd stopped grieving so much for Mary.

Not that he told Kate everything. Not that he admitted the reason he'd worked so hard for her was to please her, to win her admiration, her respect. Not that Kate confided in him. But she listened, and he felt a deeper closeness to her.

The evening would have been ordinary, had his feelings for Kate not been so dazzling that even the ordinary became wonderful. After they ate, he called Maggie and made sure she didn't mind Bobby Lee's sleeping over. Then he drove Kate down to Galveston, and they walked along the beach, talking still. Later he took her to a nightclub to dance. And all too soon he found himself inside her elegant sky-rise apartment, sipping Scotch from her expensive crystal as he held her in his arms and looked out upon her magnificent view of the sprawling city and the Galleria. Then he was kissing her, and her body was melting into his, her mouth and skin sweeter and more intoxicating than the smoothest, hottest liquor.

He had no idea how he negotiated the dark halls and circular stairway as he carried her up to her bed, nor how he got her undressed and into that bed. All he knew was that when he fitted her naked body to his, when her legs wrapped around his waist and her voluptuous lips caressed his mouth and throat, this was what he'd craved from the first moment he'd set eyes on this lush, vibrant, passionate creature.

Her careful control was gone. She was writhing and twisting; and her warm flesh stirring against his thighs set him aflame. He caught her to him and held her tightly as she impatiently urged him into that final, most intimate embrace. He kept trying to go slow, and she kept passionately urging for more. Only in that last moment, when he was ready to plunge deeply inside her, did he remember that he had to protect her.

"Just a minute, honey," he murmured, his heart thudding violently as he released her.

Leaning across her trembling body, he fumbled for his wallet on the floor. He had the thing out of the wrapper and was pulling it on when her velvet-soft voice stopped him.

"No," she whispered in that same beguiling tone that had tempted him to come out with her tonight, gently trying to push his hand away. "You don't have to put that on."

Her soft, warm, soothing lips moved along his neck while her seeking hands explored his body, tempting him from his purpose, and for an instant he did forget everything except the exquisite torture of those slim hands circling his manhood.

Then he was on fire to enter her. But he had always taken responsibility for any woman he'd ever made love to, and not even passion could make him set aside his fierce principles. He had to protect her from the consequences of tonight's lovemaking.

You don't have to put that on, she had said.

Why the hell not? he wondered.

Her fingertips lightly stroked his silken male flesh in delicate circular motions until he shivered, tightening, until he felt he'd burst in her hand if he didn't get inside her.

He was panting hard—dying for her. Every nerve cell in his body urged him to take her.

She opened her body so that he could slide inside her.

"Are you on the Pill?" he demanded.

He felt her tense before she reluctantly whispered, "No. But it doesn't matter, darling." She reached for him with trembling hands and tried to coax him forward into the velvety warm, satin softness he was aching for.

But he couldn't. Not till he knew why she didn't want him to protect her.

He saw her radiantly tender face when she was with his son, and stronger than Keith's passion to have her was the sudden, coldly intelligent realization that she wanted far more from him tonight than mere sex.

Very gently his hard hands wrapped hers and wrenched them from his waist. She gasped as if in pain. His own loins cramped as he bolted out of the bed and strode angrily toward her window.

"What's wrong?" she called to him.

"You tell me."

"I don't know."

"Don't lie to me, damn it. This is some sort of setup. I want to know what's going on. Why did you ask me out? Ask me here? To your bed? What do you want?"

"You."

The husky torment in that raspy sound tore his heart, but he laughed harshly, bitterly. "Are you so desperate for a husband that you'd try to manipulate me into getting you pregnant, so I'd marry you?"

Silent tears leaked from the corners of her eyes as she turned her face away. "No."

"Honey, that's a lousy way to trap a man."

"I—I never wanted to trap you. I just wouldn't mind having a—" She stopped herself as if she realized it would be stupid of her to admit anything.

And suddenly he knew, and the truth chilled him more than the thought she might want to marry him.

She wasn't after him. She had never wanted him. Why should she? On that first day she'd seen him as some immoral, oversexed, low-class stud. As some failure. Despite his work to win her respect, that's probably how she still saw him.

Hell, she'd bought him, hadn't she? How could she respect him? Especially when he'd even taunted her that he'd throw his body into the bargain if she chased him hard enough? Maybe that gibe put him partly at fault, but he was furious at her anyway. Furious and hurt because all her heated passion tonight had been a lie... to trick him, to use him.

"You just wanted a baby? So—that's what tonight was about?"

She was sobbing.

"My baby?" he demanded cruelly. "Or just any dumb stud's baby?"

"I—I didn't think it out."

"Like hell." He didn't flatter her or himself by giving her the benefit of the doubt. "If you'd gotten pregnant, you wouldn't have even thought I deserved to know. You wouldn't have told me, would you?"

As she continued to weep soundlessly, he scooped up his slacks and shirt and stalked furiously out of her bedroom.

He would never have thought that a woman who'd been so softly willing could have made him feel so lousy and hurt and cheap—so bruised to his very soul.

Maybe he deserved this. Every intelligent instinct had warned him to stay the hell away from Kate Karlington.

And in the future he damn sure would.

Chapter Seven

The week since Keith had stormed out of her apartment had been busy and very confusing for Kate. Keith's fury, which she considered unreasonable, had persisted. He hadn't come to work for three days, and when he finally did, he worked with a cold, silent efficiency that terrified her.

Not once did he so much as look at her, nor voluntarily speak to her, or refer to that night, but she knew that the injury she had done him had made him as miserable as she was. She wanted to go to him—to apologize, to beg his forgiveness. At the same time she didn't quite know what to say or how to say it.

What had happened had made her realize how desperately she wanted him, and how much she really did want a baby—before it was too late. And somehow when he'd been making love to her, these two longings had forged themselves into one. It wasn't as if she'd deliberately seduced him to get pregnant. It was just that after they'd ended up in her bed, and he'd made her aware of that possibility, she'd hadn't wanted to do anything to prevent it.

Which had started her thinking.

Was it really so terrible that she'd wanted his baby? It wasn't as if she'd intended to hold him responsible. She had thought he would be happy to have sex with no strings attached. What other man had ever wanted a deep involvement with her?

Her father had never wanted a real relationship. Nor had Edwin, who had married her only for her money. When she had been in the hospital after miscarrying their child, never once had either of them come to see her. She had felt so lonely then she had wanted to die.

Was Keith a different breed?

Every time she looked at Keith, she remembered how wild and dark his flushed face had been right before he'd sprung away from her. He'd wanted her badly, as badly as she wanted him. And even now, when he was so cold and sullen, she knew he avoided her because he still wanted her. So they stayed apart, each a tightly coiled bundle of nerves, each lashing out at everybody else until the entire office staff was as cross and irritable as a spring forest full of grumpy bears.

Thus, when Esther walked into Kate's office frowning late on that rainy Friday afternoon, to tell her that a female tenant had been robbed of her rent money and then pistol-whipped while using a pay phone outside the project to call the police, Kate had lashed out at her secretary unfairly.

"Well, what are you telling me about it for? Isn't this the sort of thing that gives you the excuse to go running into Keith's office for a long private chat behind closed doors?"

"For your information, I have tried to reach him. Not that I'm the one who's so interested in him. Only I can't get him on his car phone. He's supposed to be in Spring at Mr. Stewart's shopping center, but Mr. Stewart says he never showed up."

"Then I'll go," Kate said, jumping up restlessly.

"Keith'll be furious. You know he doesn't want any of the women on that property—especially this late in the afternoon." It was the project where Kate had first met Keith.

"Good! I hope he does get mad! I'm sick and tired of his chauvinism."

"Honey, you've had him mad night and day ever since last Friday."

"Oh—so you noticed!"

"Yes, and it's time you two started snapping at each other instead of at me!"

"You're so right!"

Kate wasn't so eager for a fight by the time she reached the project. In the dark the shabby project looked more ominous than it had the day she'd met Keith. When she saw several shadowy figures lurking in the dark alley behind the apartments, smoking under the eaves, she shivered.

A spray of sparks showered to the earth as the men flicked their cigarettes to the ground when she parked her Jaguar. They moved toward her, only to stop when a tall man yelled from the back of a building and yelled. "Yo!"

Keith stepped out of the shadows.

He had obviously beaten her here. He went over to them. When they finished talking, their lighters flashed as they lit fresh cigarettes and Keith rushed angrily through the misting rain toward her.

"What the hell are you doing here?" he demanded, yanking her out of her car.

"I heard about the robbery—"

His large possessive hand crushed down on her shoulder as he shoved her against her car. "I already took care of that. I gave the tenant two rent-free months and put her in an ambulance headed to the hospital. Which brings us back to why you're here when I told you to stay the hell away from this side of town."

"You just manage this property. I own it, or have you forgotten—"

"Never for a minute."

"And I'm the boss—your boss—or have you forgotten?"

"Maybe not for long. I don't want to work for anyone who makes stupid, self-destructive decisions."

In a quieter tone, she said, "I didn't think you'd care—now."

His fingers ground into her upper arm. "What the hell is that supposed to mean?"

"You know. After our date last Friday—"

With a longing that bordered on pain, her silent green eyes rose to his. His dark face was set in hard, unreadable lines.

"If you think I want you riding around in that flashy car in a neighborhood like this when it's getting dark and a woman was just assaulted for a lousy few hundred bucks, you're crazy."

In spite of his anger, she felt a tiny thrill at his obvious concern.

"Get back in your car," he ordered. "I'll drive you home."

"What about your car?"

"I'll come back for it later."

"I—I don't want to put you to that much trouble."

"Honey, that's all you've ever done." But his deep voice no longer sounded quite so stern. In fact, it was almost gentle.

"I'm sorry for Friday, Keith," she whispered, gathering her courage.

"Yeah. So am I, honey." Lightly his hands touched her damp cheek, and the warmth of his fingers flooded her with rich bittersweet yearning. "I wish we'd met some other way. I wish you were some ordinary girl. Or I wish I was some rich guy... rich enough to date you on equal terms. But I'm not. As you just so sweetly reminded me, you repossessed everything I owned, and you're my boss now. And that's that." He opened her door. "Get in the car, Kate, before you get soaked."

"So, it's over," she whispered.

"You know as well as I do it wouldn't work. You're too damned rich, and I'm too damned proud."

She nodded reluctantly.

The windshield wipers slashed back and forth. He drove fast, even though it was pouring and the freeway was under construction—he drove as if he was very angry and wanted to be rid of her as soon as possible.

"But I—I can't forget what a wonderful time I had with you that night," she murmured.

"You will," he said grimly. "We have to, but it was good, too good. You know, Kate, Esther told me about Edwin and...the baby you lost. I'm sorry...."

"I—I didn't realize how much I still want a child...."

"I figured that one out, too, honey." Again his voice was curiously gentle.

"I was so happy when I was pregnant. It was like I already knew the baby and loved it. Maybe all new mothers feel that way, or maybe it was just that I've never had anybody all my own."

"Find a rich guy the next time. Have his damned baby."

"I didn't mean to use you. I—I didn't even think about getting pregnant till you stopped to get that thing—"

"Okay. Maybe I can buy that."

"But I thought you'd be getting something out of, er, the encounter, too."

"You don't just go to bed with some jerk and have his kid because you want a kid that day," he said tightly as he drove up the ramp into her parking garage and eased her car into its numbered space and cut the headlights.

"You're not some jerk, and I do want a child. Is that so wrong, Keith?"

"Yes! Think of the kid. You should get married first. Kids need fathers, too."

Not the kind of father she had had.

But as she looked at Keith, she felt an involuntary twist of tender longing. He cared a great deal about

Bobby Lee. She had always known that not all fathers were like hers. She remembered how jealous she'd felt of school acquaintances who spoke adoringly of their fathers.

It was utterly dark, so all she could see of Keith was the shadowy outline of his carved profile. Maybe if she had been able to see him better, she would never have been so bold.

"*I should get married.* . . . Is that a proposal?" she whispered.

"Hell, no."

"Then you're going to make me humble myself and beg you for it—again?"

"What?"

"I'm asking you to marry me, you big, beautiful, hunky, poor-boy Neanderthal," she said, shocked and embarrassed by her own forwardness even as she touched his cheek. Even as her mouth fused hotly with his.

A wave of shockingly intense desire pulsed through them both as he curved his hand around her neck and slanted her tantalizing lips against his.

From deep in his throat he groaned, "Oh, God. . . . Kate, what are you doing to me?"

"I assure you my intentions are most honorable this go-round."

Her proposal of marriage tempted him even more than her generous salary had tempted him three months ago when she'd asked him to go to work for her.

"No!" Keith thundered ten minutes later when they were alone in her luxurious apartment and he'd downed his second Scotch. "No way! Kate, are you crazy? You don't love me. I don't love you. The last thing you want is to be stuck with me for life when all you really want is a baby."

"You were the one who informed me that babies need fathers and so honorably suggested marriage," she said primly, defending herself. "Not me. I was perfectly willing to forgo that sacred institution and just try to get pregnant on my own."

"That wouldn't be fair to the...to *our* baby."

"Okay. So, I'll concede that point—I believe you did tell me once that your morals were more old-fashioned than mine," she agreed sweetly, pouring him a third glass of Scotch. "I didn't believe you at the time. But I'm beginning to see that you're not the man I thought you were at all."

"If you're trying to get me drunk, I can hold my liquor," he growled, not trusting her. Not trusting himself.

"I know."

"How would it be fair to me or you if we married each other when neither of us really want marriage?"

"What if marriage gave us something we did want? And what if it was only for a year?"

"What?"

"Maybe less than that. And why wouldn't it be fair—if we both got something we wanted? I know you're attracted to me, and I... Well, you know I feel the same way about—"

He felt a hot shiver of unwanted excitement go through him.

"You little fool, that's not enough to base a marriage on."

"Okay, but it would be a big perk . . . at least for me."

In spite of himself he smiled.

"And suppose I agreed to tear up the foreclosure papers on your properties and extend your loans with a very generous interest rate—say over the next five years—if you married me for that year. . . ."

"You'd go that far—"

"I want a baby . . . more than anything. *Your baby.* The second I'm pregnant, you can pack your bags and I'll grant you a divorce. You'll have your property back. And I will retain all rights to the child."

All rights to his child! She wanted to have his child and then to be rid of him. Suddenly the smooth Scotch scalded his throat like acid. *Nothing had changed.*

"Why, you make it sound as simple as just another . . . foreclosure deal." His voice was so low, at first she didn't catch the soft menace in it. Then his hand jerked, and the crystal glass he'd been holding flew wildly against the wall where it exploded into millions of sparkling, razor-edged pieces. His deep voice exploded with the same violence. "Why am I surprised you think I'm that low? When that's what you've thought since the day you met me? You think because you took my properties so easily, you can take everything else just as easily . . . including my self-respect."

"Keith, I—I . . . I didn't mean . . ."

"Goodbye, Kate. I'd be willing to do a lot of things to get my properties back, but I'd never sink so low as to sell my own child."

Desperate to prevent his going, she raced in front of him and threw herself in front of the door. "All right. All right. I hadn't thought of that—that you'd feel like that."

"Why the hell not? Because you see me as some subhuman?"

If she hadn't looked so utterly desperate, he would have shoved her aside and walked out for good.

"Keith . . . I—I think I'm beginning to see that you're really nothing like any man I've ever known. Not my father . . . not Edwin. . . . They didn't care about women or relationships or children or . . ."

Words could never have stopped him, but that look of forlorn agony in her beautiful eyes made him hesitate a second longer. Then he tried to push her roughly aside.

But she clung to his arm.

"Save your strength for the next man on your list of contenders to be your . . . your baby machine," he roared because the mere thought of other men ever touching her stabbed him with jealous anger.

"I don't have a list," she said very softly. *"There's only you."*

She felt the strong grip of his hands on her arms, pulling her against him.

"Why me?" he demanded gruffly as she nestled instinctively against the hard comfort of his warm, muscled chest and listened to the thudding rhythm of his heart. "Why me, you little fool?"

"I'm not sure. For one thing, I trust you. And I do respect you. You've earned every dollar I've ever paid you and more. You didn't sleep with me when you could have. You don't pretend you feel more than you do."

"Maybe I just thought you were smart enough to see through me if I did."

"Keith, all my life I've been so lonely and so terrified of loneliness," she whispered. "The other girls at my boarding school went home on the weekends, but I never could. I just want somebody of my own, somebody I can love who maybe someday will love me. I know most of the men I might marry would really be marrying me for my money, and I don't want that kind of marriage again...where I think I'm loved, and I'm not. I—I promise you I won't be the indifferent kind of parent my father was. And if you wanted the baby as much as I do, I would never take it away from you. You could see it, and love it as much as you wanted to. I would want you to. I just never imagined..."

And Keith, who understood loneliness and need, was lost.

"Kate. Oh, God, Kate." Maybe she'd had money, but she really hadn't ever had much else. Maybe there was something of real value that she needed from him.

The hot moistness of his breath comfortingly touched her nape. Slowly he squeezed her slim shaking body more tightly against his as his own emotions raged out of control.

She shivered as his lips moved burningly through her hair, across her cheek.

"I must be getting as crazy as you," he murmured. "The answer's yes."

Then his mouth claimed hers in a shattering kiss that brought something far deeper and more mysteriously profound than mere physical pleasure. It seemed to her that when his mouth touched hers, his soul touched hers. But, of course, such a thought was ridiculous. She didn't love him. And he certainly didn't love her. Hadn't he said she could have his body—but never his soul?

But after the kiss was over, her eyes remained blissfully closed, her body warmly aflame, her thoughts sweetly tumbled and hazy. As he held her, she could feel the steady hammering of his heart, the disturbed huskiness of his breathing. He was every bit as aroused as she.

"Kate?"

She opened her eyes drowsily when he shook her and stared at his smoldering gaze and darkly carved features. "You're so good-looking," she said dreamily. "So—so sexy."

"I'll marry you, honey—but on my terms. Not yours."

He really was the most impossible man. She licked her lips. *But he was terribly handsome. And he did kiss divinely.* She forgot everything when he kissed her. She pursed her lips expectantly.

"First," Keith began sternly, "Bobby Lee will move back in with Maggie. I will live with you during the week, but I will visit him every Saturday and Sunday during the daytime hours and come home to you after five."

"But I don't mind him living with us. In fact I would love having him around—"

"Kate—no! He hardly remembers Mary, and he already sees you as more of a mother figure than I like. I don't want him becoming too attached when you'll be so temporary in his life."

She felt oddly hurt. Left out.

"That's not all. You will give me control of my former properties as well as your company for the year we're married. And we stay married, not till you get pregnant but until the baby's three months old. And if you do get pregnant, when you're three or four months along, you'll stay home and take care of yourself while I work...."

"That's impossibly chauvinistic...."

"If you're determined on this crazy plan, I won't have the mother of my child or my child at risk, while you drive yourself at the office. I know how hard you work. I know what happened to you the first time, how terribly hurt you were. Honey, you would never have come up with this crazy scheme if you were over that miscarriage."

That much was true.

"And," he continued, "when we do divorce, I'll pay child support, and I'll want generous visitation rights."

"Is that all?"

He nodded.

Strangely enough she wasn't nearly as furious at his preposterous terms as another woman might have been. She remembered how tired she'd gotten in the fourth month, how indifferent Edwin had been about her health. She heard herself agree weakly, wantonly. "Oh, all right." She sighed. "But only if you kiss me again."

"I think kissing has landed us both into enough trouble for one day."

"But we're formally engaged now," she protested, her heart pounding.

Apparently he wanted her lips as much as she wanted his. And when that devastating kiss had turned into a dozen expertly placed all over her body and she found herself sprawled half-undressed beneath him on her couch, again he refused to let her seduce him.

"Stay the night," she begged, loosening his tie.

"No, Kate."

She pulled his tie through his collar and let it fall to the floor. "Why not? We're getting married."

He got up and moved to another chair. "Because if you got pregnant first, you might welsh on me. Then I'd lose you, my property and all rights to my kid."

"You're tough."

"So are you, honey. This is probably not much more to you than just another foreclosure deal. But I'm risking everything I care about."

After he left, she felt lonely and dissatisfied. But for some reason as she crawled into bed, aching for the feel of his arms around her, his parting words brought more comfort than pain. Every time she remembered the way his eyes had seared her, a tremor went through her. Because in that last moment he had made her feel that she meant everything to him.

Chapter Eight

"Well, it's about time you showed up," Kate said softly, fighting to conceal her ripple of excitement as she closed her desk drawer quickly. She didn't want Keith to see her mirror and comb and lipstick tube and realize she'd been anxiously primping because of him.

Keith's avid black gaze burned across her face and then down her body, but he said nothing.

"I left word with your secretary hours ago that all of the prenuptial documents were ready. I thought maybe you were going to change your mind and...jilt me," she said quietly.

"No way," he whispered but with such force that he startled her.

For an instant his eyes locked on hers again with that unnerving intensity. She wondered what he was thinking, what he was feeling when he moved toward her.

"Here are the papers...." she began, leaning down to pick them up.

"They'll wait," he murmured tightly, tossing them back down on her desk. They scattered messily, several white pages falling to the floor.

Before she could stoop to retrieve them, he gathered her hands and pulled her to him, holding her so close, she felt the dizzying heat of him deep inside her body. "You look especially beautiful today. So beautiful, it's hard to concentrate on the business aspects of our marriage."

She had dressed carefully to make him think that, and yet the passion in his voice was so much more than she had expected, and she was filled with a strange longing that made her feel awkward and unsure.

"Keith, you don't have to woo me," she said in a strangled tone.

"Maybe I want to," he muttered harshly.

A shadow of pain crossed her face and she turned away from him. "But you don't have to. You know this is a done deal."

"I bought you something," he said, his voice tighter and harder as he slipped a tiny velvet box into her fingers before he let her go.

She opened the box and could not quite suppress a gasp of pleasure when she saw the small but very lovely diamond winking at her from the black satin interior.

Humbly she touched the stone and then jerked her hand back. She was stunned by the thoughtful, romantic gesture. And happy. So happy, she was afraid.

"Do you like it?" he asked in a low, guarded tone, taking the ring out and slipping it on her finger. "I know it's not very big."

His ring on her finger felt far more binding than the fat stack of documents her lawyers had compiled. And far more wonderful.

"You . . . you shouldn't have. I mean you can't possibly afford it," she whispered, striving for control.

"You didn't have to..." Then she blurted, "You know this isn't a real marriage."

His hand tensed on her wrist and he yanked her nearer. "I know, damn it. But maybe I could forget it—if you didn't constantly remind me."

Did he want to forget it? As much as she did?

Before she could ask or argue further, his hard mouth was on hers, kissing her angrily at first and then with surprising gentleness. When his warm lips played across hers and opened them, a moan of unadulterated pleasure escaped her.

He pulled back but continued to hold her so that her face was nestled against his throat.

"Kate, are you going to throw my poverty up to me for the rest of my life? Do you ever think of us as two human beings? As just a man and a woman?"

She turned pale and began to tremble. How could she ever explain that she was far too terrified of dreams of such happiness to ever hope they could feel that way about each other?

"I'm sorry," he muttered when she didn't answer. His dark face was grave. "I shouldn't have asked. I shouldn't push you. Like you said, this is a done deal. You spelled out the rules, and I agreed to them. You don't want me. Just a kid. Let's leave it at that."

He let her go and, ducking his dark head, charged through the door and slammed it.

After he was gone, she stared miserably down at her slim hand, turning his ring so that it flashed and hating herself for making him unhappy. She had stupidly spoiled a moment he had tried to make special.

She halfway expected him to back out of their "done deal." But five minutes later his secretary was at the door with a terse note from Keith demanding the legal documents.

Within minutes he had signed them, and they were back on Kate's desk.

As she stared at his bold black signature, she remembered the day he'd coldly signed over his properties to her. Suddenly she was more frightened than ever.

Not that he gave her time to be afraid for long. Keith rushed her to plan the wedding quickly.

So they could get it over with, he said brutally when she asked why he was in such a hurry.

And one week later they were married.

Still, in that limited time, Kate had made sure that her second wedding was far grander than her first. She made all the lavish arrangements to prove to her wealthy family that she was proud of her new husband and future marriage, never realizing that her groom might find the ceremony stilted and their elegant reception at the city's poshest country club pretentious and stuffy.

Keith, bored and weary from the much-rehearsed ceremony, from the long photographing session afterward and then from standing more than an hour in the receiving line, ignored several icy looks of disapproval from his new family and bride and excused himself, leaving a white-faced Kate behind while he wandered restlessly through the well-heeled throng.

His tux was rented, and his black tie felt itchy and tight around his neck. Maybe this was what a real wedding was supposed to be like, but it was beginning to feel as dreary as a funeral. Maybe that was because Kate's family didn't try to conceal that they thought he wasn't good enough for her.

He felt their eyes boring into his back as he made his way cynically to the tables piled with elegant food. He thanked the Lord for his uncle John, who was laughing too loudly from the champagne and drawing some of the stuffy Karlingtons' disapproval away from himself. Bobby Lee was taking his share of the heat, too. More Karlingtons were frowning at the boy for chasing several of his Jones cousins at the far end of the ballroom.

At one point Keith had offered to corral the children, but Kate had smiled and said she wanted Bobby Lee to be happy at their wedding.

Keith was about to pick up a fancy fried chicken leg when he caught the disdainful sound of his own name drip like acid from a cultured, feminine tongue.

He whirled. But saw no one. For a second he thought the wedding was making him paranoid.

"Her father would roll over in his grave," drawled another haughty voice from behind a trellis laced with white roses.

"How could she marry so far beneath herself? Again? This one's even poorer than the first."

There was muffled laughter.

"I—I, uh, I think this one's rather more attractive than Edwin," a third woman's voice countered timidly. "And his little boy is absolutely adorable."

The others pounced.

"Of course, *you*, Mathilde...would notice that the scoundrel's attractive...in a vulgar, primitive sort of way! Gold diggers usually are—as *you* should have learned from your own disastrous marriages! And as for being adorable, his brat is a little savage!"

Keith downed a glass of champagne in one gulp. Then he seized a second glass and made his way to the other side of the trellis.

The stoutest of the three blue-haired biddies almost dropped her glass when she saw him. But he gallantly caught it. Managing a cynical little bow, he replaced it in her much-beringed fingers.

"Why, thank you, ever so," she said in a chilly tone.

"My pleasure—*ladies*."

They blushed like girls.

Keith smiled boldly and lifted his goblet. "To the bride.... To her good fortune. And to her future happiness...with me." He clicked his glass to each of theirs. "Weren't you just saying that I, uh, was a lucky man?"

The stout one almost choked.

"Don't let me interrupt your conversation," he continued.

"It wasn't important," one of them snapped.

"Indeed," he purred, his steely voice softening only because Kate had come up and shyly taken his arm.

"We were saying we thought your wedding was lovely, dear," Mathilde said timidly.

"Be happy for me, Aunt Mathilde," Kate whispered, casting a radiant glance at him.

The ladies' faces froze. So did Keith's smile as he wondered why Kate's entire family believed that the only reason he could want her was for her money.

"I feel happy, too," he murmured very tenderly, very protectively, concentrating solely on his bride. His fingers tightened against the back of her satin gown as he crushed her closer. And as his lips brushed hers, he felt the primitive thrill of male possession.

She was his. And he was glad. Neither she nor the Karlingtons would have believed the truth—that neither her money nor the return of his properties had anything to do with his marrying her. She was a beautiful, desirable woman. He wanted her for herself alone. He had wanted her so much, he would have made a bargain with the Devil to have her.

And in a way that's what he had done.

Their honeymoon hideaway was an ultramodern, two-story beach house with high sloping roofs and skylights loaned to Kate by one of her wealthy relatives. Located on Bolivar Island and, therefore, vulnerable to the violence of hurricanes from the Gulf of Mexico, the mansion stood on high concrete pilings that had been sunk deep into the soft sand.

Standing on the wooden deck, Keith stared out at the silver rollers that swept the beach. The view was no better than that from his own rougher beach house on the same island. The same surf caressed the same sand with the same constant roar. The same salty breeze rushed around both houses. The same moonlight lit the night. And yet the two houses, his so shabby and this one so elegant, seemed worlds apart.

He wondered suddenly about the woman he'd married. She had played a CD of Ravel while they'd eaten lobster; he would have been just as happy with country-western music and hamburgers. She had served him the finest, driest French wine; he was so used to Texas beer, he was still thirsty.

Was there any way a man of his simple tastes and common background could ever understand a well-educated woman who'd been to every glamorous city in the world? All he knew was that he suddenly wanted to.

More than anything.

If he had acquired this sudden taste for an elegant woman, maybe he could just as easily learn to like very dry Chablis.

Who was he kidding? Why would it even matter?

Wasn't he only a male body she had bought to satisfy this need for a child she had not been able to satisfy in any other way? Wasn't she going to ditch him the second that was accomplished?

Not if he played this hand for all it was worth.

Slowly he turned his back on the dark water and walked across the deck to go inside where Kate was waiting for him.

Tonight was their wedding night. It was high time he started finding out who she was and what she really wanted from him.

Kate was sitting up in bed scribbling enthusiastically. Her brows were drawn together, her mouth pressed into a tight line as if she was concentrating very hard. He smiled. Was she composing one of her know-it-all columns for the newspaper?

He would have liked to tell her that just because she and her snooty clan had been born rich and had had opportunities, maybe they weren't all that much smarter than he was. Maybe Kate was just lucky; maybe her money had shielded her from the hard knocks that would have taught her nobody knew as much as they thought they did.

His gaze was drawn to her dark curling lashes resting on her smooth pale cheeks like tiny fans.

He had expected fancy, impractical lingerie, but her shoulders were bare above the white sheets. In the dim golden light of the bedroom, she looked fragile and innocent, incredibly lovely and as pure and sweet as a virgin.

Even if she'd bought him, even if she thought that meant she owned him, even if he were no more than that body she had temporarily hired for stud services, it had become impossible for him to hate her.

She moved, and the sheet slipped and he saw the lush curve of her breasts. He felt a sudden raw eagerness. His heart surged with what he told himself was nothing more than the most natural and selfish male desire.

Besides, it had been a long time since he'd had a woman. Too long. If she was using him, he was using her.

He closed the door heavily, so she would look up at him. But when she did, her expression was so uncertain as she bit her lip that he wondered if she felt humiliated because she'd been the one to propose. He realized he was just as unsure of his feelings for her.

Nervously she set her tablet aside and turned the light off when he began to undress. As he ripped his trousers off, he tried not to think of all that was wrong in their relationship. This beautiful, assertive woman would be his till three months after she gave birth to his child. He had a year.

If she couldn't learn to love him, so what? He'd learned the hard way that this was no fairy-tale world. Maybe he wasn't ready for love, either.

She turned him on. By marrying her, he would get everything back that she'd taken from him. She'd get something she wanted, too.

Even if he couldn't win her, their marriage was a mutually profitable business deal. Even if their relationship didn't work out, this was a no-lose situation.

All this seemed so simple until he got into bed and caught the scent of her expensive perfume. Until he saw the tears in her shining eyes and the sudden quenching of her smile as her lips began to tremble. Until he felt the warmth of her body clinging to the sheets. Until he took her into his arms, and her slim body slid warmly against his own, arousing something deep and eternal in him that was so much more than simple desire.

His hands raced over her hot naked skin, pausing on the almost flat curve of her abdomen.

She wanted a child.

His child.

She wanted his child more than she wanted anything else in the world. Didn't she know that his child might tie her to him?

Her hands came around his neck and sifted through his thick black hair. He touched his lips to hers ever so softly, and was surprised by the sweet emotion that filled him. Then his tenderness was followed by fiercer emotions and fiercer needs. His shaking hands tangled in her long, flowing hair as he dragged her nearer.

She moaned as he ran his mouth over her, kissing her throat, her breasts, kissing her everywhere until the tart taste of her womanly essence filled him. His pulses began to throb.

And suddenly she was writhing and moaning, and the whole thing spiraled out of control as is often the case in human relationships.

Mating and creating could form the deepest of human bonds.

Her satin-smooth skin was as sweet as warm honey.

God, he wanted her so much.

He had sworn to himself he would be able to keep his distance from her—even in bed. But the passionate melting together of their bodies carried their souls, as well, and what followed between them brought a bewildering tide of glorious new feelings and hungers. As he was caught up by the force of forbidden needs, he knew that all the boundaries in his life had suddenly been shattered forever.

He had been alone.

He was alone no more.

It was as if he were her first, and she were his. It was as if all their lives they had been looking for each other. Neither understood the wild rapture that possessed them the moment that they began to make love. But the incandescent emotion that thrilled every cell of their beings utterly overpowered them.

He took her a second time, so that he could savor the wonder of her more slowly, so he could savor the glowing emotion he felt when he was inside her. She did the same, running her hands with guiltless wonder over the muscular contours of his magnificent bronzed body, reveling in him like a wanton, kissing him everywhere as he had kissed her the first time, but again it wasn't long before that strange sensual rhythm of their bodies and minds became a vital power that drew them out of themselves and swept them away from all their previous realities and carried them to a new one that was theirs alone.

When it was over, Keith fell back into himself and was terrified. He wanted to crush her close, to beg her to forget their stupid bargain and to love him.

But she believed in buying and selling. She wanted his baby—not his love. So he got up without a word, pulled on jeans and a shirt and stormed barefooted out to the beach.

He meant only to get some space and then return to her.

But she pulled on a white robe and followed him, calling to him from the balcony, and suddenly the terrible need he felt for her was way too much. He knew he would break and confess his true feelings. If she even believed him, she would probably despise him. So, instead of returning, he started running, his feet digging desperately into the wet cool sand as he sprinted away to escape the opulent mansion and the lovely woman who called down to him.

He didn't know if he would ever be strong enough to go back. Suddenly he knew this marriage could turn out to be the biggest mistake of his life.

Chapter Nine

*K*eith had left her. Maybe forever.

Kate had grown up in the South, but the modern South. Not being a southern belle, she had not simpered, played hard-to-get games or denied her true needs when she had been with Keith.

No, she had chased him by asking him out first, by proposing. Nor had she hidden her eagerness for him in bed.

And now he was gone.

Where was he?

Had he really found her so hopelessly undesirable that he never wanted to see her again? Had her desperate need for him driven him away? Was he going to disappear like everyone else she had tried to love?

Not even the thought that Keith had made love to her twice and might have given her a baby softened the blow of his leaving.

She'd watched him run down that beach until he'd become a fleck and dissolved into nothingness. Then she'd crept back to bed and lain in the dark, straining to hear the sound of his return above the roar of the surf, feeling even more desolate when he didn't come back than she had the night she had lost her baby.

The sun was blazing when she finally forced herself to rise lethargically from her bed. That single glance in her bathroom mirror at her hollow-eyed, soulless white face had been so terrible she had not dared look at herself again.

Their honeymoon was to have lasted a week. No way could she return to Houston and face the humiliation of everyone knowing that Keith had left her after one night.

So she stayed at the house, somehow living through the heavy hours. In the afternoon she went out on the deck and listlessly watched the endless roll of the surf as the sinking sun turned the tips of the waves and the clouds to flame.

She wished she could be numb inside. She wished that she could stop thinking, that she could stop feeling. That she could regain some control.

But it was no use. The sun disappeared, and the waters darkened quickly as the last of the pinkness vanished in the sky. And she stayed outside shivering in the lonely darkness.

The moon came up, and she thought its silver glow on the waves looked the same as it had in Keith's hair when they'd been in bed. She remembered the way he'd touched her nipples with his callused fingers. Her skin began to burn as she remembered how his mouth had roamed her body.

No!

Her anguish was suddenly so great, she wanted to scream. To die. She had to stop torturing herself by thinking of him.

She glanced away from the sparkling water to the beach where she had last seen him. Suddenly she saw a tall figure running toward her from the beach.

It couldn't be Keith.

But her heart began to pound. Thinking herself crazy, she forced herself to look away. Then she turned back, unable to resist watching the man.

There really *was* something familiar about those broad shoulders.... About the way the moonlight glowed in his black hair.

Then the man turned from the beach and headed toward her.

And she knew.

"Oh, Keith," she moaned softly, thankfully, closing her eyes and leaning back against the house, willing herself not to act too eager. But when she felt the heavy tread of his footsteps on the stairs, her eyes flew open. Her pulse raced.

He came to an abrupt stop ten feet away from her.

Shyly she lifted her head and fought to manage a haughty, controlled Karlington look.

Across the darkness he whispered huskily, "Forgive me."

How could she do anything else?

"Why did you go?" she asked, her haughty air crumpling, her false voice shattering.

His face was as gray and lined with exhaustion as her own. His deep voice cracked in an equally betraying manner. "I...I didn't think that my leaving might hurt you."

"I—It didn't...." But her voice broke again.

"Okay." In his blazing eyes she saw the most powerful emotion. "I was so afraid you'd be gone," he said humbly, holding his arms out to her. "I wouldn't have blamed you. I behaved wretchedly. You deserved better."

How could she resist such sweetly sincere humility? From a man as proud as Keith? And since she was no southern belle, she came flying into his arms.

He crushed her to him, shuddering as if just holding her aroused powerful, uncontrollable needs. Then he shoved her up against the wall of the house, and their bodies melted together.

His thrilling salty mouth was wet and hot and seeking as it covered hers. He hadn't shaved, and the rough new growth of his beard burned her skin and lips. But she was clinging, sighing, surrendering to the volcanic tide of emotion his hard lips and hands so magically aroused.

Within seconds they were both on fire.

Very gently she wrapped her legs around his waist, and he walked, carrying her like that, inside.

He ripped her clothes off and then his and made love to her in the moonlight on the thick carpet by the fireplace. He was wilder and more primitive than the night before, and he stirred her to new heights of passion that left her quivering and spent and utterly and completely his. And when it was over he didn't get up and leave her. Instead he picked her up in his arms and carried her to bed, pulling her to him beneath the sheets so that their bodies curled together like two perfectly matching spoons. They stayed that way for the rest of the night and long into the morning. And when they finally awoke, their arms and legs warmly entangled, the first thing he did was make love to her again.

He never told her where he had gone that first night nor why, and even though it worried her, she was too afraid of spoiling their new happiness to ask. And although she masked it, another dark, unspoken fear took root and grew in her heart.

If he could leave her once like that without a word— he could do it again.

But in spite of that dark, festering fear, she fought to savor every bright moment of happiness he was willing to give her, and even living with that doubt, she was happier than she'd ever imagined she could be with anyone. She grew to love everything about him, even his faults, and even his little annoying ways—like the way he always left her bathroom trashed every time he took a shower. Like the way he always tore the plastic wrapper off the newspaper and threw it absently onto the carpet.

She didn't mind that he was always grumpy until his first cup of coffee, that after work he needed thirty minutes of solitude to decompress. It didn't bother her that he couldn't hang a towel straight or that he couldn't seem to remember how to load the dishwasher right. He threw his clothes all over the living room furniture every night when he came home. But his presence was so dear, she couldn't scold him for such habits. Not when he loved to cook. Not when he sang to her as he cooked, and quite charmingly, especially since he couldn't carry a tune.

Their life together quickly fell into a pleasant routine. He followed her to work every morning, and at work he found a thousand excuses to seek her out. They threw themselves into every project with more enthusiasm and energy than ever before. He wanted her opinion and approval on every decision he made. His hands-on approach to management left her the freedom to do what she loved—juggle numbers.

But much as she loved working with him, she looked more forward to their workday ending.

They would come back to her apartment together. When she closed the front door, and Keith would begin ripping off his tie and jacket, she would feel a leap of excitement. *For the first time, she felt as if someone belonged to her.*

They would cook dinner together, eat together, and she would usually do the dishes. They would talk, and before long—always when she had begun to monopolize their discussion or win their argument—he would start kissing her. Every day he gave her more pleasure than the day before. And it was only after he had fallen asleep in her arms that she would think of that awful first night when he had left her without a word. Then she would think of the future and the day he would walk out like that again—forever.

Besides that bleak future, what bothered her most about their life was that Keith stuck to his rule about Bobby Lee. Except for the times that Maggie brought

Bobby Lee to the office, Kate didn't see much of the little boy. Some evenings after supper Keith would kiss Kate goodbye and go over to Maggie's to see his son. When Keith spent those first few Saturdays and Sundays away from her doing things with Bobby Lee, she missed them both unbearably.

She was feeling very depressed and lonely one Sunday when Keith came home early and found her. He saw her sad face and stunned her by asking her if they could have Bobby Lee over to eat supper and spend the night the next Friday night.

She was overjoyed and planned their supper down to the last detail. Then when Bobby Lee said what he really wanted was to go out for hamburgers, they went out instead. The evening went so wonderfully that Bobby Lee begged to stay the entire weekend with them. She begged, too, and Keith had reluctantly agreed.

After that weekend, Keith refused to let Bobby Lee spend another. Even so, Kate began to dream that Keith might really come to love her, that they might become a real family.

Keith teased her, he charmed her, he seduced her. But never once did he tell her he loved her. Sometimes when she was feeling down, she wondered if he made love to her so often because he wanted to get her pregnant so he could be rid of her. She began to wish she wouldn't get pregnant immediately, that their life would follow this idyllic pattern long enough for him to fall in love with her.

But one Monday morning she walked into the kitchen as Keith was frying bacon, and the thick sickening smell of bacon grease hit her like a heavy wave. For a second or two, as she groped to open the window and turn on the exhaust fan, she couldn't breathe.

As she gulped in fresh air, she thought she'd be okay. Then a second later, a stronger bout of nausea hit her. She swallowed and then dashed for the bathroom.

When the humiliating spasm had passed, Keith helped her up. She felt even weaker and paler when she realized he had seen everything.

His handsome face was ashen. "So—are we going to have a baby?"

"I—I think so."

When she stared up at him forlornly, he pulled her into his arms and held her for a long moment as if she and the child were very precious to him. She clung, liking the way his hard hands were so gentle as they stroked her hair, wishing with all her heart that he would say he wanted to stay with her forever.

Instead, he let her go, his dark face tense again. "Well, it looks like things are working out the way you wanted."

"For you, too, I imagine."

"This was your idea—not mine, remember?" he said bitterly.

"Yes."

And without another word, he turned and left her.

In spite of her joy over the baby, she felt doomed.

Chapter Ten

Keith had changed toward her drastically as soon as he'd learned about the baby. A new silent darkness had crept into their relationship.

Not that Keith was ever deliberately unkind. Not that Keith didn't support her in every imaginable way. Not that he hadn't helped her select a doctor and driven her to her checkups. Not that he wasn't endlessly patient with her mood swings and morning sickness. Not that he wasn't endlessly helpful when she was too tired to shop or do housework.

But there was a brooding quality about him now, a profound lethargy that seemed to drag him down. And her, too. He didn't laugh as much, and he was guarded and less spontaneous than before. Keith didn't insist she had to quit working as he had vowed he would, but as the months passed, she gradually turned more and more of her business affairs over to Keith and spent more of her time preparing for their baby.

With every day, Keith seemed to withdraw from her more. He came home later. He never initiated a conversation with her, and when she entered a room, he no longer looked up and smiled in the old way that had made her feel special.

Only at night, when they were in bed, did he now seem to belong to her. And even then, when he took her in his arms, she thought he did so reluctantly, as if he were fighting some part of himself, as if he were willing himself not to want her. But always when her mouth sought his, when her body surrendered to his, he melted, too, and their lovemaking bound some deep part of him to her, if only for those few fleeting moments of ecstasy. But afterward, he withdrew again and became that courteous stranger, who said the right things and did the right things. She would lie in the darkness, knowing that she was losing him and wondering what she could have done differently to have made him love her, wondering what was so wrong with her that no one had ever wanted her for herself alone.

Edwin had married her for her money, and so had Keith. The only difference was that Keith had been more brutally honest. He had never bothered to lie and say he loved her.

Even worse than her sleepless nights were the lonely weekends when Keith visited Bobby Lee. As the months sped by, her misery grew. Every Saturday morning when Keith left, she felt more abandoned than the one before. But she said nothing until one fateful Saturday a week or so before her due date.

That morning she felt heavy and irritable and dangerously moody and sorry for herself as she followed Keith to the living room. As he put his hand on the door to go, the pressure of the last few unhappy months mushroomed inside her. Suddenly she rushed up to him and, putting her hand on his, begged him to take her with him.

"Look," Keith began patiently enough. "I hate leaving you all day—especially now, but you have my number...."

His number! Because her pregnancy played havoc with her hormones, she could swing from mildly dependent and needy to wildly hysterical at the speed of light. *She didn't want his number. She wanted him!*

You just don't get it, do you? She didn't speak aloud, but her sulky glare spoke volumes.

Her mind whirled even as she fought for control. How could he be so calm, so infuriatingly rational? It maddened her that his body wasn't bloated, that his emotions weren't in turmoil. Her whole life was changing and he was acting as if his wasn't and as if they still ought to be playing by the same old rules.

Not that it occurred to her that *she* had made the rules. In that self-pitying instant she hurtled over some precarious emotional edge. Suddenly she wanted to stomp up and down like a spoiled child and scream wildly. When her bottom lip curled sullenly, she bit down hard on it.

"Surely," he continued in that same, very male, hatefully rational tone, "you can see that your coming would just make this whole impossible situation more difficult—for all of us."

That did it!

Some tinsel-fine thread sheared at her emotional center.

"Impossible situation?" she shrieked. "I—Is that how you see our marriage? How you see me?" Then she began to weep, thinking even as the thick tears flowed down her puffy cheeks that the last thing she had wanted to do was scream and weep.

"And how do you see it, Kate?" he thundered, losing his patience at last. "I've often wondered. You made it damn clear that you didn't want a real marriage with me. Never—not once...except when we're in bed...have you ever acted— You're always so cool...so controlled." He started to say more and stopped himself. "I'd better go—before I do or say something we'll both regret!"

"Say it! Do it! What could be worse than the way you've been torturing me with your fake kindnesses, with—"

"Fake— Damn you, I'm not your robot, Kate— though I've tried to be. I'm a man, and I'm sick and tired of playing your game. You think you own the world...that you own me. You've told me about your father buying women. Are you really so different from him?"

"How...how can you say that?"

"Kate, I don't know if I can take another three or four months...." He turned to go.

"How can you just walk out?"

"With two feet, one after the other—darling."

"Oh, I—I do hate you."

His black eyes narrowed. "Is that really how you feel?"

She was too wild with her own pain to deny it. "Yes! Yes!"

His handsome face darkened. "Well, cheer up," he said quietly. "You will be rid of me soon enough. I regret this sham of a marriage every bit as much as you do.'' Without another word he stormed out, so anxious to leave he did not even bother to shut the front door.

She rushed after him and slammed it. Then in the next moment she pulled it open again. She wanted to call him back, to tell him that she didn't hate him, that she could never hate him, that she had only said that because he'd accused her of being like her father and because she was too proud to admit the truth—that she loved Keith and couldn't contemplate life without him.

But a savage pain tore through her middle and cut her in two. Gripping her distended abdomen in agony, she sank to the floor, calling after him helplessly.

But he had gone.

It was too late to tell him she loved him. She had lost him.

''Dear God, please don't let me lose his baby, too!''

She tried to get up, but a second fiery thrust slashed through her. She lay on the floor, panting breathlessly, fighting not to panic. But the pains were coming too hard and too fast, and she was terrified she would never make it to the hospital in time.

''Keith . . . I—I'm so sorry.'' Her voice was a whisper in the empty room. She shut her eyes and prayed silently.

From a long way away a deep voice said tenderly, ''I'm sorry, too, my darling.''

As if in a dream, hard, strong arms lifted her and cradled her close. She opened her eyes, and Keith was there. His dark face was quiet and grave.

He was her love. Her rock.

She reached for him and struggled to say something, but the pain cut off her breath.

"Don't try to talk," he whispered as he carried her out the door. "I'm taking you to the hospital."

The walls were white in the delivery room. Everyone wore blue. Even Keith, who was pressing her hand very tightly in his, was in blue.

A frightened voice cut through the haze of pain. "Doctor, I'm losing the baby's heartbeat!"

Kate clutched Keith's hand frantically and then started to scream. "No—not again!"

A mood of professional panic descended upon everyone.

"We're going to have to do a C-section."

A plastic mask was placed over Kate's face. She fought to shrug it off, but a gentle voice said firmly, "Sing the alphabet to me like a good girl."

When she got to the letter *C*, Keith's ashen, craggy face began to blur and float away. In a panic she realized she hadn't ever told him she loved him.

But when she tried to say the words, her voice died soundlessly. Then the lines of his dark face began to dissolve, and she was sliding away from the lights and the pain into a darkness that was total and eternal....

"You'll have to go now, Mr. Jones," a nurse ordered.

Keith nodded miserably even as he clutched Kate's lifeless hand more tightly. This was a thousand times worse than Mary because this was his fault. He had lost his temper and brought on the terrible fight that might end in Kate's death and his baby's. As he held on to her limp fingers, he vowed that if she lived, he would never allow himself to lose control again. He would stick to the idiotic bargain she had forced him to make—no matter what it cost him.

"If there's a choice, save *her*," Keith whispered desperately, knowing he was probably overreacting because of all the hospitals and all the surgeries he'd gone through with Mary. "Take the baby. But don't let her die. Please don't let her die."

"She's going to be fine, Mr. Jones."

Fighting to believe that, Keith leaned down and kissed Kate's cold pale cheek one last time. "Don't let her die—because I love her," he whispered.

But the woman who would have given anything for those words was asleep and did not hear them.

Chapter Eleven

"Where did you put my suitcase, Kate?" Keith called from the living room.

The long-expected question jolted through Kate as if it were a bolt out of the blue.

The sun was sparkling outside. Houston looked lovely. Kate had been leaning toward her mirror, running a brush nervously through her hair. At his simple query, every warm feeling inside her turned to ice. Her brush fell from her shaking fingers and clattered onto the bureau, scarring the fine glossy wood.

So today was to be the day he would walk out of her life forever.

Why today?

Heidi was four months old.

Kate had lived with the dread of this moment every day since Keith had brought her home from the hospital, her fear having intensified until that terrible third-month birthday.

But the dreaded date had come and gone, and although the day had been tense and she'd felt hysterically close to losing control, Keith had said nothing and done nothing. She had been too afraid to ask why because she might cause the very thing she feared most. And three days later Keith had even lovingly given her red roses on Mother's Day.

And now, suddenly, he was leaving her.

For a long moment she couldn't trust herself to answer in that cool polite manner that had become their custom—except for that one fight—ever since she'd gotten pregnant.

With the uncanny timing all babies are born with, Heidi started to cry.

Thank goodness! Relieved at the excuse not to answer him, Kate rushed to their daughter, only to find that Keith had gotten there first.

Kate paused at the door, unable to join him by the crib. "I just fed her and changed her." Her voice sounded lost and far away, not so carefully controlled—a stranger's voice.

Keith nodded absently and then grinned at the tiny redheaded being he gently lifted into his arms. "There, there, my sweet darling," he said to the baby in that husky, warm voice he never used with his wife—except in the dark when they made love.

Keith held the little girl close and continued to whisper soothingly. Only when Heidi began to coo did he speak to Kate again in that coolly polite tone. "I don't think she wants anything but love."

Dear God. Kate struggled to smile bravely in that cool way he was smiling at her, but her lips quivered.

Her heart was breaking. She was flying to pieces inside. The Karlington control, which had been her first line of defense against loneliness and despair, seemed to be shattering forever.

Not that he noticed. He had looked down at Heidi again, his entire cherishing attention focused on their daughter, who had wrapped her tiny fingers around his larger one.

Kate was not jealous of his love for Heidi. Kate simply wanted his love, too. And seeing how wonderful he was with their daughter always made Kate all the more sharply aware of his indifference to her.

Ever since Keith had brought them home from the hospital, he'd treated Kate as gingerly as she were made of eggshells. As if she were a stranger he was forced to live with and make polite conversation with. And she had played along, careful not to expose all her vulnerable new needs.

Not that he hadn't been wonderful. Those first weeks when she'd felt too weak and sick from the surgery, he had done practically everything for her and the baby. He allowed Bobby Lee to come more often now—to visit his sister. While Kate had been overly anxious about the baby because Heidi was her first, he, the more experienced parent, had been self-confident and relaxed. With every passing day, Kate had come to rely on his help and upon his steadiness and strength.

With every passing day she craved his love more.

"It's going to be hard not to see her every day," Keith murmured.

His low, polite voice sent a searing flash of pain through her. *It's going to be horrible not to see you every day, too,* she thought.

"I—I'll get your suitcase," Kate whispered and then stumbled upstairs to her hall closet, where she'd stashed it neatly all those long months ago. Frantically she began tearing boxes down from the packed shelves until she found it. Feeling wild and desperate, she tossed the hateful thing onto the landing, not caring when it rolled to the edge of the top stair, teetered and fell, end over end, banging loudly all the way down the winding stairs.

Miserably, Kate watched Keith come out of their daughter's room, lean down calmly and pick it up.

"Thanks. I guess I overstayed my welcome," he murmured mildly, not bothering to look up at her.

Thanks? After they'd lived together for more than a year?

Just go, if you're so anxious to! She wanted to shout at him. She wanted to run down the stairs and throw him and that awful suitcase out. But she was determined to avoid another wild humiliating scene like the one that had brought on her premature labor when he had said that he regretted their sham of a marriage.

Knowing she was on the verge of tears, Kate ran into her bathroom and locked the door so he wouldn't see. There she hugged herself against the wall and wept soundlessly as she listened to him throwing things into his bag. But as the tears rolled down her cheeks, in an odd way she was almost glad this thing she had dreaded had finally happened.

Because only now, when he was actually leaving, did she realize how unbearable the silent explosive tension between them had become. How had she borne needing him and wanting him this long while pretending that she was an aloof creature made of ice?

It seemed an eternity later that he uttered a muffled curse as he slammed his suitcase closed. Then she heard the sounds of his footsteps coming up the stairs.

She held her breath, struggling for control when he hesitated before her door. After a long time he knocked gently.

"Kate—"

"Go away!" she whispered.

"I wanted to say...goodbye."

"Fine. Goodbye."

"You were the one who said that all you wanted from me was the baby."

"Yes," she whispered desperately, sinking to the floor like a broken lump, dying inside as she wondered how she would live without him.

"And that is still all you want, right? You want your perfect, neat life back, right?"

She choked on a sob. "Yes! Yes! Just go," she ground out in an agonized tone.

He hesitated and then she heard his retreating footsteps. They sounded like leaden weights going down.

The minute her front door slammed behind him, she unlocked the bathroom door and came flying out of it. Stepping onto the landing, she saw the heap of tangled boxes and hangers she'd thrown out of the closet. The silence in the vast apartment held a new and crushing loneliness. Gone were Keith's clothes thrown messily over the back of her couch.

Her gaze ran fondly to the plastic newspaper wrapper he'd left on the floor. More hot tears filled her eyes. It was the dearest thing in that room filled with priceless Karlington antiques.

Without Keith, the baby she had wanted so desperately would never be enough. The Karlington money meant nothing.

She hadn't ever wanted him to go. She had always wanted him. As much as she had ever wanted their baby. *More.*

Then why hadn't she broken down and begged him to stay?

Because from the first she had been the one to chase him. Because she didn't want him to stay for any other reason except that he loved her. Because he had once said, "I regret this sham of a marriage...." Because she loved him enough to sacrifice her own happiness for his.

She was reasonably sure she could have used the baby and several other arguments to get him to stay. She had the Karlington money after all. She could have offered him the use of it, the power that came with it for as long as he stayed married to her.

She thought of the nights they shared in bed together. Of his final tendernesses to her when he'd taken her in his arms only the night before. Of his seeking mouth and roaming hands, his flaming passion. Of her own. But such passion was not love. Hadn't he told her she could have his body anytime—but never his soul?

She wanted all of him—desperately.

She wanted him to stay because he loved her.

Heidi began to cry.

Never again would she rush to her child and have the added pleasure of finding Keith there, too, to share her joy.

After a long moment Kate ran down the stairs. But when she opened the door to the nursery, Keith stepped coolly out of it.

Startled, caught completely off guard, she felt terribly vulnerable—exposed. Her voice came out harshly, defensively. "What are you still doing here?"

But he was different, too. The cool stranger was gone. She saw an agony as wild and profound as her own in his piercing black eyes as he stared at her tear-streaked face.

"Why are you crying?" he demanded in a gentle, compassionate tone.

"I—I'm not...cry...ing," but the words came out in a horrendous very un-Karlington-like blubber. "I don't want you to pity me...."

In the next minute, his arms came around her, and his searching mouth claimed hers hotly, passionately—adoringly.

"God, Kate, I tried to leave you—"

Heidi made a muffled, indignant sound.

"What about the baby—" she whispered brokenly as he propelled her into the hall and slammed the door.

"The baby is fine. We've both spoiled her—that's all."

"I don't understand. Why...why are you still here?"

"Because, damn you, I'm not a high-class Karlington who can say goodbye to you through a locked door. Because I can't play by your rules another miserable second," he said brokenly, angrily. "Because I want you too much to let you go without a fight. I don't care if you despise me because I'm poor...and you're rich. If you despise me because you think you bought me or because you think I'm a failure or because I made this stupid idiotic deal. Or because your family thinks I'm a gold digger—"

"But I—I don't think any of those awful things. I—I don't despise you. I—I made all those stupid rules to protect myself...because I'd been hurt before. I—I thought you regretted our marriage."

He didn't seem to hear her. "I want to help you raise Heidi. I feel like a heel leaving you to face it all—practically alone—even if it is your idea. I don't go for the mother of my kid raising my kid alone when she doesn't have to."

"You don't have to go," she said, no longer caring that she was chasing him again. "I never wanted you to."

"I thought you just wanted me to serve as a baby machine."

"No. I love you, Keith. I've always loved you. That's probably why I wanted your baby that first night, why I asked you to marry me. Why I did all the stupid things I've done."

"I'm glad you did those things. Because I love you, too," he said simply. "I have for a long time."

"Are you sure you want me...and not my money?"

"Damn your money and your father and Edwin for making you think money is everything. I wish you were poor. That we were equal."

"We are equal," she whispered. "More than equal. I think you're wonderful."

He kissed her mouth softly, reverently. "I love you for yourself alone. You are everything to me."

A long time later, after many fervent kisses, she asked, "If you loved me so much, why didn't you ever tell me before?"

"Because I was playing by your rules. Suffering under them. Dying under them. When I gave you that ring, you reminded me we wouldn't have a real marriage. After that... Then the one time I broke down, we had that terrible fight and you went into labor. I was so afraid you might die... that the baby might die...that it would be all my fault...that I decided to stick to your stupid rules till you told me to go. I did it for you. I didn't want to ever hurt you like that again."

"Oh, my darling. I thought... you were just marking off the days till you could leave me."

"After you got pregnant, I hated every day and every night we had together, because time was our enemy. Then, when Heidi was three months old and you didn't throw me out, I began to hope you felt something for me, too. But you never said— Not even when I gave you the roses on Mother's Day. You were just this exquisite polite stranger who said, 'Thank you, darling.'"

"You didn't say anything, either. Why did you pick today to leave?"

"Today?" He raked his hands through his hair. "I just couldn't take it anymore. I couldn't live with you—loving you, wanting you to love me. And I could see what this was doing to Bobby Lee. Every time he came to stay, he begged to stay. He feels left out."

"I do love both of you. I wanted him with us so much. But I was afraid to show it...especially after you left me on our wedding night. I thought maybe I'd chased too hard and been too eager...."

"I left because I realized I was madly in love with you, and I didn't know how I could live with you and not let on. I left because I loved you, but I came back for the same reason. It's why I couldn't walk out the door today."

"And I was too proud to confess how much I loved you partly because I'd chased you so blatantly, so shamelessly."

"Honey, I want you to chase me—for the rest of our lives. I like it when you're shameless."

And the incredible warmth in his voice lit a tiny spark of happiness within her that soon grew into a fire that raged out of control when he carried her up to bed. For the first time in a long time they made love in the middle of the day with the sunlight streaming through the high windows. And she lost all control, gave herself to him more shamelessly than ever before.

Afterward she wouldn't let him go until he admitted that at last she did possess every part of him—not only his body but his soul, as well.

And he possessed every part of her, too.

Keith loved her. She was the mother of his children.

But most of all, she was his beloved wife.

* * * * *

Ann Major

Ann Major was born and raised in warm, semi-tropical Corpus Christi, Texas. She lives there now in a yellow house with white shutters, with her husband of twenty-four years. (She fell for him when she was sixteen and married him seven years later.) She has three children: David, Kim and Tad. She has three cats: Holmes, Willie and Slim. Ann allows her husband and children to own one dog: Benji. Benji spends his time trying to figure out how to get out of the backyard.

Ann likes to feed birds and squirrels in her backyard. She likes water and mountains, especially when they come together. She sails, windsurfs, kayaks and swims. Hiking and tennis are two of her favorite sports. She plays the piano and enjoys all kinds of music.

Favorite things: conversations with good friends; good books, especially romance novels; travel; research.

Least favorite things: On the grand scale—crime and child abuse. In her own life—parties that she has to go to because if she doesn't, she'll hurt someone's feelings; watching television with her husband when he's feeling trigger-happy with the remote; a blank computer screen coupled with her empty, self-doubting mind; and the question *When are you going to write a real book?*

Secret things she feels guilty about: That she hates to cook. The the weeds in her flowerbeds are taller than the real plants.

Bad habits: The telephone and television.

Secret nightmare: That filing cabinets will take over every room in her house.

While avoiding her flowerbeds and stove as diligently as possible, Ann has written nearly thirty romance novels.

Cullen's Child

Dallas Schulze

A Note from Dallas Schulze

"Write an anecdote to go with your short story," my editor said casually. I tried to muffle my whimper of dread. Give me a choice between writing about myself and walking barefoot over hot coals, and the coals win out every time.

It's just so hard to know what to say. I haven't lived in exotic places or done exotic things. I've lived in California for over twenty years now, most of them spent married to a really terrific guy who makes my life complete.

I have more hobbies than you can shake a stick at, assuming you had a stick you wanted to shake. I like to cook, especially to bake. If there's a needlecraft I haven't tried, it's only because I haven't heard of it yet. My current passion is quilting, but I also cross-stitch and knit. I collect dolls and dress them—the fancier and the more intricate the garment, the better. I love to garden, though I don't have as much time for it as I'd like. My reigning passion is writing, of course. Give me a notebook and a pen and I can occupy myself for hours.

When I was asked to contribute to *Birds, Bees and Babies,* my first response was, "Me?" After all, I'm not anybody's mother, unless you count my very spoiled calico cat, and I think she considers me more slave than parent.

Then my editor told me the theme for the book was babies, and I thought that here was something I could sink my teeth into—metaphorically speaking, of course. Who can resist a baby? Who'd want to? So I thought up a story about a woman who thinks she has a very good reason for resisting a particular baby, and I put a baby smack-dab in the middle of her life. I hope you enjoyed reading the end result as much as I enjoyed writing it.

Dallas Schulze

Chapter One

A baby had never been part of the bargain.

Darcy Logan's expression was grim as she stared out the car window at the rain-washed scenery. The weather matched her mood, bleak and gray. She'd never been to Washington before and she hadn't seen anything yet to make her regret that lack. Oh, it was green and lush all right, but in the week since she and Cullen had arrived, she hadn't gotten more than a glimpse of the sun. It had been raining when they'd landed at the airport. It had been raining when they'd attended Susan Roberts's funeral and it had continued to rain in the five days since then. She was starting to think it never did anything else.

Of course, the weather was appropriate, considering the event that had brought them here. Cullen's sister had been two years short of her fortieth birthday when she died from cancer, leaving behind a six-month-old baby girl.

Darcy shivered. She'd never met Susan but her heart ached for what the other woman must have gone through. How terrible to be facing your own death when you should have been dealing with 2:00 a.m. feedings and diaper rash.

Cullen had taken his sister's death hard, she thought, glancing at him. Grief had carved lines that bracketed his mouth and had left a dulled sheen in his eyes. He hadn't been sleeping. She knew that because she hadn't been, either. Especially not the last couple of days since Cullen had told her that Susan had left her baby in his care.

Darcy's first reaction had been disbelief. And when Cullen had made it clear that he had every intention of fulfilling his sister's request, panic had taken over, closing her throat and making her heart pound.

"I owe it to her," he'd said before she could get out any of the words of denial.

"Don't make any quick decisions." She was amazed by how level her voice was. You'd never know that she felt like screaming her denial to the world.

"There's no decision to make. Susan made me the baby's guardian. She trusted me to do what's right for her."

"That doesn't necessarily mean that *you* have to raise her yourself," Darcy had protested reasonably. "Susan trusted you to make the right decision for her baby, but that could mean that somebody else—"

"There is no one else."

The flat statement had made her feel like an animal in a trap.

"What about your parents? Susan lived with them. She must have trusted them. They're the baby's grandparents. They might welcome a chance to raise her."

"No." Cullen had turned away from the window of their hotel room and looked at her, his eyes bleak. "The last thing she would have wanted was for my parents to raise her baby. That's why Susan made me her guardian, because she knew I'd never let that happen.''

Darcy had stared at him, bewilderment and panic churning inside her. ''But you said she lived with them.''

''Because they made sure she was incapable of doing anything else,'' Cullen had said bitterly.

''I don't understand.''

''You will when you meet my parents. I don't think I can explain it to you before then.'' He'd picked his denim jacket up off the bed. ''Let's get some lunch.''

And Darcy, too shaken to pursue the discussion, had followed him from the room and eaten a meal that could have been sawdust for all the attention she'd paid to it.

That had been yesterday and now, here they were, about to pick up Cullen's niece. About to destroy the happiness she'd found these past few months.

''This is it.'' Cullen's flat announcement dragged her out of her thoughts. He pulled the car over next to the curb.

Darcy glanced at the house, seeing a neat, two-story brick building bracketed by tidy flower beds. The white trim extended to the perfectly centered wooden porch, which housed a metal glider covered in pastel floral cushions. All in all a pleasant, if not particularly inspired, picture. Certainly nothing to cause the bleak expression in Cullen's eyes. He couldn't have looked more grim if the view had been a bombed-out inner city block rather than a plainly affluent suburban neighborhood.

She struggled with the urge to reach out and smooth the lines from beside his mouth. Despite the fact that they'd been lovers for eight months and had lived together for the last five of those months, she wasn't sure she had a right to try to soothe his pain.

They'd met at a party given by a mutual friend. By the end of the evening Cullen had persuaded her to go out with him, despite the fact that she'd avoided even the most shallow of entanglements for the past six years. But she'd been alone so long and he'd refused to take no for an answer. He'd made her laugh, something she'd done precious little of lately. So she'd agreed to go out with him, telling herself that her agreement had nothing to do with the fact that he made her heart beat a little too fast.

A week later she'd found herself in bed with him. Three months after that, when he'd found out that her apartment building was about to be turned into condos, Cullen had suggested that she move in with him. She'd refused, feeling that odd little flutter of panic that came with the thought of getting close to someone again. But he'd pointed out that she'd spent every weekend at his place, not to mention two or three nights a week. She was practically living there, anyway. Besides, everyone knew that two could live cheaper than one. Think of the money they'd save.

It was a silly argument. Neither one of them had any real financial worries. Cullen and his partner ran a very successful construction firm in Santa Barbara.

Darcy's salary as loan officer in a small bank might not put her in the *Fortune 500* but she made enough to be comfortable. Living together had nothing to do with saving money and they both knew it.

Still, she'd let herself be persuaded. The truth was, Cullen filled up some of the empty spaces in her heart. He was like a fire on a cold, snowy night and she couldn't resist the urge to draw closer to him, to warm herself on his heat.

Five months later her heart was still turning over in her chest every time she looked at him. Not that it came as any surprise. Cullen Roberts had probably been stirring heart palpitations in women since he'd reached puberty.

Darcy looked at him, trying to define what it was about him that made him so impossibly attractive. His dark brown hair was worn just long enough and shaggy enough to make a woman want to run her fingers through it. His eyes were a clear, vivid blue and always seemed to be laughing, even when his mouth was solemn. And when he did smile... Well, a smart woman would run for cover, Darcy thought. She'd always considered herself a smart woman but she hadn't run far enough or fast enough.

But he wasn't smiling now. He was staring out the windshield, his hands still gripping the wheel, his mouth tight, his eyes bleak. Darcy noticed that he still hadn't looked at his parents' house, the house where he'd grown up.

"It's a very pretty house," she said when the silence had stretched to uncomfortable lengths. "Looks like a nice neighborhood to grow up in."

Looks like a great place for a motherless baby, she wanted to say, but didn't.

"I haven't been back here in seventeen years," he said, finally turning to look at the house. "When I left, I swore I'd never come back."

The uncharacteristic bitterness in his voice startled her. Since he'd never mentioned them, she'd assumed he wasn't close to his parents. And the fact that they hadn't exchanged so much as a word at his sister's funeral had confirmed the accuracy of that assumption. But the old anger that roughened his voice still caught her off guard.

"I guessed there were...problems between you and your parents," she said hesitantly. "But seventeen years is a long time."

"Not long enough. I wouldn't have stayed as long as I did if it hadn't been for Susan." The name cracked in the middle, his mouth twisting with pain as he thought of his dead sister.

Darcy touched the back of his hand where it was clenched on the steering wheel. This was the first time either of them had faced any sort of personal crisis and she was uncertain about offering him comfort. She'd barely known he had a sister until the early-morning call last week that had told him of her death.

"I should have come back for her," he said abruptly. "I shouldn't have let her stay here."

"She wasn't a child, Cullen. She was four years older than you are. If she chose to stay, there was nothing you could do about it."

"You don't know Susan. She isn't—wasn't," he corrected painfully, "strong the way you are. She didn't have the ability to stand up for herself. She'd stand up for me but never for herself."

Strong like her? God, did he really believe she was strong? She must be a better actress than she'd realized, Darcy thought bitterly, if she'd kept him from seeing just how weak she really was.

"Still, she was thirty-eight years old, Cullen. And she had a job at a day-care center. She didn't have to live with your parents. She could have moved out."

Cullen was already shaking his head. He shot her a look that said she didn't understand.

"You don't know my parents." Without another word, he pushed open his car door and got out.

Darcy fumbled with her seat belt, aware that her fingers were trembling. She had to talk to him before he saw his parents. Ever since he'd told her what was in Susan's will, she'd been trying to find the words to say what needed to be said. But they needed to be the right words, just the right tone of voice.

She finally mastered the unfamiliar latch just as Cullen pulled open her car door. It was more misting than raining, just damp enough to be annoying but not enough to warrant an umbrella. Darcy could feel the moisture settling on her hair as she slid out of the rental car. Cullen's hand came under her elbow, steadying her. Just as he'd been doing since they'd met—steadying her, taking care of her. God, she couldn't lose that now. And she would if she couldn't talk him out of this. She put her hand on his arm and tilted her head back to look up at him, ignoring the dampness.

"You know, Cullen, I've been thinking about this situation." Yes, that was good. She sounded calm, no trace of the screaming panic she felt inside showed in her voice. "I know you want to honor Susan's wishes, but have you considered the possibility that your niece might be better off staying with your parents?" She saw denial flicker in his eyes and hurried on before he could interrupt. "After all, even if *you* had problems with them, this is the only home she's known. Maybe it wouldn't be such a good idea to take her away from all that's familiar. The lawyer said that your parents want to raise her and this is a beautiful neighborhood. The schools are probably terrific and—"

He put his finger against her mouth, stilling the tumble of words. "I know we haven't really discussed any of this, Darcy, and I'm probably not being fair to you to make decisions like this without your input. But Susan made me Angie's guardian and I'm not leaving without her."

"I'm just trying to think of what's best for the baby," she said. She felt her cheeks heat with shame. *Liar. You're thinking of what's best for you. You know what's going to happen if he brings this baby home. You're going to lose him.* "Are you sure she wouldn't be better off with her grandparents?"

"You haven't met my parents," he said again, and there was something in his tone that told her it would be a waste of breath to continue the argument.

"What about the baby's father?" She was clutching at straws, but when you were drowning, it was worth grabbing at any possibility.

"The lawyer said he wants nothing to do with the baby."

"He might feel that way now. But that doesn't mean he won't change—"

"He's married and has three kids, Darcy. In the letter Susan left me, she said not to contact him, that he knew about the baby and had offered her money but he wanted no actual involvement."

"Oh." Darcy spared a moment of sympathy for Cullen's sister, for the hurt she must have felt. But she couldn't help but feel a wave of panic on her own behalf. Cullen wouldn't leave the baby with his parents and the baby's father wanted no part of her. That didn't leave very many options.

"Don't look so upset, honey." Cullen smiled down at her.

"I'm not upset," she lied.

Darcy didn't know what he read in her eyes, surely not the fear she felt. She'd spent years learning to control her expression, learning to reveal only what she chose. But whatever Cullen saw, it made his face soften, one side of his mouth kicking up in a lopsided version of the smile that had persuaded her to go to bed with him barely a week after they'd met.

He smoothed one finger over the curve of her cheekbone. "We'll work everything out, Darcy. I promise. Once the three of us get back to Santa Barbara, we'll take time to sort it all out."

The three of us. Words right out of a nightmare.

Darcy couldn't force a smile but she managed to nod. Apparently it was enough to satisfy Cullen because he bent to drop a quick kiss on her cold mouth.

"Thanks, sweetheart."

Linking his hand with hers, he led the way up the cement walkway. Darcy felt like a prisoner walking to her doom. These past eight months with Cullen had been the happiest of her life. And unless he changed his mind about letting his parents raise his sister's child, it was all going to come to an end.

Cullen could feel Darcy's tension in the hand he held. He knew she was upset, knew that he was probably being unfair in making a unilateral decision on such a major issue. They should discuss the impact a baby would have on their lives, talk about what kind of changes it would mean, how they would deal with those changes. He should ask her how she felt about bringing a baby into the life they'd built together.

He *should* do all those things, but at the moment he couldn't get past the basic facts: Susan was dead and she'd left her baby to him. She'd trusted him with the most precious thing in her life. And nothing—not even Darcy—was going to keep him from fulfilling that trust.

Darcy would understand, he told himself. Once she'd met his parents, she'd understand why there had been no choices to be made about this, why he hadn't consulted her, asked her what she thought.

There was a knot in his chest as he stepped onto the porch. He'd been a scared, angry seventeen-year-old when he'd left home. That was half a lifetime ago. At thirty-four, he was a successful businessman, with money in the bank. He owned his own home, two cars and half a boat. And since meeting Darcy, his personal life was on track. He was, by any standards you cared to apply, successful.

So why was he standing in front of his parents' door with a knot in his stomach and the feeling that he'd failed in some indefinable but significant way? It was a feeling that had been all too familiar when he was growing up, a feeling he'd thought he'd left behind him when he'd left home.

Darcy tugged on the hand he was holding, making him realize that he was crushing her fingers.

"Sorry." He released her. "I'm a little uptight, I guess."

"It's been a rough week." She reached up to touch the lines of strain that bracketed his mouth. Cullen was momentarily soothed by the concern in her eyes.

He brushed his fingers across her cheek. Even after all these months, he sometimes found it hard to believe that she was really his. He'd wanted her from the moment he'd seen her. He'd gone to his friend's barbecue only because he had nothing better to do, thinking he could always leave early if he wanted. Darcy had been standing in a patch of sunlight, her hair so pure a gold it almost hurt to look at it. He'd wangled an introduction, taken one look at the smile in her pale, almost crystalline gray eyes and fallen like a ton of bricks.

Darcy's light shiver brought him back to the present, back to the task at hand, which was getting Susan's baby out of his parents' house. He gave Darcy a quick, strained smile that didn't quite reach his eyes.

"This shouldn't take long."

Cullen ignored the doorbell and rapped his knuckles against the smooth oak of the door. He was aware of Darcy glancing at him, her eyes curious, and knew that she must have a lot of questions. He'd never talked about his family with her, so she could have no idea how he felt about this homecoming. But then, he didn't know much about her family, either. Maybe he should ask—

The sound of footsteps on the other side of the door made him break off the thought. The sharp tap of high heels on polished oak floors. His mother. The only woman he'd ever known who wore high heels at home. And then the door was opening and, for the first time in seventeen years, he and his mother stood face-to-face.

She hadn't changed much. There was more gray threaded through her medium brown hair, a few more lines on her forehead. But her eyes were the same— looking at him, measuring him, finding him wanting. Just as she had when he was a boy.

"Cullen." Maeve Roberts's greeting was flat and emotionless.

"Mother." He was so tense that his neck ached.

"Come in." Her eyes, the same deep blue as her son's, flickered over Darcy. "Both of you."

Darcy felt the tension in Cullen as they stepped across the threshold. Not exactly a fatted calf kind of welcome, she thought.

The interior of the house was as neat as the exterior. Light oak wood floors, creamy white walls, a few delicately shaded watercolors on the walls—all very pale and restful. Not the kind of decor one associated with children. She felt her hopes of Cullen leaving the baby here slip a little more.

"Nothing's changed," Cullen said, half to himself. "This is just the way it looked when I was a kid."

"Your father and I enjoy our home," Maeve said over her shoulder. "We've seen no reason to change it."

She led the way into the living room, which was decorated with the same lack of color as the entryway. In here, the floor was covered with a plush carpet in a pale fawn color. Guaranteed to show every bit of dirt, Darcy thought. She resisted the urge to glance behind herself to make sure she wasn't leaving footprints.

"Cullen is here, William." Maeve made the announcement in the same flat tone of voice with which she'd greeted her son.

There was a strong resemblance between William Roberts and his son, Darcy saw as the older man set aside the paper he'd been reading and rose from his chair. It was there in the shape of his face, in the tobacco brown of his hair, still visible through the liberal sprinkling of gray. His eyes were blue, also, though a paler shade than his wife's and son's.

But where Cullen's eyes usually sparkled with life and his mouth always seemed to hover on the edge of a smile, there was a stillness about his father's face, a tightness about his mouth that made it difficult to imagine him smiling at all.

"Cullen." He nodded as if greeting an acquaintance he hadn't seen for some time.

"Dad." Cullen's greeting was just as cool. "This is Darcy Logan. Darcy, my parents."

Darcy murmured an acknowledgment, aware of William's cool eyes skimming over her and dismissing her.

"Are you my son's mistress?" Maeve asked in the same tone she might have used to ask if Darcy liked jam on her toast.

Darcy's mouth gaped in shock. She was at a loss for an answer. *His mistress?* Did anyone actually think in those terms anymore? Cullen's hand squeezed hers. In warning? In support?

"Darcy and I have been living together for the last five months," Cullen said. "Not that it's any of your business."

"I think we have a right to know what kind of moral atmosphere you're taking our grandchild into," Maeve said, pressing her lips together.

"No, actually, you don't." Cullen's tone was almost pleasant. "Susan's will gave me sole custody of her daughter."

"If she'd lived longer, Susan would have changed her mind," William said heavily. "She'd begun to realize the sin she'd committed, bearing a child out of wedlock as she had."

"I'm sure you helped her see that. I'm sure you made sure she knew every minute of every day just what a crime she'd committed."

"Unlike you, Susan had some understanding of the importance of strong moral behavior." William didn't so much as glance in Darcy's direction, but she knew the words were a reference to her presence. Clearly, as far as Cullen's parents were concerned, the fact that he had a mistress—good Lord, had they really used that term?—made it clear that Cullen didn't share his sister's understanding.

"Where's the baby?" Though she could feel the anger in him, Cullen's tone was level.

"She's upstairs." Maeve glanced at her husband. "We feel it would be better if she stayed with us. Clearly, you're in no position to be taking on the rearing of a child."

"Bring her down."

"Though your father and I didn't ask for this burden, we feel it's our duty to—"

"Are you going to bring her down or should I go up and get her?"

The steel in Cullen's voice cut through his mother's words. Glancing at his face, Darcy suppressed a shiver. She hoped never to see that look turned in her direction.

"Don't speak to your mother in that tone," William said sternly. "We've decided the child would be better off under our care. If you—"

"I don't give a damn what you've decided." Cullen's eyes blazed with an emotion perilously close to hate. "Susan made me the baby's guardian. If you want to argue with that, then you can do it in court."

"I see you haven't changed since you were a boy," William said, and the words were not intended as a compliment. "You're still overly emotional and thoughtless to a fault."

"You mean, I'm not a block of morally unimpeachable ice like the two of you. I'll take that as a compliment."

"You're thinking only of yourself here. You're not giving a thought to what's best for the child. If she stays with us, she'll have stability. She'll grow up with a firm understanding of right and wrong, with—"

"Without love, with no sense of self-worth," Cullen interrupted. "You'll break her spirit the same way you broke Susan's, the way you tried to break mine. Only I was lucky enough to have Susan to love me, to push me out before you could destroy me the way you did her." He took a short step forward, using the advantage of an extra two inches of height to loom over the older man. "Now, are you going to bring her baby down here or am I going to have to tear the goddamned house apart to find her?"

Cullen didn't raise his voice. He didn't have to. The cold rage in his eyes was threat enough. Darcy put her hand on his arm, half-afraid he might actually strike his father. His muscles were rigid as iron beneath her fingers. The silence stretched.

William looked away first, his pale eyes shifting to his wife. He nodded abruptly. "Get her."

Maeve's lips compressed. She glanced at Cullen and for an instant, Darcy saw some emotion flash through her eyes, something that could have been hatred. It was gone immediately, but the memory of it stayed in Darcy's mind, chilling her.

What kind of people were they that they could look at their son with such hatred, that they could talk about their recently deceased daughter having committed a terrible moral sin? Where was the grief they should have been feeling over Susan's death? The regret that their relationship with their only remaining child was such a shambles? Darcy shivered and drew her jade green jacket shut over the matching dress. It seemed colder in here than it did outside.

Maeve left the room at a measured pace, the skirt of her neat, powder blue dress barely shifting as she moved. She was as tidy and soulless as the house, Darcy thought. No wonder Cullen was so determined to take charge of his niece. What must it have been like growing up in such a sterile, judgmental household? She'd spent less than ten minutes here and already felt chilled to the bone.

No one spoke while they waited. The tension that stretched between the two men was at odds with the pristine, colorless room. From the little she'd seen of them, Darcy suspected that Cullen's parents were strangers to strong emotions of any sort. Unless you considered feeling morally superior an emotion.

She heard the click of Maeve's heels in the hall and then the older woman walked into the room carrying a blanket-wrapped bundle. There was suddenly a hard knot in Darcy's chest, making it hard to breathe. She let her hand drop from Cullen's arm as he stepped forward to meet his mother.

Maeve hesitated a moment, her eyes meeting her son's. Whatever she read there apparently convinced her that further argument would be a waste of time. With a look of unconcealed dislike, she allowed him to take the baby from her arms.

Cullen showed none of the hesitancy Darcy might have expected from a man who had little or no experience with babies. His hold was secure, if a little awkward. She noticed that his hand was not quite steady as he eased the blanket back from the baby's face.

Uncle and niece stared at each other with identically colored blue eyes. The baby managed to work one hand free of the soft white blanket, waving it aimlessly in the air. She gurgled a greeting.

"Hello, little one." Cullen's facial expression was nothing short of captivated.

Baby Angie, with a wisdom far beyond her six months, solidified her position by rewarding him with a grin that crinkled her small face and revealed two tiny teeth. Cullen returned the grin and Darcy watched helplessly as his heart fell firmly into the infant's tiny hands.

Chapter Two

"Are you sure she's warm enough?" It was the second time Cullen had asked the question in the twenty minutes since they'd left his parents' house.

"She's wrapped in a blanket and the heater is on. Besides, it's damp but it's not that cold outside. This is Seattle not Siberia."

"Sorry." Cullen's smile was self-deprecating. "It's just that she's so little."

"Most babies are." Darcy flicked on a turn signal preparatory to making the turn into a supermarket parking lot. Baby Angie had come with a limited supply of basic necessities like diapers and formula. Clothes could wait until they got back to Santa Barbara, but the rest of it couldn't.

Once inside, they found the baby-food aisle easily enough, but the array of choices made Cullen's eyes glaze with fear. Taking pity on him, Darcy made a few quick choices, tossing items into a cart and trying to ignore the bundle in Cullen's arms, a feat considerably more difficult than she would have liked.

At the checkout counter, Cullen tried to hand Darcy the baby so he could get out his checkbook.

"No!" The refusal was automatic and held a panic-stricken note that made his eyebrows go up. She forced a smile. "I'll pay for it. I've already got my checkbook out." She waved it for emphasis.

"Okay."

She thought he gave her a questioning look, but the clerk chose that moment to admire Angie, who was peering over the edge of her blanket to offer that irresistible two-toothed smile. The clerk smiled fatuously. Cullen looked proud. Darcy kept her eyes resolutely turned away.

By the time they reached the hotel, the knot in her stomach had grown to roughly the size of a basketball and all she wanted was to lock herself in the bathroom with a full tub of hot water and not come out until her skin looked like a topographical map of the Sierras.

But when she mentioned the idea to Cullen, he looked as if she'd just threatened to abandon him in the middle of a jungle without so much as a can of bug repellent. He ran a construction company, for heaven's sake, she reminded herself. So how was it possible for him to look so utterly helpless holding a baby?

"I think she's wet," he said, sounding every bit as helpless as he looked.

"Babies do that. We bought plenty of disposable diapers." She pulled the box from one of the grocery sacks and set it on the bed.

To his credit, Cullen didn't ask her to do the job for him. He carried Angie over to the bed and laid her down, unwrapping her from her blanket with methodical care. Darcy told herself that she should get started filling the tub, but she didn't move. Cullen's hands looked huge as he fumbled with the series of tiny snaps that ran down each leg of Angie's pink romper.

The minute her legs were freed, Angie began kicking and waving her arms in the air. She opened her perfect rosebud mouth and squealed loud enough to wake the dead. Cullen jerked back as if she were a rattlesnake coiled to strike.

"What's wrong? Did I hurt her?"

"There's nothing wrong. She's just letting you know she's here."

"As if I hadn't noticed," he muttered, warily approaching his niece once more.

It took some effort, but he managed to remove both plastic pants and wet diaper. Angie kicked harder, apparently delighted to find herself bare bottomed. Cullen disposed of the wet diaper and pulled a new one from the box Darcy had helpfully opened.

Diaper in hand, he leaned over Angie.

Both her tiny legs churned like pistons.

He gave Darcy a questioning look as if she might know the trick for getting a six-month-old baby to hold still.

Darcy shrugged.

Looking grimly determined, Cullen turned back to his niece.

Ten minutes and three ruined diapers later, lines of defeat had appeared beside his mouth. His fingers were locked around diaper number four, the knuckles white with tension as he eyed his opponent. She grinned up at him, and babbled something that sounded suspiciously like "I win."

Darcy was torn between laughter and sympathy. A heavy lock of dark hair tumbled onto his forehead. His eyes held a wild look generally only seen in trapped animals. There were damp patches on the underarms of his shirt, though the temperature in the room couldn't have been more than seventy degrees.

Darcy took pity on him. No matter how much she wanted to keep her distance, she couldn't stand by and watch him suffer. Not to mention that, at the rate he was going, they were going to run out of diapers long before they boarded their plane tomorrow morning.

"Let me try." She came forward and held out her hand for the diaper.

"I don't think she wants to wear a diaper," Cullen said as he handed it to her.

"She's just testing you to see who's the boss." She opened the diaper and set it on the bed next to the wiggling baby.

"*She* is," Cullen conceded immediately.

"Are you going to let yourself be bullied by a baby who probably doesn't even weigh as much as fifteen pounds?"

"Yes."

"Coward." She looked down at Angie, who waved her arms and babbled happily. Darcy couldn't help but grin back at her. She felt something loosen in her chest, like a key sliding into a lock that hadn't been turned in a very long time. But she didn't want to open that particular lock, she reminded herself. Not ever again.

"Your uncle is a coward," she told the baby. "Imagine a grown man like him letting a little thing like you bully him."

Angie babbled and cooed as Darcy caught both her ankles in one hand and lifted her far enough to slide the diaper under her bottom. A minute later, the baby was diapered, and a clean romper tugged on over her wiggling body.

"How did you do that?" Cullen demanded suspiciously, as if he hadn't watched the entire operation.

"You just have to be firm and remember that you're bigger than she is."

"I was afraid I'd hurt her," he muttered, staring down at his niece.

"Not likely. Babies are tougher than—" The words caught in her throat, painful, as if she'd swallowed a fishhook.

"Than I think," Cullen finished for her, apparently seeing nothing odd in her abruptly ended sentence. "I guess they'd have to be or else the whole human race would be out of business. It's just that she's so little." He leaned down to touch Angie's hand and she promptly grabbed hold of his finger. "Look at how tiny her fingers are. And did you see her toes?"

"Yes." Darcy was pleased to hear how steady her voice was.

"It's incredible, isn't it?"

"Incredible," she said dully. Cullen glanced at her and she forced a quick smile as she turned toward the

phone. "She'll probably be hungry soon. I'll call room
service and see how we go about getting her formula
heated up."

"And I wanted to call Sara and see if she'd be willing to do some shopping for us tomorrow morning."

"Shopping?" Sara Randall was Cullen's secretary.
Darcy had met her a few times and liked her.

"For baby stuff. You know, cribs and strollers and
whatever babies need. She's got three grandchildren.
She's bound to know what to buy."

Darcy nodded and picked up the phone. "Good
idea."

Shopping for baby furniture was right up there on
her list of favorite things, right next to having a root
canal or getting her hair died purple.

"I don't know what I'd have done without Susan."
Cullen's voice was low, in deference to the baby sleeping in a crib provided by the hotel. "She was the only
thing that made life bearable when I was a kid."

The two of them were lying in bed. Darcy was exhausted, physically and emotionally, yet sleep had
never seemed less likely. It was obvious that Cullen felt
the same.

"The two of you must have been close." She looked
over at his profile. He'd drawn only the sheer inner
drapes earlier and the light of a full moon shone
through them, illuminating the room with pale clarity.

"We were. I would have run away from home long
before I was seventeen if it hadn't been for Susan. I

didn't want to leave her and I knew she wouldn't come with me."

"Why? If things were so terrible, why did she stay?"

"It sounds melodramatic but I think they'd broken her spirit." Darcy heard the rustle as he shrugged. "I don't ever remember hearing a word of praise from either of my parents. From the time I was little, I was told what a failure I was, how I had to try harder to be worthy of the Lord's love. I remember thinking that I could do without His love if only *they'd* love me."

"They must have loved you." Darcy's protest was weak as she remembered the icy dislike with which they'd looked at him earlier.

"I don't think so. I'm not sure they even love each other. They're cold, soulless people, Darcy." There was no anger in his voice, only the flatness of someone stating a fact. "They never hugged us or told us we'd done a good job. If you got bad grades, you were sent to your room to contemplate your sins—their exact words—and they didn't speak to you for a week. If you got good grades, they never said a word. I think it would have been easier to deal with out and out anger. If they'd hit me, at least it would have been a reaction of some kind, an acknowledgment that they felt *something* for me."

"It sounds like a lonely way to grow up," Darcy said softly, her heart aching for the small boy he'd been.

"It would have been if it hadn't been for Susan. She was four when I was born and I think she was so desperate for someone to love and to love her that she practically adopted me as her own. She was always there for me, proud of me if I did something good, telling me I'd do better next time if things went wrong."

"She sounds wonderful."

"She was the best," he said simply. "I kept in touch after I left. As soon as I was scraping out a living, I asked her to come live with me. She always put me off and I let her." There was bitter self-condemnation in his words.

"You couldn't make her leave, Cullen," Darcy said. She reached out hesitantly and touched his shoulder, feeling the knotted muscles there. "She made her own choices."

"I think she was afraid to leave them. Or maybe she was afraid she'd be intruding on my life."

"Maybe. But she still had to make her own choices. You can't beat yourself up because she didn't take you up on your offer to help her leave."

There was a long silence and she hoped Cullen was thinking about what she'd said. He couldn't hold himself responsible for the choices his sister had made. No one could force someone else to do what was best for them.

"She didn't tell me she was sick." There was a lost sound to the words that made Darcy's heart twist.

"She probably didn't want you to worry."

"If she'd told me she was sick, I would have been here for her."

"I know you would have." Darcy eased over, closing the gap between them.

"I talked to her a month ago and when I asked if she was all right, she said she was a little tired but that was all. I was in a hurry and I forgot to tell her I loved her." His voice was suspiciously thick.

"She knew, Cullen. I'm sure she knew." She could hardly get the words out past the lump in her throat.

Acting on instinct, she slid her arm under his neck and pulled him toward her. He was stiff for a moment, rejecting the comfort she was offering. The stiffness left him abruptly and his arms came around her in a convulsive movement.

"I didn't get to tell her goodbye."

His hold on her was painfully tight, but Darcy didn't protest. She stroked her hand over his thick, dark hair, offering him wordless comfort. There was little else she could do for him. Only time could heal his wounds.

And sometimes a wound was so deep that not even time could reach it. Her eyes were bleak as she stared over Cullen's head at the crib and the sleeping baby it held.

Any uneasiness that either of them might have felt the next morning over the intensely emotional scene of the night before was swallowed up by the hustle and bustle of getting ready to go to the airport. Angie was not a morning person and she announced this fact most emphatically.

Unfortunately there wasn't much that could be done about it, so the ride to the airport was made to the accompaniment of her protests. By the time they boarded the plane, she'd begun to regain the sunny nature she'd displayed the day before. At Darcy's suggestion, Cullen gave her a bottle to suck on as they took off and it seemed to do the trick because there were no more tears between Seattle and Santa Barbara.

In fact, she cooed her pleasure as she arrived at her new home. The adults, on the other hand, were more than a little the worse for the wear. After a week of emotional ups and down, the condo looked like paradise. As soon as Darcy got out of the car, she turned her face up to the sun, letting its warmth beat down on her.

But not even the California sun could warm her all the way through, she thought as Cullen got out of the car behind her with Angie cradled in his arms. His eyes met hers and she forced a smile. He had enough to deal with, what with his sister's death and suddenly finding himself with an infant to care for. He didn't need the additional pressure of her own personal demons.

Sara Randall had proved herself more than worth her weight in gold. She'd not only gone shopping for everything a baby could need, but she'd arranged to have everything delivered. Cullen's partner, Kiel Jackson, had provided a key to the condo and the two of them had set up the spare bedroom as a temporary nursery.

Tired as she was, Darcy welcomed their presence, especially Sara's. The older woman was more than happy to hold Angie and exclaim over what an extraordinary baby she was. In the fervor of her welcome, Darcy hoped her own lack of enthusiasm would be more easily overlooked. Not that she didn't agree that Angie was a remarkably beautiful and good-natured baby. It was just that she really didn't want to get close enough to notice such things.

She only had to get through tonight, she told herself, listening with half an ear as Kiel filled Cullen in on the business of the past week. Tomorrow she'd be going back to work and she wouldn't have to deal with the painful ache that twisted her heart every time she looked at Angie.

A little time and distance, that was all she needed to get things into perspective, to settle everything in her head. A few days and she'd find a way to deal with the situation. Not that there was much "dealing" to be done. She could either adjust to Angie's presence in her life—in *their* lives—or she could give Cullen up. And since she was unwilling to do the latter, then she'd have to find some way to cope with the former.

Darcy woke suddenly, her heart pounding, her skin chilled and damp. Bits of nightmare chased her from sleep, images too thin to catch yet that left her trembling with remembered fear. It had been a long time since she'd had this particular nightmare, but the aftermath was still familiar. She'd never been able to remember much about it except for the sound of a baby crying.

A shallow wail brought her upright in bed, her breath catching in her throat. Still foggy with sleep, for an instant it seemed that the nightmare had followed her into the waking world, just as she'd always been afraid it would. But when the wail came again, Darcy realized what it was. Angie.

It was a real flesh-and-blood baby crying, not the wraith of her nightmares. Darcy sagged, her breath gusting out of her on a half sob of relief. Angie cried again and she felt Cullen stir. She started to sink back down against the pillows. He'd take care of the baby, just as he'd been doing since they'd brought her home.

Another wail, this one with a lost, inquiring sound that had Darcy on her feet before the sound died down. She could no more ignore that cry than she could walk on water. It called out some deep maternal response that couldn't be denied.

The addition of a crib had turned the condo's spare bedroom into a nursery. A heavy oak dresser served both to store Angie's small wardrobe and act as a changing table. The double bed had been shoved into a corner to make room for the crib, a stroller, a car seat, and a box of toys. Angie hadn't brought much with her by way of material possessions, but Cullen had made up for that lack.

Angie wailed again as Darcy entered the room, the sound dying down to a series of sad little whimpers. Ignoring the clutter illuminated by the night-light, Darcy walked across the room and stopped beside the crib. Angie was lying on her back, her face crumpled with tears.

"What's the matter?" Darcy asked softly.

At the sound of her voice, the baby's eyes flew open. She stared up at Darcy for a moment as if pondering her presence. In the week since they'd brought Angie home, Darcy had managed to keep her distance for the most part. After considerable thought, she'd decided that that was her only option.

It was a ridiculously simple strategy but it had worked fairly well so far. She simply did her best to be elsewhere when Angie needed attention. There were times when it hadn't worked out that way, of course. If Cullen was showering or on the phone and the baby needed something, Darcy didn't ignore her. Not only would that have been unfair to the baby but it would have made her aversion to his niece obvious to Cullen. The last thing she wanted was him questioning her feelings about Angie and babies in general.

Making up her mind, Angie lifted her arms in a clear demand to be picked up, babbling something that could probably be interpreted as "What took you so long?" Darcy wondered if Angie thought she was her mother. Or did she remember Susan, wonder at her abrupt disappearance?

Angie babbled again, jerking her arms impatiently, but Darcy hesitated. She'd done her best to avoid holding the baby if she could. It hurt too much. It was stupid really. It wasn't as if she hadn't held other babies in the past few years.

Last year, there had been a mini baby boom at the bank and it seemed as if someone was bringing in a new infant every other week. She'd held each of them, admired them and had managed to hold the memories at bay. But Angie was different. Angie wasn't just in her life for a moment. Angie was here to stay and it would be so easy to let herself forget, to let herself get too close. That wouldn't be fair to either of them.

Cullen had been so busy adapting to his abrupt introduction to fatherhood that he hadn't had time to notice anything else. He'd even been letting his partner, Kiel Jackson, run their construction company so he could devote himself completely to easing Angie's transition to her new life. But eventually things would slow down a little and he'd realize that she treated his adorable niece much as she would a python, interesting enough to look at but something from which to keep her distance. And then he'd want to know why she was so careful to keep Angie at arm's length.

And just what was she going to say? "Sorry, I just don't like babies?" Or did she tell him the truth and risk seeing the look in his eyes change to contempt? The thought caused a stabbing pain in her chest.

Angie's smile faded at the delay and she whimpered, her lower lip quivering pathetically. Darcy moved automatically to stop the howl that was sure to follow that look. Cullen hadn't had a decent night's sleep since they'd got home from Seattle. If she could help him sleep a little longer by changing a wet diaper and settling the baby back in her crib, she'd do it.

She'd held Angie before. So the solid weight of her wasn't the shock it had been the first time. Still, Darcy's heart jerked a little as she felt Angie's small body settle into her arms. She closed her eyes a moment, her breath catching on the sharp pain in her chest.

Swallowing hard, she opened her eyes and drew a deep breath, forcing her thoughts to the here and now. She carried Angie to the dresser and laid her down. She could do this. She could change a diaper and get one six-month-old child back to bed without falling apart. After all, you didn't have to become emotionally involved to change a diaper. A couple of minutes and she could crawl back into bed, cuddle up next to Cullen and hope that the warmth of his body would drive away her own inner chill. How long could it take to diaper one baby?

Longer than she'd anticipated. Especially when that baby was more interested in kicking and squirming than in getting a dry diaper. When Darcy started trying to pull off the plastic pants, Angie drew her knees up and waved her arms. A brief but vehement struggle later, Darcy was the proud possessor of both plastic pants and soggy diaper. Angie grinned at her and babbled happily.

"Don't tell me you were trying to help," Darcy muttered.

She dropped the diaper in the diaper pail and pulled a fresh one from the stack nearby. Angie kicked both legs, delighted to find herself bare bottomed, pleased to find herself with an audience at one o'clock in the morning. Or maybe just delighted with life in general.

Darcy smiled despite herself. It must be nice to be six months old and have nothing to worry about except growing up. Not that Angie's life had been picture-book perfect so far. Finding herself an orphan at six months was not exactly part of a fairy tale. But Angie had had Cullen to come to her rescue. Darcy folded a diaper and managed to get it under the baby.

Cullen had come to her rescue, too, though he probably didn't realize it. Before she'd met him, her life had been painted in shades of gray. Largely by her own choice, Darcy admitted to herself. She'd spent years building fences around herself, making sure she didn't get too close to anyone, that she didn't open herself to that kind of hurt.

And then she'd met Cullen and he didn't seem to notice the fences or, if he did, he'd chosen to cut through them. And she'd suddenly found herself living in a world of color again. Did he have any idea what he'd done? Did he know he'd dragged her out of her shell, made her feel again? Made her vulnerable again?

"You're a very lucky little girl," she told Angie. "Your uncle Cullen is a very special man and you're lucky to have him. *I'm* lucky to have him."

But would she have him much longer?

She pushed the question away as she finished diapering the wiggling baby and picked her up. Despite the tiredness revealed by her heavy-lidded eyes, Angie didn't seem to have any immediate plans to go back to sleep. Darcy couldn't help but smile at the infant's determination.

"You're a stubborn little thing, aren't you?"

Angie muttered, her eyelids drooping a little before being forced upward. Darcy rocked her gently, keeping her voice to a singsong rhythm.

"Afraid you'll miss something important if you go to sleep? It'll all still be there in the morning."

She continued to talk to the baby, nonsensical words, their meaning less important than the sound of her voice. As she spoke, she forgot about keeping her distance, about holding herself aloof. The soft weight in her arms felt sweetly familiar and right.

The dimly lit room was a pleasant haven, safe and secure. Darcy began to sing quietly to the baby, momentarily forgetting all the reasons she couldn't let herself get close to this small scrap of humanity, and allowing herself to simply enjoy the feel of having her arms full again after being empty for so long.

Chapter Three

The man standing in the doorway thought he'd never seen anything more beautiful in his life than the picture the woman and child made. Darcy was wearing a plain white T-shirt, size extralarge, that came halfway down her thighs. Cullen had never understood how something as basic as a T-shirt could look so sexy, but one thing he'd learned in the past six months was that Darcy Logan could probably make a trash bag look sexy.

But it wasn't sex he was thinking of at the moment. Or at least, that wasn't *all* he was thinking of, he amended, looking at the smooth length of leg beneath the hem of the T-shirt. Until this moment he hadn't realized just how beautiful a woman could look holding a baby. The tenderness in Darcy's expression as she looked down at Angie sparked a warmth somewhere deep inside Cullen.

She looked so utterly natural holding the baby, so right. The very picture of mother and child. For a moment he felt a piercing grief at the thought of his sister, who would never again hold her baby and sing to her. But a part of Susan remained behind in little Angie. He couldn't bring his sister back but he could do his best to live up to the faith she'd had in him.

He'd raise her child for her. With Darcy's help, he hoped.

She'd been so uncomfortable around the baby that he'd begun to wonder if Darcy was afraid of her. God knew, he could sympathize with the feeling, he thought ruefully. Angie scared the life out of him. There was no reason Darcy wouldn't feel the same.

As far as he knew, she didn't have much experience with babies. Though she'd certainly known enough to guide him through his first fumbling attempts at some of the basics like diapering and bathing and feeding. At the time he'd been too grateful for her knowledge to question its source. Vaguely, he'd thought it must be some inborn instinct that women had, but he doubted that knowing how to put on a diaper was part of the genetic code.

Now here she was holding Angie as easily as if she'd been doing it since the child was born. He envied her that look of easy competence even as he wondered how she'd come by it. It occurred to him that, despite the months they'd lived together, there was a great deal he didn't know about her. The present had been so absorbing that there hadn't seemed to be much reason to discuss past histories. Maybe it was time to think about changing that.

"You're very good with her," Cullen said quietly.

Darcy jumped and turned toward him, careful not to disturb the now-sleeping baby. The light was dim, but for an instant he thought she looked guilty, as if she'd been caught doing something she shouldn't. The guilt—if that's what it had been—disappeared immediately, replaced by the carefully neutral expression he was coming to associate with anything to do with the baby.

"It doesn't take any talent to change a diaper," she said lightly.

"I don't know about that." Cullen's smile was rueful as he came into the room. "It took me quite a few tries to master the skill, and I wouldn't have managed at all if you hadn't shown me how."

"You'd have figured it out. A man who can build a house isn't likely to be permanently stumped by a diaper." Darcy's tone was quiet but matter-of-fact.

"Houses don't wiggle while you're trying to nail up the next stud," he pointed out. "The first time I tried to change her, I'd have been willing to swear she had six legs and all of them moving at once. If you hadn't come to my rescue, I'd still be in that hotel room in Seattle trying to get her to hold still long enough for me to sort everything out."

"If you'd waited for her to hold still, you would still be waiting. Babies don't do still very well." She carried Angie over to the crib and Cullen followed, watching as she eased the infant down onto the mattress.

"So I've learned. Where did you learn so much about babies?" It was a casual question but he felt Darcy stiffen and there was a tiny pause before she answered.

"Baby-sitting," she said. "I did a lot of baby-sitting when I was a teenager."

"I didn't know that."

"No reason you should," she said, lifting one shoulder in a half shrug.

Her tone was so completely normal that Cullen wondered if he'd imagined that brief moment of tension. He reached down to tug a pink cotton blanket up over Angie.

"She'll just kick it off," Darcy pointed out.

"I know." Cullen brushed the back of one finger over Angie's cheek, marveling at the softness of her skin. "She's so small and helpless," he murmured. "It's kind of scary when you think about how dependent she is. Makes you a little nervous, you know."

"I know." Something in her tone brought his head up, but she turned away before he could see her expression. "Since she's settled, I'm going back to bed."

"I'll be in in a minute." But he was speaking to her back.

As Darcy left the room, Cullen turned back to the sleeping baby. Resting his hands on the top rail of the crib, he looked down at her, but for the first time in a week, he wasn't really seeing her. He was seeing Darcy the way she'd looked when he'd first come in, her face soft and practically glowing with tenderness. As soon as she'd realized he was there, that expression had disappeared, wiped from her face as if it had never been. As if there was something wrong with her showing affection toward Angie.

In the short time they'd lived together, he'd learned that Darcy was a very private woman. She reminded him of an iceberg, concealing so much more than she ever revealed. He had the feeling that she kept an important part of herself hidden away from him. Sometimes he wondered if he knew her at all.

Angie shifted in her sleep and the little blanket slipped halfway off. With a half smile, Cullen tugged it back over her tiny form. Brushing the tip of one finger over her cheek, he turned and left the room.

Darcy was in bed when Cullen entered their bedroom. Her eyes had had time to adjust to the darkness and she watched as he pushed the door partially shut behind him and crossed to the bed. His chest was bare and she let her gaze drift over the mat of dark hair that covered muscles hardened by physical labor. Cullen was as likely to be found swinging a hammer as he was reading blueprints.

Though she couldn't see it in this light, she knew his skin was tanned from working in the sun without a shirt. The hair on his chest tapered to a dark line that arrowed across the flat plane of his stomach before disappearing into the low-slung waist of the black, cotton pajama bottoms he wore.

Despite her emotional turmoil, she felt desire stir in the pit of her stomach. Though they'd slept together every night, they hadn't made love since he'd gotten word about his sister's death, nearly two weeks past.

He stopped beside the bed. There wasn't enough light for her to read his expression but she could see the glitter of his eyes and knew he was looking at her. Perhaps it was the darkness or the lateness of the hour or the stress of the past couple of weeks, but it seemed to Darcy that he was suddenly almost overwhelmingly male.

He seemed to loom over the bed and when he lowered his hands to shove the pajama bottoms off his narrow hips, the hunger that tightened her belly was mixed with a touch of purely feminine uneasiness. She wasn't afraid of him but she was abruptly aware of the very definite differences between a man and a woman. He was so much stronger than she. There was comfort in that knowledge but a part of her acknowledged the potential danger inherent in that strength.

Her breath caught in her throat as the black cotton slid off his hips, revealing the strength of his arousal. Cullen must have heard the revealing sound because he grinned with pure masculine arrogance. If she hadn't been melting inside, Darcy would have been tempted to sock him in the ribs as punishment for that look. The throbbing ache in the pit of her stomach urged her to pull him down to her, to let him soothe that ache as only he could do.

She might have done just that if he hadn't grinned again and set his hands on his hips, bending one knee in a classic masculine pose, flaunting himself with infuriating impudence, daring her to resist him. She couldn't and he knew it, damn his blue eyes. But that didn't mean she had to give in without a fight.

Darcy eased out from under the covers and stood up. Without a glance in Cullen's direction, she grasped the hem of the plain white T-shirt and eased it slowly upward, baring her body an inch at a time.

Cullen felt his mouth go dry as she drew the shirt up over her hips, exposing the triangle of soft blond curls at the top of her thighs. The slender curve of her waist and the inviting hollow of her belly button were next and then she paused. She gave him a sidelong glance that he felt all the way to his toes.

She inched the shirt a little higher, baring her midriff and the beginning swell of her breasts. His fingers curled into his palms as he fought the urge to grab her and rip the shirt from her before tumbling her back onto the bed. She looked at him again, as if measuring his desire. Apparently satisfied with what she saw, she drew the T-shirt the rest of the way off.

Cullen stopped breathing. It didn't matter how many times he saw her like this, he was never prepared for the impact she had on his senses. Her full breasts swayed as she tossed the T-shirt away. She lifted her hands and ran them through her hair, turning slightly so that he had a perfect view of the inviting thrust of her breasts as her arms lifted.

It was a game they'd played before, teasing each other with pretended indifference, driving each other crazy by looking but not touching. The game had only one ending, but there was pleasure in drawing it out, in building the fires slowly, letting the heat climb.

Tonight, Cullen wasn't in the mood to draw things out. It seemed as if it had been months since he'd touched her, forever since he'd touched that smooth, golden skin.

Darcy gasped when his hands closed over her hips, his fingers curving into her soft bottom as he pulled her up against his hard body with almost violent force. She threw her head back, her urgency rising to meet his. His mouth came down on hers, his tongue plunging into her mouth with no preliminaries, only a stark, driving hunger that added to the ache in her.

Her fingers dug into the rock-hard muscles of his upper arms. She twisted herself closer. His arousal was hot and hard against the softness of her belly, making her whimper with hunger. It seemed as if it had been so long since he'd held her like this, loved her like this.

Cullen lowered her to the bed, bracing his arm against the mattress as he followed her down. His knee slid between hers, and Darcy opened her legs to him, the tension inside coiling almost painfully tight.

"I don't want to wait." His voice was husky as the tip of his erection brushed against the dampness of her most sensitive flesh.

"Who asked you to?" she got out breathlessly. The arch of her hips was an irresistible invitation.

Cullen's first thrust took him deep within her, filling the emptiness. Darcy sucked in her breath and arched her body to take him deeper still. She needed to feel him all the way to her soul, needed to know that he was hers and hers alone.

Cullen groaned as he felt the heated dampness of her surround him. He felt completed, made whole in a way only she could do. He caught her hands in his, pinning them flat to the bed as he withdrew and thrust again.

Darcy dug her heels into the bed and arched to meet him. He lowered his body to hers, the muscular width of his chest crushing her breasts, the crisp mat of hair abrading her tender nipples. There was a tightly coiled spring low inside her belly and every thrust, every brush of his body against hers drew the coils tighter still until it seemed as if the pressure of it was more than she could bear.

And then Cullen's hands slid under her, his fingers digging into the soft flesh of her bottom, pulling her up to meet his solid penetration of her, deepening an embrace that couldn't possibly get any deeper, making her his all the way to her soul.

And the tension inside her shattered into tiny fragments of sensation. If she'd had the breath to do so, Darcy might have screamed. But he'd stolen her breath, her soul, her heart. She dug her fingers into the damp muscles of his shoulders, sobbing with the force of her pleasure.

Cullen groaned as he felt her climax take her. She shuddered beneath him as tiny muscles rippled and contracted around him, dragging him headlong into his own satisfaction. He pulled her higher on his invading flesh, feeling Darcy's nails bite into his shoulders as the movement prolonged her own pleasure.

And then he gave himself up and let the heavy pulse of release take him.

Through eyes blurred with tears of pleasure, Darcy saw Cullen's face above her, the skin tight across his cheekbones, his lips drawn back from his teeth, a guttural groan bursting from him. She lifted her legs and locked her ankles across his lower back, arching her body into his. He shuddered against her as the movement deepened their already impossibly deep embrace. The pleasure seemed to go on and on, long rolling waves of sensation.

It was a long time before Darcy gathered the strength to open her eyes. She felt heavy with exhaustion yet so light that it seemed possible she might float up from the bed without Cullen's weight to hold her down. There was a pleasant tingly feeling to her skin.

Cullen shifted, easing his weight onto his elbows and looking down at her. It was too dark for her to read his expression but she caught the white gleam of his teeth as he smiled.

"That'll teach you to tease, Ms. Logan."

"I've certainly learned my lesson, Mr. Roberts." Her voice was almost as steady as his.

"See that you don't forget." The last word ended on a groan as she tightened certain muscles, demonstrating an admirable grasp of the situation.

"I certainly wouldn't want to tease," she said, widening her eyes in a show of innocence at odds with the far from innocent movement of her body.

"I can see that you wouldn't." Cullen flexed his hips, letting her feel his growing arousal.

"I wouldn't want to disturb you." It took considerable effort to keep her voice steady.

"I like being disturbed." Cullen wrapped his hands in her hair, using the hold to tilt her head back. Darcy shivered as she felt his teeth against the taut line of her throat.

It wasn't as urgent this time. Arousal built slowly, drugging her senses, melting her body into his until it was hard to tell where one stopped and the other began. Her response to Cullen never failed to surprise her. She'd always thought of herself as a rather cold person. But Cullen brought out a fire in her that sometimes threatened to consume her.

She moaned, her fingers clinging to his shoulders as the world rocked around them once more.

And for a little while Darcy could push aside her fears that she was going to lose him.

Chapter Four

"I can't believe that one baby requires all this stuff just to go out to dinner. A small army could march across the Gobi with less."

Darcy grinned as she watched Cullen struggle with the car seat and a bulging diaper bag. It was the first time they'd ventured out of the house with Angie in the two weeks since they'd picked her up in Seattle.

"An army doesn't have to cater to the needs of a baby," she told him.

"Well, if this is what it takes, there'd be a lot fewer wars if they did. Three months in boot camp couldn't prepare a man for carting all this stuff around," he groused. "Not to mention they'd be too tired to fight because they'd never manage to get a decent night's sleep."

The last was a mutter as he walked out the door to put his burdens in the car. Darcy was left alone with the baby. She looked at Angie, who was lying on the sofa with pillows mounded around her to keep her from rolling off. Having pulled one sock off, Angie was doing her best to bite her toes.

Darcy's hands twitched with the urge to pick her up but she resisted. She'd had plenty of time to think about the situation. Since coming back from Seattle, she'd thought of little else. The situation seemed impossible: she wanted nothing to do with having a baby in her life but Cullen now came with a baby attached.

And the one thing she was absolutely sure of was that she *did* want Cullen in her life. The realization of just how much was rather frightening to someone who'd spent the past six years carefully wanting nothing and most especially wanting no one. She'd lived with Cullen almost six months, but it had taken Angie's arrival to make her realize how much she'd come to depend on him, how much she needed him.

Her first reaction to the baby had been denial. If she told herself he didn't matter so much, then he wouldn't. But she'd never been much good at lying to herself. The truth was that she couldn't bear the thought of going back to the sterile, empty, *safe* existence she'd led before Cullen had come into her life. The happiness she'd found with him might be fragile—he'd surely hate her if he ever learned the full truth about her. But fragile or not, she didn't want to give it up, didn't want to give up the man who'd given it to her.

And since she couldn't ask Cullen to give up his sister's child, she was going to have to find a way to come to terms with Angie's presence in her life. Not so complex really, she told herself as she watched the baby contentedly playing with her own toes. Cullen hadn't noticed anything odd about her behavior toward his niece so far. And if he did, she'd just tell him she wasn't the maternal type. Then all she had to do was keep a little emotional and physical distance between herself and Angie.

How hard could that be?

Losing interest in her toes, Angie looked around for a new distraction. Her flailing hand found the stuffed cloth block she'd been playing with before discovering the delights of toe chewing. She lifted it and studied it with a seriousness worthy of an entomologist examining a new species of beetle. Her eyes were exactly the color of her uncle's, that same clear, heart-melting blue. Darcy found herself smiling at Angie's serious expression.

"Ready?" Cullen's question preceded him. Darcy's head jerked toward the door as he entered.

"Yes." *There was nothing to feel guilty about,* she scolded herself.

"How are my two best girls?" At the sound of Cullen's voice, Angie abruptly lost interest in the block. Her head turned until she found him. Immediately her small face creased into a two-toothed grin and she began to kick both her feet in excitement.

Cullen's answering grin was nothing short of enthralled, Darcy thought as she watched him walk over to the sofa. Despite the lack of sleep he'd complained about, he looked devastatingly handsome. A shock of dark hair fell onto his forehead, emphasizing the blue of his eyes. He was wearing black jeans and a blue shirt almost the exact shade of his eyes. She'd bought him that shirt for Christmas. Now she almost wished she hadn't. He didn't need anything to make him look more attractive. The man practically qualified as a lethal weapon as it was.

"How's my girl?" he asked Angie as he leaned down to pick her up. His hands looked huge against her small body but he held her easily, with none of the uncertainty he'd shown at first. Held in midair, Angie babbled happily, both legs churning with the excitement of having Cullen's attention.

I know just how you feel, Darcy thought wryly.

The restaurant was new to both of them, a family kind of place with a menu that ran more toward hot roast beef sandwiches with mashed potatoes than filet mignon with tiny vegetables.

"I didn't think Angie was ready for Chez Bev," Cullen said, mentioning a restaurant they'd been to several times.

"I doubt they're ready for her, either." Darcy's tone was dry, but she didn't look particularly disappointed by his choice of restaurants, Cullen thought, glancing at her as he settled Angie into a high chair.

"You could be right. Imagine the waiter's expression if she spit a mouthful of baby carrots at him." He latched the tray in place before sliding into the red vinyl booth.

"It would cause a major crisis," Darcy agreed. "The chef would probably come out to ask her what it was about his special recipe that didn't appeal to her."

"I'm not sure her French is up to task," Cullen said seriously.

Angie babbled something and slapped both hands against the metal tray of the high chair as if demanding to know where dinner was.

"I don't know. I think she could get her message across in most languages," Darcy said dryly.

"You could be right." Cullen found a toy in the bulging diaper bag and handed it to his niece to distract her from the delay with mealtime. Angie promptly began to gnaw on the plastic ring.

Seeing that she was occupied, at least momentarily, he turned his attention to Darcy. One thing he'd learned about babies was the truly amazing amount of time they required. It seemed as if he hadn't had time to draw a breath. He'd been telling himself that he and Darcy would talk, that they'd discuss the changes Angie had made in their lives. But it had been two weeks and they'd yet to talk.

He'd never realized just how big a job it was to take care of a baby, especially since he'd been thrown in at the deep end without the slightest preparation for the task. Without his secretary, who'd been willing to extend her job description to include shopping, and Darcy to show him the fine points of diapering, among other things, he doubted if either he or Angie would have made it to the end of the first week.

He thought he was starting to get the hang of it now, but it still seemed as if most of his waking hours were spent dealing with the minutiae of life with a baby. And the brief bits of time he had for anything else were spent trying to keep up with his business. Kiel hadn't complained about dealing with his partner's work as well as his own but Cullen didn't expect him to keep doing it. Besides, there were decisions that took the two of them to make. Add Darcy's job to the mix and the end result was that the two of them hadn't had a moment to themselves.

Except in bed. They communicated just fine there. But when he was in bed with Darcy, his urges ran to something more elemental than discussing life changes.

But now, here they were, alone, unless you counted Angie and the couple of hundred other patrons in the restaurant. It wasn't exactly intimate and he hadn't planned on starting a serious discussion tonight but maybe they could talk without too many interruptions.

"Darcy, I—"

"What can I get for you?" Their waitress looked about eighteen. She wore the same nondescript brown and white uniform the other waitresses wore but she'd accessorized hers with black ankle socks, combat boots and a small gold stud through one nostril.

Cullen managed to keep his expression under control until the girl had taken their order and left. Once she was gone, he leaned across the table.

"Who do you think does her makeup?" he asked, keeping his voice low.

"Lon Chaney. I'm sure I saw that same look in the original *Phantom of the Opera*. It's the hair I'm not sure about."

"You mean that spiky thing on top of her head is her hair?" Cullen widened his eyes in mock disbelief. "How does she get it to stand up like that?"

"Years of practice and a can of mousse."

The girl returned with their drinks. Once she was gone, Cullen's eyes met Darcy's and she dissolved in giggles. His rich chuckle joined her laughter. Angie chortled happily, unconcerned with the cause of the adults' good humor.

"We haven't laughed much lately, have we?" he said as their laughter faded.

"Things have been a little hectic." Darcy reached for the pottery cream pitcher and added a generous dollop to her coffee.

"That's an understatement." Angie threw the purple plastic ring onto the table and Cullen automatically returned it to her.

"I'm a banker. We're supposed to understate things." Darcy reached for her spoon. The plastic ring landed right next it and Darcy picked it up and set it on the high chair's tray.

"I know I said we'd talk—about the baby and everything. We need—" This time Angie threw the ring on the floor and then leaned over to look at the results of her effort. Cullen bent and scooped it up and started to hand it to her.

"She'll put it in her mouth," Darcy commented.

"What?" His thoughts on other things, he stared at her blankly.

"She'll put that in her mouth." Darcy nodded to the ring. "It's been on the floor."

"Oh. Right." He turned and stuffed the ring back into the diaper bag and came up with a cloth ball. Angie took it from him with a squeal of delight.

"Not that it really matters."

"Not that what matters?" he asked, feeling as if he'd lost the thread of the conversation.

"Whether or not she put that in her mouth after it had been on the floor. If she can survive chewing on her own feet, I suspect she's tough enough to survive the little bit of dirt it might have picked up."

"Then why did you stop me from giving it to her?"

"Because there's a grandmotherly looking type at the counter who's keeping an eye on us, and I was afraid she'd slap your hand if you did something she disapproved of."

Cullen looked in the direction she'd indicated, his glance colliding with that of an older woman who was sitting at the lunch counter. She beamed at him. He smiled in return and then turned back to Darcy, who was watching him over the rim of her coffee cup, her gray eyes bright with humor.

"Why is she looking at me like that?" he asked sotto voce, as if the woman might actually be able to hear him from fifteen feet away.

"She's impressed by how good you are with the baby."

"I haven't done anything." He returned the cloth ball to Angie, who'd flung it into the middle of the table. She promptly threw it again. Fetch was one of her favorite games, as long as someone else was doing the fetching.

His patience with Angie was so effortless that he wasn't even aware of it, Darcy thought. He'd turned his entire life upside down without a second thought to give his niece a home. And he didn't even see anything extraordinary about what he'd done. Watching him with the baby, it occurred to her that he was born to be a father. The role fit him like a well-tailored suit.

The realization seemed to open a gaping chasm between them, with her on one side and Cullen and the baby on the other. The bright lights suddenly seemed a little blurred and there was a constriction in her throat. She lowered her head and pretended to search for something in her purse while she got her emotions under control.

"Are you all right?"

Cullen leaned across the table and Darcy didn't have to look at him to know that he was looking concerned. Why couldn't he do things the way men were traditionally supposed to do them? Why couldn't he be an insensitive lout, oblivious to her feelings?

"I'm fine," she said, dragging a crumpled tissue from the bottom of her purse and dabbing it against one eye. "I just had something in my eye. It's out now."

She lifted her head and gave him a bright smile to show that everything was peachy keen. Cullen looked doubtful and she had the feeling that he might have pursued the issue if the waitress hadn't chosen that moment to return with their order.

"Here you go."

If Darcy had been starving to death, she couldn't have been any more grateful to see a waitress. Spiky hair, nose stud, combat boots and all, the girl couldn't have looked better if she'd been wearing white wings.

"Here's our food," she said cheerfully, just in case Cullen hadn't noticed the plates being set in front of them. She knew, even if Cullen hadn't yet figured it out, that there wasn't much chance of having an intelligent conversation while feeding a six-month-old baby.

He might want to talk about the changes in their situation, but she didn't. She didn't want to have to try to find a way to tell him that she'd continue to live with him but that she wanted to have as little as possible to do with the baby. He was sure to want to know why and she didn't have the words to give him. Unless she told him the truth and that was out of the question.

Apparently, Cullen realized that serious conversation and feeding a baby were not compatible activities. Darcy gradually relaxed as the conversation stayed on relatively neutral ground. She told him what had been going on at her job. He mentioned a new construction project that he and Kiel were going to bid on.

It was so much the kind of conversation they'd always had that if she closed her eyes, Darcy could almost have believed that it was B.B.—Before Baby.

She watched with admiration as he managed to eat his meal while feeding Angie. She'd never been half so good with— She cut the thought off, turning her thoughts from that particular path. It wasn't difficult, she'd had years of practice.

They were nearly finished with their dinner when the older woman who'd smiled at Cullen earlier approached the table.

"I hope you don't mind, but I just had to get a closer look at your baby."

"Not at all," Cullen said, casting a quick look in Darcy's direction. She shrugged. He'd learn that babies had a way of starting conversations between total strangers, whether you wished it or not.

"I couldn't help but notice her when you brought her in." She leaned over to peer at Angie, who gave her a cheerful smile. "Not a shy bone in her body," the woman said delightedly. "She's the spitting image of my Wanda. Not now, of course, because she turned forty-eight this last March. She says she's only forty-one but that's not something a mother's likely to forget, now is it?"

She fixed Darcy with bright blue eyes and Darcy nodded obediently. "I can't imagine how."

"Exactly what I told Wanda. Besides, I have her birth certificate," Wanda's mother said triumphantly.

"I doubt these folks want to hear about that, Millie." Millie's husband had been standing behind her, looking mildly embarrassed by his wife's chatter.

"I suppose not, but it's just so exasperating. I mean, she can have all the nips and tucks she wants and dress up like a teenager and I don't say a word about it, but it seems to me she's going a bit far when she starts lying to her own mother about her age.''

Silence seemed the only safe response. Darcy saw a suspicious tuck in Cullen's cheek and knew he was struggling to hold back a laugh. Obviously he was in no hurry to leap into the conversation.

''Millie.'' Mr. Millie was starting to look as if he wished he were somewhere else.

''All right. I'll stop nattering on.'' Millie smiled down at Angie again. ''I just had to tell you two what a beautiful little girl you have here. Not that I can't see that you already know that,'' she added. ''She's lucky to have parents who care for her the way you two obviously do.''

''Oh, but—''

''Thank you.'' Cullen's voice cut across Darcy's automatic attempt to correct the woman's assumption that they were Angie's parents.

With a last smile at the baby, Millie departed. At another time Darcy would have been amused to see that Mr. Millie had his hand firmly around his wife's upper arm as if to prevent her from dashing back to talk some more.

But there was a funny ache in her chest that made it difficult to see the humor in the scene. It was silly to let something so small cause her pain. What did it matter that Millie-Wanda's mother thought Angie was her child?

It didn't matter at all except that, for a moment, she'd have given almost anything for it to be true.

"I didn't see any reason to get into explanations," Cullen said.

"No, of course not." Darcy forced a smile as she looked at him. "She was quite a character, wasn't she?"

"I think her husband was about ready to gag her."

"I have a sneaking sympathy with poor Wanda." Darcy wondered if it was her imagination that made Cullen's humor seem a little forced. "All that nipping and tucking and then betrayed by your own mother."

"Must be rough."

They finished their meal, though Darcy could barely remember what she was eating. She refused dessert with a smile. The tightness in her stomach made her wonder if she'd be able to keep down what she'd already eaten.

Angie was asleep almost as soon as Cullen strapped her into her car seat. The drive home was silent, with Darcy pretending an intense interest in the scene outside her window. She knew, with an instinct she didn't question, that Cullen had every intention of having that long-delayed talk tonight. The one that would inevitably involve some discussion of the future, of Darcy's place in the future he and Angie were bound to share.

Logically, she supposed such a discussion couldn't be postponed forever, not when it involved Angie's future. But surely it could be delayed just one more night.

Cullen turned the car into the slot in front of the condo and it had barely stopped moving before she reached for the door handle.

"I'll get the diaper bag," she said, snatching it up and making her escape.

It took time to get a baby out of a car seat. Maybe she could be in the shower by the time Cullen reached the condo. She might have succeeded in doing just that if it hadn't taken even more time than usual to dig her keys out of the bottom of her cavernous purse. She was going to get a smaller purse, she promised herself as Cullen joined her on the porch, the baby asleep in his arms. Or a bigger key chain.

"I'm going to hop in the shower," she said without looking at him.

"Darcy." Cullen's voice halted her flight across the living room. "I'd like to talk to you."

"Could it wait?" she asked without turning.

"I think it's waited long enough."

"I was just—"

"Please."

The single word was more effective than if he'd shouted. She stopped and turned to look at him, trying to keep the uneasiness from her voice.

"It's getting late—"

"It's not even nine o'clock."

"I have to get up in the morning."

"It's Saturday. You can sleep in."

He wasn't going to give up. Darcy sighed.

"Why don't you put Angie to bed?" She ran her fingers through her hair, letting it tumble back to her shoulders like a pale gold curtain. "I'll put some coffee on."

"Thanks." They both knew he wasn't thanking her for making coffee.

Chapter Five

Cullen stopped in the kitchen doorway and indulged himself by simply looking at Darcy. The warm scent of coffee filled the air. She was getting mugs from the cupboard. Their position on the second shelf meant she had to reach to get them and her T-shirt rode up, baring a swatch of pale skin above the waist of her jeans.

He knew the taste of that skin, knew that if he dragged his tongue along the length of her spine, she'd tremble with need. He knew the way the soft flesh of her bottom yielded beneath his fingers. Knew that kissing the back of her knee made her giggle. He knew every inch of her, every muscle, every nerve, just where to touch her to have her dissolve in his arms.

She was his. He hadn't been her first lover but he'd been the first to satisfy her, the first to show her the potential of her own body. He'd never asked about her past lovers, any more than she'd asked about his. Never questioned her shocked surprise the first time she'd come apart in his bed.

Whoever the man was—and he had the feeling there'd only been one—he'd been a fool. But Cullen admitted to a sneaking feeling of gratitude toward the unknown fool. He liked it that he'd been the one to introduce Darcy to passion. He didn't care if he was first but he damn well wanted to be last.

As if sensing his gaze, Darcy turned suddenly to face him, her fingers tight around the cups she held.

"I didn't hear you," she said, her voice a little sharp with surprise.

"Sorry. I'll try to learn to stomp." Cullen pushed himself away from the door and came farther into the kitchen. "Coffee smells good. Thanks for making it."

"You're welcome. It's decaf. I didn't think either one of us needed caffeine at this time of night."

"You're probably right." He certainly didn't need anything to keep him awake and she looked tense enough to shatter at any moment.

She set the mugs on the counter and poured coffee in them while Cullen got a carton of half-and-half from the refrigerator.

"Did you get Angie to bed all right?"

"Out like a light."

Cullen poured a dollop of half-and-half into the mug decorated with a lavender and white carousel horse. The other mug displayed a folk-art-style painting of a cat. The mugs were among Darcy's contributions to their living arrangements. Before she'd moved in with him, he'd had two plates, two forks, two knives, two of everything. And the only coffee cup he'd owned had been a chipped white cup that looked as if it had been recovered from the wreck of the *Titanic*. Darcy's collection of colorful mugs was only one of the many ways she'd brightened his life.

Without discussing it, they took their coffee into the living room. Darcy curled up on the sofa. Cullen chose the big leather chair that sat at an angle nearby. He took a sip of his coffee and then stared down into it. Darcy took a sip of hers and then studied a piece of lint on the arm of the sofa.

The silence was deafening.

"I wanted—"

"You said—"

They both broke off and looked at each other. Cullen nodded. "You first."

"I was just going to mention that you'd said you wanted to talk to me."

"Funny. I was just going to mention the same thing." His smile was rueful. Darcy's was uncertain. But the tension that had been threatening to suffocate both of them was broken.

Cullen set his cup down on the thick sheet of glass that formed the top of the coffee table. It was supported by a gnarled piece of driftwood. He was going to have to get a new coffee table, he thought absently, noting the sharp corners of glass. Either that or find a way to pad the edges of this one. Angie was already standing up with a bit of support. According to what he'd read, it wouldn't be long until she was trying to walk and he didn't want her to crack her head open on the coffee table.

He said as much. Darcy looked surprised but she glanced at the table and nodded.

"The edges could probably be padded, maybe tape some old towels to the glass." She shook her head, her mouth curving in a half smile. "Early American Baby decor."

"Not likely to start any new trends."

"Well, it might not attract the designer crowd," she agreed.

"Do you mind?" he asked abruptly.

"That *House & Garden* isn't beating a path to our door?" She raised her brows.

"That there've been so many...changes because of the baby." He saw her fingers tighten around the mug and her eyes shifted away from his.

"I think it goes with the territory," she said lightly.

"Yes. But I couldn't blame you if you resented it." He set down his barely touched coffee and stood up. There was too much churning inside him for him to sit still. "You didn't ask for any of this."

"You didn't, either."

"No. But Susan was *my* sister, not yours." He turned and paced to the sliding-glass door that led out onto the patio. Twitching aside the curtain, he stared out into the darkness, half wishing he hadn't brought the subject up. They'd been rubbing along together all right. Why rock the boat?

Because you don't want it capsizing under you when you least expect it. Because you don't want to lose the best damn thing that's ever happened to you.

He turned back to her with an abruptness that made Darcy jump. "Look, I know I didn't give you any choice about this. And I know I should have. I had no right to throw your life into turmoil without even discussing it with you."

"What was there to discuss?" She leaned forward to set her cup down, the faint tremor in her hand belying the calm reason of her voice. "You couldn't leave Angie where she was and there was no one else who could take her."

"Yes." They were the same arguments he'd used on himself and the logic of them sounded just as inescapable as it had then. But that didn't soothe his conscience. "I should have—"

"You did exactly what you should have," Darcy interrupted. She stood up and walked over to where he stood, setting one slim hand on his arm and looking up at him. "I'm not upset or angry that you didn't discuss this with me, Cullen. The decision was only yours to make and you couldn't have made any other."

He stared down at her, an uncharacteristic brooding look in his blue eyes. She was so good at hiding what she was thinking, what she was feeling. It could have been a natural part of her makeup but he'd always suspected that it was something she'd learned through hard experience.

From the first moment he'd met her, he'd seen the shadows in her eyes. Someone or something had hurt her in the past. Hurt her badly enough to put those shadows there. They'd begun to fade over the past few months, as if she were—very slowly—starting to forget whatever it was that had marked her. Or if not forgetting, then at least putting it behind her.

But just lately the shadows were back, turning her clear gray eyes smoky, muting the sparkle he'd come to love. He was afraid she was slipping away from him and if he lost her, he'd lose the best part of his life.

"You're not happy."

The flat statement hit Darcy with the force of a blow. She let her hand drop from his arm as she took a quick step back, grateful that the light from the single lamp wouldn't be enough to reveal the way the color had drained from her cheeks.

"I don't know what you mean." It was a weak response, but it was the best she could do. She'd been so sure that she'd concealed her feelings from him, so careful not to allow even the smallest crack in the facade.

"I mean, you're ... uncomfortable around Angie." Cullen hesitated over the choice of words. The feeling he got from Darcy wasn't discomfort. It was more like fear, but that sounded too ridiculous to say out loud.

"I haven't spent a lot of time around babies, that's all."

"You said you'd done some baby-sitting," he reminded her.

"Baby-sitting is a little different from having one around full time," she said lightly.

"True."

But he continued to look at her, those clear blue eyes asking questions she couldn't—wouldn't—answer. If he knew the real reason ...

"I—I guess I'm not really the maternal type," Darcy said, lifting one shoulder in a half shrug. "I mean, I think Angie's adorable and all that, but she doesn't *do* a whole lot, if you know what I mean. You can't talk to her or anything."

She shrugged again, keeping her face turned from the light to hide the color burning in her cheeks. She hadn't realized she had it in her to sound so completely shallow and inane. *You can't talk to her.* As if she expected to be able to discuss Dostoyevski with a six-month-old baby. If Cullen hadn't despised her before, he probably would now.

"I guess that sounds pretty stupid," she muttered when he didn't say anything.

"No. I think I understand what you're saying." What he didn't understand was why she was telling him such a barefaced lie. He didn't doubt that there were a good many people who felt that way. He could even understand it to a certain extent. But he'd have bet any amount of money that that wasn't how Darcy felt.

"I used to think I wanted to be a mother," Darcy said, almost choking on the words. "But I guess maybe I don't have the requisite genes. I know that's not what you want to hear. Obviously you'd like me to say that I'll be a terrific mother to Angie, but I don't think I'm cut out for the job. I know that's a real problem."

She stopped and swallowed hard. It required every bit of self-control to keep her voice level while she said what had to be said. "If you want me to move out—"

"No!" Cullen's response was reassuringly quick and emphatic. "That's the last thing I want."

He reached out and caught her hand in his as if afraid she might dash out the door that instant. Darcy drew a deep breath and closed her eyes for a moment, relief so powerful inside her that her knees actually felt weak.

"I don't want you to go," Cullen said firmly. He pulled her into his arms and Darcy went willingly, resting her head against his chest and feeling the strong beat of his heart beneath her cheek.

"I don't want to go," she said, and Cullen knew the admission didn't come easily.

She guarded herself so carefully, he thought, bending to rest his cheek against the top of her head, inhaling the soft scents of shampoo and soap. Darcy rarely wore perfume and he'd decided that the natural smell of a woman was far more erotic than the most expensive perfume could ever be.

"We'll work things out," he told her.

"But Angie has to come first. I wouldn't want to hurt her."

"We'll work everything out. If the fact that you can't talk to her really bothers you, just wait a year or so. According to Sara Randall, she'll be talking like a magpie by then."

Darcy's laugh was choked and she closed her eyes to hold back tears. What had she ever done to deserve a man like Cullen Roberts? But there was something to what he said. If she could hold on until Angie was a little older, until she wasn't quite so afraid of—

She blocked the thought, focusing instead on the feel of Cullen's arms around her. She always felt safe when he held her.

"We'll work everything out," he said again.

If she'd just tell him what was really bothering her, maybe he'd be able to do something about it, Cullen thought. He felt as if he was shadowboxing. He could get glimpses of the enemy but there was nothing to catch hold of, nothing to tell him what he was fighting.

But he wasn't giving up. He was going to find out what was behind those shadows in Darcy's eyes and he was going to banish them forever.

Cullen rearranged his work schedule, bringing most of his paperwork home with him so that he could take care of Angie. When he had to be out on a site, he left her with Sara Randall's youngest daughter. Divorced, with two children of her own, Marie welcomed the extra money and Cullen knew Angie would be well cared for.

Though it had been less than a month, it was already impossible for him to imagine his life without Angie in it. Until his sister's death, he hadn't given much thought to fatherhood. He'd had a vague idea in the back of his head that he might like to have a child someday but, at thirty-four, he hadn't felt that there was any rush to make plans.

Now, abruptly, he found himself plunged into the deep end of parenthood and enjoying it more than he'd ever have imagined. Every day was a new discovery, for himself as well as for Angie. She'd filled a gap in his life he hadn't even realized was there.

With her and Darcy, his life was complete. All he had to do was figure out a way to prove to Darcy how right the three of them were together.

Darcy had mixed feelings about seeing the ties grow ever stronger between Cullen and his niece. She couldn't wish anything less for either of them, but with each day that passed, it seemed clearer that she didn't—couldn't—fit into the tidy picture before her.

Still, things were better than they had been. Talking with Cullen had helped. She hadn't told him the truth—at least not all of it—but she'd made it clear that he'd better not count on her to round out the happy family picture. And it seemed as if he'd accepted that. He certainly didn't thrust Angie into her arms in an attempt to encourage some kind of bonding between them.

Without the pressure of expectations—even if they had been strictly her own—Darcy found herself, paradoxically, more comfortable around the baby than she had been. She relaxed enough to allow herself to enjoy the innocent pleasure Angie took in everything that happened into her field of vision.

She'd almost forgotten the sheer fun to be had in watching those moments of discovery that came so often for an infant. Angie was fascinated by everything she saw and innocently confident that the world was her personal oyster.

It would have taken a much harder heart than Darcy's not to be touched by the baby's pleasure in life. There was a certain pain in watching Angie, but it wasn't as sharp as she'd expected it to be. Apparently, time really did, if not heal, then at least numb all pain.

As long as Cullen didn't expect her to be responsible for Angie, she could almost let herself believe that things might work out, after all.

The early-summer days slipped by in a not unpleasant pattern. An evening in early June found Darcy and Cullen both at home. Darcy had fixed dinner and afterward they'd settled in the living room. Cullen was reading a list of recent changes in the building code that could affect projects he and Kiel had coming up. Darcy had a new mystery open in her lap, but her attention kept wandering from the book.

After twenty minutes on the same page, with not a word of it sticking in her head, she gave up. She looked up, wondering if Cullen's building codes were as boring as her novel. If they were, maybe he'd be interested in watching an old movie on cable. He was sound asleep, which answered her question about how boring the building codes were, she supposed.

Darcy's features softened as she looked at him. He probably needed the sleep. Between running J&R Construction and taking care of Angie, he was handling two full-time jobs. It was no wonder he was dozing off at seven o'clock.

She caught a movement out the corner of her eye and turned to see Angie crawling in her direction.

Well, "crawl" wasn't an entirely accurate description. It was more a series of belly flops, but what she lacked in coordination, Angie made up for in determination. Since discovering this new method of locomotion a few days before, she'd become an indefatigable explorer, which had required some hasty redecorating to get every possible danger out of her reach.

Now Angie was making her way toward Darcy with solemn perseverance, her blue eyes fixed on Darcy's bright purple socks. Smiling, Darcy wiggled her toes a little. With a grunt of effort, Angie heaved herself the last few inches and flopped onto her belly in front of her goal. Her tiny fingers closed over Darcy's toes, her grip surprisingly strong.

Darcy wiggled her toes again, enjoying the little girl's intent frown as she studied this new toy. Having examined with sight and touch, there was only one choice left, which was taste.

"Hey." Darcy laughed softly as she leaned forward to scoop the baby up. "It's one thing to chew on your own toes but you can't go around munching on other people's. It's just not done in polite society."

Angie was willing to give up the purple sock in exchange for being held. Besides, her new position put her in reach of other interesting objects. Chubby fingers closed around the gold chain Darcy wore around her neck. The chain had been a birthday gift from Cullen not long after she'd moved in with him and she rarely took it off.

"That was a present from your uncle," she told the baby. Angie didn't lift her eyes but continued to study the chain very seriously. After a moment she leaned forward to taste it. Laughing, Darcy pulled her back. "You're going to have to get over this tendency to put everything in your mouth, punkin."

Deprived of the chain, Angie reached for Darcy's nose. Darcy shook her head free and caught one little hand in hers. Bringing it to her mouth, she nibbled on the tiny fingers, drawing a rich baby chuckle. For a few moments she completely forgot all the reasons she needed to keep her distance, for Angie's sake as well as her own, and she let herself simply enjoy the small person in her arms.

From his position on the sofa, Cullen watched the two of them through slitted eyes. He knew that the instant Darcy realized he was awake, she'd get that oddly guilty look on her face and hand the baby to him.

No maternal feelings, his Aunt Fanny. In the rare moments like this, when she forgot whatever it was that haunted her, she was as natural a mother as it was possible to imagine. Her quiet laughter mixed with Angie's fat chuckles and he thought he'd never heard a sweeter sound in his life.

She loved Angie, whether she knew it or not. And though she'd never said the words, he knew Darcy loved him. And God knew, he loved her more than he'd ever dreamed possible. He'd cajoled her into moving in with him, then he'd waited for her to open her eyes and see that what they had was too special to give up. His becoming Angie's guardian had thrown a monkey wrench in the works, but only for a little while. Surely Darcy was starting to see that they could work things out.

Smiling, she buried her nose in Angie's neck, eliciting squeals of delighted laughter as Angie's chubby hands caught fistfuls of Darcy's pale gold hair. Cullen felt his heart swell with love for them both and he was unashamed of the sharp sting of tears at the backs of his eyes.

He was willing to admit to a few doubts, but now he knew that it was going to be all right, after all.

Chapter Six

"What have you got planned for today?" Cullen asked. He was sitting at the table, feeding Angie her breakfast when Darcy walked into the kitchen.

"Shopping. And I wanted to catch up on some paperwork I brought home with me yesterday. Everyone and their dog wants a loan. There aren't enough hours in the day to get everything done."

She opened the refrigerator and peered inside, hoping for inspiration. The sight of last night's leftover pizza made her stomach churn sluggishly and she shut the door. Maybe she'd just have a cup of coffee this morning.

She'd awakened in the middle of the night again last night and had been unable to resist the need to go into the nursery and stand next to the crib, watching the steady rise and fall of the baby's breathing. Reassured, she'd gone back to bed, only to wake an hour later, trembling in the aftermath of a nightmare. It was the third night this week that her sleep had been chopped up and the strain was starting to tell. She felt gray and worn.

"You look tired," Cullen commented as she poured herself a cup of coffee and sat down across the table from him.

"Thanks," she said dryly. "Nice to know I'm looking my best."

"I didn't say you looked bad. I said you looked tired." He fed the baby a spoonful of carrots, deftly scraping the excess off her chin.

"There's a difference?" She took a sip of coffee, hoping the caffeine would jump start her sluggish brain.

"I heard you get up last night."

"I had a little trouble sleeping. Too much going on at work, I guess." She shrugged. To her relief, Cullen accepted the explanation for her insomnia without question.

"You need a day off."

"This *is* my day off."

"Not if you've brought home paperwork." He managed to sneak another bite of carrots into Angie's mouth. She pursed her lips as if to spit them out, saw Cullen watching her and grinned instead. He shuddered.

"You have disgusting table manners," he told her firmly. She banged her spoon on the metal tray of her high chair and squealed her delight at this description.

"I don't think she believes you," Darcy commented.

Hearing her voice, Angie turned and favored Darcy with the same carrot-smeared grin. Darcy smiled back, feeling that odd little twist in her chest that had become so familiar in the weeks since Angie had come to live with them. She was such a beautiful little girl. It would be so easy to love her. If only she dared take that risk.

"Can your paperwork wait?"

Cullen's question drew her attention back to him. He'd dampened a cloth and was busy wiping carrot off of Angie's face and hands.

"I suppose it could. Why?"

"Because we're going on a picnic."

"A picnic?"

"You know, one of those meals where you sit on the cold, hard ground, fending off wasps and ants and getting sunburned. A picnic."

She wrinkled her nose at him. "You make it sound so appealing."

"The challenge is half the fun," he said briskly. He stood up and lifted Angie out of her high chair. She kicked madly. "I've arranged for Marie to take Angie for the day."

Darcy hesitated over the refusal she'd been about to give him. "Just the two of us?"

"I thought it might be nice for a change."

"I don't mind if Angie comes along," she said quickly. "She's a good baby."

"She's a pest." Since he was tickling Angie's toes at the time, it was clear that "pest" was not the pejorative it might have been. Settling the baby in one arm, he looked at Darcy, his azure eyes holding an expression that made Darcy's heart beat a little faster.

"I want some time without distractions. And being a distraction ranks high on Angie's best talents."

"I really should do some of that paperwork," she said slowly.

"The paperwork won't go anywhere. Come on, Darcy. Play hooky with me."

The coaxing tone was more than she could resist, as was the thought of having him to herself for a whole afternoon. She didn't resent Angie's demands on his time but she wouldn't have been human if she didn't miss the times when it had been just the two of them.

"Okay. A picnic sounds like fun, ants and all." Besides, who knew if there would be another time.

Darcy leaned her head back against the seat and let the wind from the open car window blow through her hair. It would look like a haystack by the time they got to whatever spot Cullen had chosen for their picnic, but she didn't care. She'd made up her mind that she wasn't going to worry about anything today. Not the future, not the past, not even the present that was all tangled up in both of them. Today, she was simply going to enjoy the moment.

She'd been mildly surprised when Cullen headed the car north out of Santa Barbara, but when she asked him where they were going, he shook his head and said it was a surprise. The idea of a mysterious destination fit right in with her mood so she simply leaned back to enjoy the trip.

They were driving up the coast highway and the Pacific sparkled on their left. A few miles above Santa Barbara, Cullen turned inland, driving between rolling hills that still showed green from the winter rains.

Live oaks dotted the land, their heavy trunks and twisted branches revealing their age. He turned onto a gravel road, drove a couple of miles and stopped the car in a tiny valley that nestled between two hills. As soon as he shut the engine off, silence washed over them.

"What do you think?" There was a certain tension in his voice as if her answer was important to him.

Darcy looked from him to the emptiness around them. "I think it's beautiful," she said truthfully. "But it seems like a long drive for a picnic."

"I'm going to build a house here." He pushed open his car door and got out. Darcy followed suit. She looked at the site again, visualizing a house cradled against one of the hills, the little valley stretching out from the front door.

"It's a wonderful place for a home."

"I don't want to disturb the site any more than necessary, so it may take a little longer than usual because we won't be bringing in as much heavy equipment."

Darcy came around the car to help him unload the picnic things from the trunk. Cullen continued to talk about his plans for the house as they headed for the shade of an ancient sycamore, laid out a blanket and spread their picnic items along one edge of it.

By the time they'd eaten the sandwiches they'd bought in town, Darcy felt as if she could see the house he'd described. Redwood and glass, a style somewhere between traditional and modern, with plenty of light filling the rooms and a big deck carefully fitted around the existing oak trees. The house wouldn't blend in with its surroundings right away, but in a few years when the sun had weathered the redwood to a soft, faded gray, you'd probably have to look twice to know there was a house there.

"It sounds beautiful," she said wistfully. She drew her knees up to her chest and narrowed her eyes as she pictured how the house would look. "I envy the people you're building it for."

"Don't."

"Don't what?" she asked, still looking out at the imaginary house.

"Don't envy them."

"Why not?" Now she turned to look at him, her brows raised in surprise.

"Because it's us. Or maybe, we're them."

"We're who?"

"We're the people who are going to live in that house." Cullen had been leaning back on his elbows but now he sat up, close enough that his shoulder almost brushed hers. "It's my lot, Darcy, and it's our house I was describing. If you like it, that is."

"If I like it?" She stared at him.

"If you don't, I'll come up with another design."

"No. No, the design sounds perfect." She turned and looked back at the spot where he'd planned to build. The house was still there in her mind's eye, only now it was her house—her's and Cullen's.

And the baby's.

She shivered a little, the image blurring around the edges. He was asking for a bigger commitment than they had now. He hadn't said it yet but the question was there.

"I don't know, Cullen." She shook her head. "It's a beautiful place and the house sounds wonderful but I— Oh."

Her words ended on a squeak of shock as she turned back toward him and saw what he was holding out to her. It was a small black box. A jeweler's box. Just the size box to hold a ring. Darcy stared at it in shock, her mind spinning. When she didn't reach to take it from him, Cullen brought up his other hand to open it. Nestled on a bed of black velvet was a diamond solitaire, utterly simple, utterly beautiful. Utterly terrifying.

"Marry me, Darcy."

"Oh, God." She lifted one hand to her mouth, still staring at the ring like a rabbit mesmerized by the glare of headlights on a country road. Realizing that "Oh, God" was not exactly an intelligent response to a proposal, she tried again. "Why?"

"Because I love you."

It was the first time either of them had spoken the words out loud and the simple beauty of them made tears well in Darcy's eyes.

"Oh, Cullen. I love you, too."

"Good." His grin was a little crooked around the edges. "That makes the feeling mutual. Say yes and everything will be perfect."

The word trembled on the tip of her tongue. *Yes, she loved him. Yes, she would marry him.* It seemed such an obvious progression.

But it wasn't simple at all.

Darcy scrambled to her feet and turned away from him. She pressed her forearms against her diaphragm, trying to still the flutter of panic there.

"I can't marry you."

"Why not?" Cullen asked calmly as he stood up behind her. "You love me. I love you. What could be simpler?"

"I wish it was that simple but there are things you don't know about me."

"There are things you don't know about me. That's one of the things marriage is for, so you can get to know everything about the person you love."

"No. There are bad things you don't know," Darcy said, her voice so low he had to strain to hear it over the whisper of the breeze in the grass.

"Like what?" Maybe, finally, she'd tell him what it was that tortured her so. He closed his hands around her upper arms, trying to reassure her without words that he was there for her. "Tell me, Darcy."

"I was married before."

Cullen's fingers tightened momentarily in surprise. He hadn't been expecting that. A part of him instantly rejected the idea that she'd ever belonged to anyone else, bound by ties of man and God tighter than any he'd yet claimed.

"That's not a crime," he managed to say calmly. "Are you divorced?"

"Yes," she said indignantly. She pulled out of his hold and turned to look at him. "Do you think I'd be living with you if I were still married?"

"I don't know. You said there were things I didn't know. Being divorced isn't a crime, either." His eyes searched her face, searching for something he didn't want to find. "Are you still in love with him?"

"No! God, no." It was her turn to take hold of him. "I don't love anyone but you, Cullen. I don't think I ever loved him. I was lonely and he seemed kind and...we got married. But I didn't feel anything for him that was even close to what I feel for you."

"I believe you." He felt the knot in his stomach uncoil a little as he drew her close and stroked his hand over her pale gold hair. "You haven't told me anything to make me regret proposing, Darcy. Is that all there is?"

It wasn't her marriage she'd been afraid to confess to, Darcy thought as she pressed her face against the soft cotton of his shirt and felt the reassuring thud of his heart. Her marriage was the least of the secrets she was keeping.

"You can tell me, Darcy."

Maybe she could. If she could tell anyone, it would be Cullen. But what if she told him and then he looked at her the same way Mark had? Mark had promised to love, honor and cherish her, but in the end he'd hated her, blamed her for what had happened. Maybe he'd been right to blame her. She'd managed to survive it when Mark looked at her that way. But if she ever saw the same look in Cullen's eyes, she knew something vital would shrivel and die inside her.

"Darcy? Is there something else?"

"No." She closed her eyes as she whispered the denial. She couldn't take the chance.

"Then there's no reason why you can't wear this," Cullen said, his voice husky as he slid the ring on her finger.

She curled her fingers as if to stop him, but it was too late. Opening her eyes, she stared at her hand where it rested on his chest. The diamond glittered back at her, warm with promise, glittering with hope.

"What about Angie?" she whispered, still staring at the ring.

"We've managed so far, haven't we?"

"Yes, but—"

"Then we'll keep managing."

He made it sound so simple. Darcy moved her finger, hypnotized by the rainbow lights that danced from the ring. Was it possible it really was that simple? And she was simply complicating things unnecessarily?

"Stop trying to complicate things, honey." Cullen's words matched her own thoughts so closely that Darcy wondered if he could actually read her mind. "We can make this work if we want it bad enough."

"I don't know."

"I know." He slid his fingers under her chin and tilted her face up to his. His eyes were so bright and clear that it seemed as if the sunlight was caught in them. "I love you, Darcy."

"I love you, too," she said, her tone more despairing than happy.

"You're going to have to work on that," he chided. "You're not supposed to sound so gloomy about it."

"I'm sorry." She summoned up a smile. "I do love you, Cullen."

"That's better. Not perfect, but better. You'll have years to practice after we're married."

"I haven't said I'll marry you," she protested in a panic.

"You haven't said you won't, either."

Her eyes searched his, wondering how it was possible that she was the only one with doubts. But there was no trace of doubt in his eyes. He looked as if he knew exactly what he was doing. She only wished she felt the same.

"I think it's traditional to kiss right about now," he said lightly.

But there was nothing light about his kiss. The kiss was pure hunger and need. Darcy could have resisted the hunger, but she wasn't proof against the need. Her head was still spinning with doubt as her hands slid into the thick, dark hair at the nape of his neck.

Cullen groaned and crushed her closer still, deepening the kiss to passion. Darcy answered with a passion of her own, her mouth opening to his, welcoming the invading presence of his tongue. The kiss went on and on until she felt almost light-headed from lack of oxygen. They broke apart at last, stepping back to stare at each other.

"Darcy?" He made her name a question. For answer, she reached for the buttons on his shirt.

She didn't notice the roughness of the blanket against her back. All that mattered was the solid weight of Cullen's body above her, the feel of him within.

Lying there in the open with no witnesses but the sun and the wind and a hawk tracing lazy circles in the sky, they confirmed their love in the most elemental of ways. In the final moment, as her body arched taut as a bowstring against his, the sun caught on the ring he'd given her and the resultant rainbow seemed dazzling with the promise of dreams fulfilled. If only she dared to reach for them.

The trip back to Santa Barbara passed in almost complete silence. Darcy alternated staring at the ring on her finger and staring out the window, between elation and terror.

Angie greeted them both with her usual good cheer, clearly holding no grudge for having been abandoned for the better part of a day. Darcy hung back, as usual, watching as Cullen picked Angie up and swung her over his head. There was a familiar ache in her chest, but for the first time she recognized it for what it was. It wasn't a longing for the past, it was a hunger for the present, a need to be part of the picture, a yearning to come in out of the cold.

Though the day's heat lingered on the evening air, Darcy shivered, frightened by the depth of her need. Inside her, a little voice was saying that she didn't deserve to step into the warmth, that she could never make up for her terrible failure.

She was careful to keep her left hand hidden while they chatted with Marie. She wasn't at all sure about her engagement. The last thing she wanted to do was accept congratulations. She was grateful when Cullen didn't say anything to the other woman, but then on the way home she wondered if that had been out of consideration for her or because he was having second thoughts.

But when they went to bed, he turned and drew her into his arms, and he certainly didn't feel like a man having second thoughts. Having burned away some of the urgency earlier in the day, this time around their lovemaking was full of tenderness. Soft sighs, gliding touches, a slow build to a shivering completion that left them both replete.

"I love you," Cullen whispered against her hair.

"I love you, too."

Darcy lay awake long after he'd gone to sleep. Staring into the darkness, she realized that she couldn't marry him without telling him the truth. The thought sent a chill through her but she knew it had to be done. She couldn't keep a secret like that for the rest of her life and it was better that it come out now, before the ties between them were woven any tighter.

She tried to tell herself that it would be all right. He wasn't anything like Mark. If anyone could understand, it would be Cullen. Tears burned her eyes and wet her cheeks as she stared into the darkness, the weight of old guilt so heavy on her chest that it actually hurt to breathe.

God help her, how could she expect anyone to understand that she'd been responsible for her own baby's death?

It seemed as if she'd barely dropped off to sleep when the nightmare grabbed her. There was the crib, all draped in black ribbons. Somewhere a baby cried— her baby—but she couldn't get to him. Something held her feet in place. The cries went on and on and she tried to lift her hands to cover her ears, but the same force kept her hands captive. She could only stand there, listening to the crying, struggling to break free.

And then Mark was standing in front of her, his pleasant face twisted with grief and hatred, his mouth an ugly slash, the words spilling out like venom-tipped darts. *What kind of mother are you? This was your fault. Your fault... your fault... your fault...* And then he was gone and the crying stopped and there was only silence. She was free to move at last, but it was too late. She crumpled to the ground, sobbing. She was alone. Alone. Just as she'd always be, just as she deserved to be.

"Darcy! Wake up!" Cullen's voice was mixed with the sound of her own sobs as Darcy swam up out of the depths of the dream. Her fingers dug into the muscles in his arms as she pressed herself against him, drawing strength from his solid warmth.

"It's okay. I've got you safe," he murmured, stroking her hair, holding her until the tremors eased. "That must have been one hell of a nightmare."

Darcy said nothing. She felt the weight of his ring on her finger and opened her eyes to stare at it in the darkness. It might have been her imagination but she thought she could almost see a flicker of light in the heart of the stone. But it was gone in an instant, as if it hadn't been there at all.

Her thinking, which had been muddled from the moment Cullen had said he was building a house for the two of them, was suddenly crystal clear. The dream had been a reminder, a warning. She'd almost let herself forget, almost let herself believe that she could leave the past behind. But it couldn't be done. Some things just couldn't be forgotten. Or forgiven.

"You want to tell me what it was about?" Cullen asked, his hand stroking her back.

"I can't marry you."

His hand froze for an instant. "You mean, you dreamed you couldn't marry me?"

"No. I mean, I can't marry you." Darcy pulled away from him and he let her go without a struggle. She could feel his eyes on her as she slid off the bed and groped for the robe she'd draped over the foot of the bed. She slid it on just as he turned on the lamp next to the bed.

"Why can't you marry me?" He sounded more curious than hurt, but Darcy knew it was because he didn't believe she meant it. But she meant it. She knew what she had to do and this time she wasn't going to persuade herself otherwise.

"I just can't. It would be a mistake." She belted the robe around her narrow waist and ran her fingers through her hair to comb it into a rough sort of order.

"Does this have something to do with your nightmare?" Cullen slid off the bed and she averted her eyes from his naked form, not looking at him again until she heard the whisper of jeans being pulled on and the rasp of a zipper.

"It's not the nightmare." A partial truth, anyway. "I just realized that it would be a terrible mistake if we got married. It wouldn't be fair to you."

"Let me be the judge of what's fair to me," he snapped.

"And it wouldn't be fair to the baby," she continued as if he hadn't spoken.

"I thought we'd settled that issue."

"No. We just postponed it. I know you think we could work things out, but the truth is that I can't be what you want, Cullen."

"You *are* what I want, dammit! Why would I ask you to marry me if I wanted something else?"

"You want a mother for Angie and you think I'll become that if you just give it a little time."

The color that stained his cheeks confirmed the accuracy of her words.

"I'll admit that I've got my fantasies of the three of us as one big happy family," he admitted gruffly, "but if that doesn't work out, that's okay. What's important is that we love each other. Or have you changed your mind about that, too?"

"No. I love you." She bent her head to stare at the ring she'd twisted off her finger. "It's because I love you that I can't marry you. And I can't live with you anymore, either."

"Oh, for chrissake! Don't give me a bunch of psycho babble. You don't *not* marry someone because you love them."

"That's exactly what I'm doing." She tossed the ring onto the bed, where it lay between them. All the life seemed gone from it. It was suddenly just a band of gold with a lifeless rock in it.

Cullen lifted his gaze from the ring to Darcy's face. He was chilled by what he read there. She meant it. She really intended to leave. He drew a slow, steady breath. She was upset. He'd rushed her this afternoon, just what he'd promised himself he wouldn't do. Whatever her demons were, he'd known they couldn't be conquered easily. Obviously the nightmare had shaken her badly. In the morning, when she'd calmed down, they'd be able to talk about this. He'd give her more time, if that's what she needed. But he wasn't going to lose her. Not without a fight.

He bent to scoop the ring off the bed, closing his fingers so tightly around it that the setting dug into his palm.

"It's late. We're both tired. Why don't we go back to bed. I'll sleep on the sofa," he added quickly, seeing the objection in her eyes. "You can't move out in the middle of the night, anyway," he added, striving for a reasonable tone and finding it with considerable effort.

Darcy nodded slowly. "I should be the one to take the sofa, though. It's not big enough for you."

Cullen wondered if it struck her as ironic that she'd just driven an emotional stake through his heart and now she was worried about the sofa being too short. But it probably made perfect sense to her since in her mind she was doing this for his sake, anyway.

"I'll take the sofa." At least that way he knew she couldn't sneak out in the middle of the night because he'd be between her and the front door.

He walked past her but stopped in the doorway and turned to look at her. She stood beside the bed, her arms at her sides, her head bent so that a curtain of pale hair fell forward to conceal her profile. He was hurt and angry and there was a part of him that would have liked to shake some sense into her. But she looked so lost and alone standing there.

Ridiculous as it was, he knew she really believed she was doing this for his own good. In a bizarre way, he supposed this was proof that she loved him. And he didn't doubt that she was hurting every bit as much as he was.

He ran his fingers through his hair, aware that they were not quite steady. When he spoke, his voice reflected the weariness he felt. "Look, I know I rushed you this afternoon. I'm sorry."

"You don't need to apologize." Her voice was so low, he had to strain to hear it. "This afternoon was wonderful."

If it had been so wonderful, then why was she leaving him tonight?

"I thought so, too," he said mildly. "What I'm getting at here is, don't make any hasty decisions. It's late. You're tired. It was an emotional day. You just had one hell of a nightmare. It's not a good time to be making life-altering decisions. Let's sleep on it and we'll talk in the morning."

He waited, but there was no response, unless he counted a faint movement of her head that could have been either a nod yes or a shake no. He chose to interpret it as the former. Not that it really mattered because they were going to talk in the morning, if he had to tie her to a chair to get her to listen.

He sighed. "I'll see you in the morning, then." He turned and left without waiting for a response.

Cullen didn't bother turning on any lights in the living room. Sinking onto the sofa, he set his elbows on his knees and let his head drop forward into the support of his hands. He sat there for a long time, listening to the rhythm of his own breathing and the soft sound of Darcy's muffled weeping from the bedroom.

Chapter Seven

Cullen hadn't expected to sleep at all, but he dozed off sometime around six in the morning, only to be awakened at seven by Angie's announcement that she was ready to get up. Bleary-eyed, he rolled off the sofa, groaning at the stiffness in his back, and stumbled into the nursery. Angie stopped crying as soon as she saw him, giving him that cheery, two-toothed grin that never failed to melt his heart.

"Good morning, imp." She babbled happily in reply, lifting her arms to be picked up.

Cullen changed her and dressed her in a pair of cotton rompers. He carried her out to the kitchen, eyeing the bedroom door as he went by. There was no sign of life behind it. Maybe Darcy was still sleeping. Maybe some sleep would make her see how ridiculous the whole idea of her leaving was.

He fed Angie her breakfast, his attention a little more absentminded than usual. He was just wiping traces of cereal off her hands and face when the doorbell rang.

"Who do you suppose that is?" he muttered as he hoisted Angie out of her seat. Eight o'clock on a Sunday morning wasn't exactly a normal time for drop-in visitors.

"Kiel. What are you doing here?"

"Good morning to you, too." Kiel raised one dark eyebrow as he walked past his partner into the living room. Cullen shut the door and followed him. "You look like hell," Kiel said bluntly.

"Thanks." Cullen thrust his fingers through his hair and ran a hand over his unshaven jaw. "What are you doing here?"

"Darcy called me." Kiel seemed surprised that Cullen didn't know. "She said you had some things you needed moved. Said it was urgent."

"She called *you*?" Cullen repeated, feeling as if he'd just been kicked in the gut.

"Yes, I did."

He looked past Kiel to see Darcy standing in the archway that led from the living room to the rear of the condo. She was wearing a pair of jeans and a white T-shirt—one of his T-shirts. Her hair was pulled back from her face in a ponytail, and he was uncharitably pleased to see that she looked every bit as lousy as he felt.

"Why did you call Kiel?" he demanded.

"Because my things won't fit in my car," she answered reasonably.

"Your things?" That was Kiel, looking startled. "Are you leaving?"

"Yes."

"No." Cullen's answer overrode hers. "I thought we were going to talk this morning."

"There's nothing to talk about." Her voice was steadier than he would have liked. She sounded so damned sure.

"There's plenty to talk about." Angie wiggled impatiently, tired of being held when no one was paying any attention to her. Cullen bent to set her on the floor, reaching to hand her a cloth ball to play with. "You can't just leave like this," he said to Darcy as she straightened.

"It's for the best."

"Best for *who?* You? It sure as hell isn't best for me."

"Maybe I should come back later," Kiel said, looking as if he'd like nothing more than to disappear in a puff of smoke. Neither of them heard him.

"You don't understand. I tried to explain."

"Explain? You didn't explain anything. Dammit, Darcy, you can't do this."

"I am doing it." Her voice shook with suppressed emotion. "Someday you'll—"

"If you say I'll thank you for this, I swear to God I won't be responsible for my actions," he snarled.

"Look, it really does sound like you two have things to discuss." Kiel edged toward the door, stepping over Angie, who'd abandoned the ball in favor of exploration.

"Don't go." Darcy took a quick step forward, her hand lifting as if she were a shipwreck victim and Kiel was her last hope of rescue.

"Do go," Cullen said, stepping back to clear a path to the door.

Kiel looked from one to the other, clearly torn. Before anyone could say or do anything, there was an odd sound from Angie, who was sitting on the floor next to the sofa. All three adults looked at her. She looked...odd, Cullen thought. Suddenly afraid, he started toward her.

"What's wrong?"

"She's choking!" Darcy was across the room in a heartbeat and had Angie up and facedown across her lap. Using the flat of her hand, she struck the baby four quick blows across the back. When there was no response, she repeated the maneuver.

Afterward, Cullen could have sworn that he actually heard the pop as the object she'd inhaled popped loose. It dropped from her open mouth and fell to the carpet. There was a moment of utter stillness and then Angie drew a ragged breath. She drew a second and expelled it with a frightened wail.

Cullen sank to his knees, shaking with reaction.

Darcy pulled Angie up and into her arms, rocking her, murmuring soothingly to her as Angie cried out her fright. Kiel bent to pick up the near fatal object and Cullen wasn't surprised to see that his friend's fingers were unsteady.

"It's a button," Kiel murmured, sinking into a chair. "Just a button." He held it out to Cullen.

"I noticed one was missing off one of my shirts a couple of days ago," Cullen said. He closed his fist over the button as if he would crush it. "I thought it had probably come off in the washer."

"A button," Kiel said again, sounding dazed.

Angie's sobs didn't last long. She'd had a fright, but she wasn't hurt and, with no real concept of death or dying, the memory of her fear faded quickly from her mind.

"Here. You should hold her." Darcy's voice sounded thin and her face was almost as white as the T-shirt she wore.

Cullen took the baby from her, closing his eyes for a moment as he felt the wonderful *alive* weight of her. When he opened his eyes, he saw Darcy halfway to the bedroom, her uncertain stride evidence that her knees were no steadier than his. The door closed behind her with a quiet click.

"Maybe you should go after her. She looks pretty shook up," Kiel said.

"Yeah." Angie wiggled to tell him that he was holding her too tight and Cullen loosened his hold. He looked down at her, confirming that she was really and truly all right. Her thick dark lashes were still spiky with tears, but she smiled at him as if she hadn't a care in the world. Which, he supposed, she didn't. He only wished he could forget the terror of the last few minutes as easily as she had.

He stood up and Kiel did the same. "Here. Look after her for a few minutes."

"Me?" Kiel automatically closed his hands around Angie as Cullen thrust her against his chest. "I don't know anything about babies."

"Neither did I," Cullen said over his shoulder.

"But..."

The bedroom door cut off the rest of Kiel's protest. Cullen wasn't worried. He knew his partner would manage. What concerned him now was Darcy.

She was sitting on the edge of the bed, her arms wrapped around herself, rocking back and forth while slow tears seeped down her white cheeks.

"Are you all right?"

She shook her head without speaking, her face twisted with pain. Moving slowly, Cullen crossed the room and knelt down in front of her.

"You did an incredible job, Darcy. I wouldn't have known what to do for her."

"It was my fault," she said, the words choked.

"Your fault? How do you figure that? It was a button off my shirt."

"All my fault," she moaned, unhearing. "Mark said it was and he was right."

"Mark? Your ex-husband?" It was a stab in the dark but it was obvious that the close call with Angie had triggered some old memories.

"He said it was my fault," she said again, her eyes staring at something he couldn't see. Whatever it was, it was obvious it was tearing her to pieces. Taking a chance, Cullen reached for her hands, prying them loose from where they gripped her elbows and closing his fingers around them, trying to tell her without words that she wasn't alone.

"What did he think was your fault, Darcy?" he asked quietly, wondering if he was finally going to get an answer to the demons that preyed on her.

She blinked and suddenly seemed to see him. He expected to see the shutters come up in her eyes, blocking him out again, but there was nothing but pain and a kind of weary acceptance in her eyes, as if she'd run as far and as long as she could.

"It was my fault our baby died."

Cullen's fingers tightened over hers, his eyes going momentarily blank. A baby? She'd had a baby? He felt as if he'd just received a kick over the heart. He struggled to keep the shock and hurt from showing in his face, but he must not have succeeded.

"I'm sorry, Cullen. I should have told you."

"You're telling me now," he said, his voice steadier than he'd expected. "Tell me what happened."

"We... I guess it never was a very happy marriage," she said in a voice drained of emotion. "We got along okay but there was never really any spark between us. I think we both knew it was a mistake, but then we found out I was pregnant. Things seemed to get better between us and we were happy for a while. Even after the baby was born. Mark was so thrilled that it was a boy."

"What was his name?" His voice was raspy but she didn't seem to notice.

"Aaron. We named him Aaron. He was a beautiful baby. Quiet but happy." She smiled dreamily, lost in memory.

"What happened?" Cullen asked, knowing that if there was any chance of healing, it could only come after the wound was completely exposed.

Darcy's smile faded and her eyes darkened from smoky gray to almost black. "He died. I put him in his crib one night and in the morning he was...gone. Sudden Infant Death Syndrome, the doctor said. He said it just…happens sometimes. Nobody knows why for sure." She sounded almost clinical now, but Cullen could feel her nails digging into his hands where she held him.

"Did the doctor say it was something you'd done?"

"No. But I knew it was. And Mark knew it, too. 'Babies don't just die,' he said."

"But didn't the doctor say that that was exactly what did happen sometimes?" he asked gently.

"Yes."

"Then why don't you believe him? Because Mark said it was your fault?"

"There had to have been some reason," she said fiercely.

"Do you think the doctor was lying to you?"

"N-no," she admitted hesitantly.

"Is this why you don't want anything to do with Angie?" Her hands jerked convulsively in his, but he refused to release them, just as he refused to let her look away from him. "Is it?"

"Yes!" The word exploded from her. "What if it happens again? What if it *was* something I did? And even if it wasn't, what if something else happened? I couldn't go through that again. I couldn't."

She began to cry, not the silent tears she'd shed before but deep, gut-wrenching tears. Cleansing tears. Or at least, that's what Cullen hoped. Standing, he scooped her into his arms and settled down with his back against the headboard and Darcy cradled in his lap.

He let her cry, holding her and murmuring softly to her but not trying to stem the flood of tears. When they'd finally subsided into hiccuping sobs, he handed her a fistful of tissues and waited until she'd mopped her eyes and blown her nose.

"What happened to Aaron wasn't your fault."

"You don't know that," she muttered thickly.

"Yes, I do. The doctor told you it wasn't your fault. If Mark said differently, he was speaking out of pain." It took a considerable effort to speak calmly about her ex-husband when what he really wanted to do was demand his address so he could go and beat him to a pulp. "Sometimes things happen and there's no reason for them. That doesn't mean you stop living."

"What if it happened again?" She sounded like a child, afraid of the dark.

"Are you sorry you had Aaron? Do you wish he'd never been born?"

"No! He was the most wonderful thing that had ever happened to me."

"But you could have saved yourself a lot of pain by not having him," he pointed out.

"But I'd have missed out on so much." Her voice trailed off as the shock of her own words went through her. "I'd have missed out on so much," she whispered again.

"If you try to protect yourself completely, you're not living," he said quietly.

"I don't think I could bear it if it happened again," she said, and they both knew she was talking about Angie.

"It won't. But if something, God forbid, were to happen to her, we'd get through it. Together."

Together. When he held her like this, it was possible to believe that they could get through anything together. She closed her eyes and pressed her face closer against the bare skin of his chest. She felt Cullen shifting but she didn't open her eyes until she felt him lift the hand that lay against his chest.

"Will you wear this?" The ring looked small in his hand, a fragile circle signifying commitment and promise. "We don't have to get married right away. You can take as long as you want to think about it. And if... if you really feel you have to move out, I'll help you." She could hear how much the words cost him. "But as long as you're wearing this, I'll know that you're still mine."

For answer, Darcy spread her fingers so that he could slip the ring in place. She knew it was her imagination, but it seemed as if the sparkle was back. Hope and promise in rainbow sparks. They lay there without speaking, savoring the feeling of being together—really together this time.

A muffled thud from the living room broke the quiet moment. "I suppose I should go rescue Kiel from Angie," Cullen said. "He looked as if I'd handed him a live bomb."

Darcy followed him from the room, smoothing her tangled hair back. It must be obvious that she'd been crying but Kiel was a good friend. And she wasn't quite ready to let Cullen out of her sight. When he was with her, she believed in the future he saw so clearly, but she wasn't sure the magic would linger away from him.

The look of gratitude on Kiel's face when he saw them was comical. His dark hair looked as if it had been combed with a hand mixer and there was a wildness in his eyes, as if his sanity was starting to crack. He was on his hands and knees behind the arm of the sofa and Darcy assumed he'd been playing peekaboo with Angie.

"She never stops moving," he said, climbing to his feet as Cullen bent to scoop Angie off the sofa. "And she can just about outrun me."

"She can't even crawl decently, yet," Cullen said, giving his partner an unsympathetic look.

"She's still fast," Kiel said darkly. He glanced from Cullen to Darcy. "You two work things out?"

She held up her left hand by way of answer and he broke into a grin. "I take it you don't need any help moving?"

She caught Cullen's questioning look and shook her head. She wasn't moving out. He was right, a life without taking chances was no life at all. Drawing a deep breath, she came forward and held out her arms.

"Let me hold her, please." With a look that combined both pleased surprise and concern, Cullen handed Angie over to her.

Darcy cuddled the baby against her heart. It felt so right to be holding her like this, to let herself feel the love she'd been trying to keep locked in her heart all these weeks.

"Do you think she's old enough to be a flower girl?" she asked, lifting her head to look at Cullen, letting all her love shine in her eyes.

"I think we could set a trend for flower girls in strollers," he said, his voice shaky with emotion.

He put his arm around her, pulling her against his side. The shadows were gone. All that was left was love.

* * * * *

Dallas Schulze

loves books, old movies, her husband and her cat, not necessarily in that order. She's a sucker for a happy ending, and her writing has given her an outlet for her imagination. Dallas hopes that readers have half as much fun with her books as she does! She has more hobbies that there is space to list them, but is currently working on a doll collection. Dallas loves to hear from her readers, and you can write to her at P.O. Box 241, Verdugo City, CA 91046.

What's next...

from the romantic, tantalizing *Birds, Bees and Babies* authors?

NIGHT SMOKE
Nora Roberts—(Fourth book in the *NIGHT TALES* series)coming in October 1994 from Silhouette Intimate Moments

It was up to investigator Ryan Piasecki to catch the arsonist before more Fletcher buildings burned—and before his desire for Natalie Fletcher blazed out of control. For playing with fire was painless compared to the passion that consumed him with Natalie.

THE ACCIDENTAL BRIDEGROOM
Ann Major—coming in November 1994 from Silhouette Desire

Silhouette Desire's November *Man of the Month* is Rafe Steel—a man with adventure on his mind, and an impossible bride in his arms! Don't miss Rafe and Cathy's story of magic, destiny...and romance.

SNOW BRIDE
Dallas Schulze—coming in August 1994 from Silhouette Intimate Moments

Colleen Bryan had loved gorgeous Gun Larson forever, but to him, she was only his best friend's baby sister. Now that they were snowed in together, she could finally show him that she was no longer a little girl!

Only from

Silhouette®

—where passion lives.

BBB94AUT

Fifty red-blooded, white-hot, true-blue hunks
from every State in the Union!

Look for MEN MADE IN AMERICA! Written by some of
our most popular authors, these stories feature fifty of
the strongest, sexiest men, each from a different state in
the union!

Two titles available every other month at your favorite
retail outlet.

In May, look for:

KISS YESTERDAY GOODBYE by Leigh Michaels (Iowa)
A TIME TO KEEP by Curtiss Ann Matlock (Kansas)

In June, look for:

ONE PALE, FAWN GLOVE by Linda Shaw (Kentucky)
BAYOU MIDNIGHT by Emilie Richards (Louisiana)

You won't be able to resist MEN MADE IN AMERICA!

If you are looking for more titles by

DALLAS SCHULZE

Don't miss this chance to order additional stories by
one of Silhouette's most popular authors:

Silhouette Intimate Moments®

#07377	THE BABY BARGAIN	$3.25	☐
#07414	EVERYTHING BUT MARRIAGE	$3.29	☐
#07462	THE HELL-RAISER	$3.39	☐
#07500	SECONDHAND HUSBAND	$3.50	☐

(limited quantities available on certain titles)

TOTAL AMOUNT	$
POSTAGE & HANDLING	$
($1.00 for one book, 50¢ for each additional)	
APPLICABLE TAXES*	$_____
TOTAL PAYABLE	$_____

(Send check or money order—please do not send cash)

To order, complete this form and send it, along with a check or money order
for the total above, payable to Silhouette Books, to: **In the U.S.:** 3010 Walden
Avenue, P.O. Box 9077, Buffalo, NY 14269-9077; **In Canada:** P.O. Box 636,
Fort Erie, Ontario, L2A 5X3.

Name:_____

Address:_____City:_____

State/Prov.:_____Zip/Postal Code:_____

*New York residents remit applicable sales taxes.
 Canadian residents remit applicable GST and provincial taxes.

DSBACK1

Silhouette®

Rugged and lean...and the best-looking,
sweetest-talking men to be found in the
entire Lone Star state!

In July 1994, Silhouette is very proud to bring you
Diana Palmer's first three LONG, TALL TEXANS.
CALHOUN, JUSTIN and TYLER—the three cowboys
who started the legend. Now they're back by popular
demand in one classic volume—and they're ready to
lasso your heart! Beautifully repackaged for this
special event, this collection is sure to be a
longtime keepsake!

"Diana Palmer makes a reader want to find a Texan
of her own to love!"   —*Affaire de Coeur*

**LONG, TALL TEXANS—the first three—
reunited in this special roundup!**

**Available in July,
wherever Silhouette books are sold.**

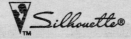